INHERITANCE

INHERITANCE

Selections from the South Carolina Fiction Project

edited by
Janette Turner Hospital

Spartanburg, South Carolina
2001

ISBN 1-891885-18-9, soft cover
ISBN 1-891885-19-7, hard cover
First printing, April 2001

Cover artwork, *Ashes, Ashes, We All Fall Down,* by Judy Hubbard
    1993 Mixed media, 14" x 20" x 2.5"
    South Carolina Arts Commission State Collection
Cover and book design by Mark Olencki
Proofreaders, Betsy Wakefield Teter, Lisa Isenhower, and Angela Kelly
Immediate family support, Diana,Weston, Carlos, Sweety, and DaveCat
Extended family support, Uncle Johnny and Ellie Mae
Printed and bound by McNaughton & Gunn, Inc. in Saline, Michigan

Hub City Writers Project
Post Office Box 8421
Spartanburg, South Carolina 29305
(864) 577-9349 • fax (864) 577-0188
www.hubcity.org

TABLE OF CONTENTS

PREFACE

Inheritance: Selections from the South Carolina Fiction Project, a collaboration between the South Carolina Arts Commission and the Hub City Writers Project, is an anthology celebrating seventeen years of this annual short story competition.

Since 1984, the Fiction Project has showcased new and emerging, as well as established South Carolina writers. The South Carolina Arts Commission and *The Charleston Post and Courier* have co-sponsored the South Carolina Fiction Project since 1993. Before that time, *The State* newspaper co-sponsored the literary competition.

The mission of the South Carolina Fiction Project is to support the growth and development of the state's literary community, writers and readers alike. More than two hundred extraordinarily diverse and creative writers have received cash awards, and their stories have been published by these newspapers. Many of these writers have gone on to publish widely, receiving regional and national awards, as well as the Arts Commission's Literature Fellowships. The anthology includes an appendix listing all of the writers who have been selected for the South Carolina Fiction Project.

Judges for the Fiction Project, distinguished writers themselves, have included: Blanche McCrary Boyd, Alan Cheuse, Peter Cameron, Ellen Alexander Conley, Percival Everett, Patricia Griffith, Josephine Humphreys, Edward P.

Jones, Joanne Leedom-Ackerman, William Henry Lewis, Ralph Lombreglia, Faye Moskowitz, Gloria Naylor, Anne Whitney Pierce, and Valerie Sayers. These judges are responsible in important ways for the quality and significance of the Fiction Project.

The anthology reflects the superb editorship of Janette Turner Hospital, author of nine books, including short stories and novels, who had the challenging task of selecting thirty-six stories for inclusion in *Inheritance*. The vitality of the collection and its literary excellence are reflections of her fine work in this capacity. We feel especially fortunate to have had the perspective of a gifted writer who comes to us from a rich cultural background. Born in Australia, Janette has lived and worked in India, London, Paris, as well as Canada, Boston, upstate New York and, of course, Columbia, South Carolina. We reached out to Janette, who is currently professor and distinguished writer in residence at the University of South Carolina, feeling that her passionate interest in the culture of our state would yield an extraordinary volume. Our hopes have been, if anything, exceeded.

This anthology owes most, of course, to the talent and imaginative power of the writers whose work is collected here. It has been a privilege to work with the program, to reconnect with many of the writers after a fairly long period of time, and to help facilitate the creative collaboration of many individuals and organizations that led to the publication of *Inheritance*.

Sara June Goldstein
Literary Arts Director
South Carolina Arts Commission

Janette Turner Hospital

INTRODUCTION

Tonight Rachmaninoff played Columbia.
So begins Thomas L. Johnson's haunting story
"Nocturne on a Winter's Night." "If someone were to say
to me in a few weeks or months or years," his narrator
continues, "that the great Russian pianist and composer
had actually come to give a recital in South Carolina,
I should scarcely believe it." The night, for more reasons
than one, will never be forgotten. The year is 1942, and
the narrator is an enlisted man stationed at Fort Jackson.
Earlier in the day, he has been assigned to accompany his
lieutenant on a painful military detail: the announcement
of the death of their only son to a man and his wife. There
are rules for such announcements, and military protocol
will permit no deviation.

> The secretary of war desires to express his deep
> regret that your son, Darden E. Genillat, was killed in
> action in defense of his country in the Philippine
> Islands, January 2, 1942.

The lieutenant reads his stark message, then he and
his two sergeants salute, execute an about-turn, click heels,
and march from the house. Hours later, at the concert, the
narrator remains stunned by the impersonal brutality of the
incident and by his own complicity in it. Rachmaninoff plays

Bach, and the narrator thinks of Bach's many children. *(Did he ever lose one...?)* In the boxes of the auditorium, he sees the Fort Jackson brass and their wives. *(I wonder which of them first received the message for the Genillats, and which of them have children.)* The ravages of war and Rachmaninoff's playing of a Chopin Nocturne are interwoven in a meditation which is itself a nocturne on loss.

Cecile Hanna Goding, in "Inheritance," writes of the aftermath of a different war. As always, on all sides, the innocent pay. "Lost my best buddy over there in Nam," says a vet who has just been laid off. That should be enough, he rages. Vets should not have to keep paying, back home, by losing their jobs to non-unionized refugees. But there is no triumph for Tu, one of the replacements, in this unskilled job. In his own country, he had been a doctor. He had had a family back then too.

> Tu said people would talk about us. That it was too soon after the war. So we met at my place instead, where there was no war. There was just quiet. There was just Tu—not talking, sometimes sleeping in the next room.
> Sometimes he cried in his sleep.
> He had dreams, he said...
> "Tell me about your family," Tu said suddenly.
> "Okay," I said. "Papa's Irish—from Chicago. Ma's from Mexico City."
> ...I watched him bring the cigarette to his mouth, holding it between his thumb and finger. His mouth was smiling, but his black eyes stayed sad. I looked through the smoke into Vietnam. I saw the street. I saw the absence of light.

Distant wars and recent wars with the same unanswerable questions, the Old South and the New South, tradition and turbulent change: all are represented in this collection which might be seen as a map of the psyche of South Carolina. For a newcomer to the state, the 204 short stories which I was asked to read have been a crash course in the cultural history and secret inner life of a place mythic in its dimensions, a dark and violent and beautiful place that is full of unexpected moments of grace.

The stories, which consist of all the prize winners from the South Carolina Arts Commission's fiction contest over the past seventeen years, reveal a complex world, a world full of slippage and bewilderment, where the old binary oppositions between southerner and non-southerner, urban and rural, black and white, safe and unsafe, no longer apply. Loneliness is an epidemic. Possible harm lurks everywhere and respects no race, no income group, no gender, no age. But hope also is ubiquitous. A life can be transformed by one moment of compassion from a stranger on a bus. It can just as swiftly, just as randomly, be derailed by violence or disaster. *One November afternoon, my father watched from a sandbar as my brother fought for his life in a river that, like my father's life, was moving in the wrong direction.* (From "My Father Like a River" by Ron Rash). Life moves toward death at high speed and one-way only. Against the rush of the current, people cling to whatever spar comes to hand: memory, tradition, a redemptive moment, a stranger's concern. *Inheritance* is an album of such moments.

The writers of these stories have made me laugh and made me cry. Often they have left me sitting for a long time in silence, in that awed, meditative state which the best works of art arouse in us. I felt myself to be suspended in a transfigured South Carolina, one that hovers above the palmetto state that is marked on the map. It exists in a parallel universe. This other South Carolina is timeless, its spatial boundaries so fluid that they stretch from sea to sea and beyond, to Europe, to Africa and Asia. Its languages and accents are multiple, as are its ethnic allegiances. Its native sons and daughters may leave, but they usually come back, and if they don't, South Carolina is always in their baggage. Strangers arrive from far places and begin to call the place home. It is a dream state, a pure and mystical distillation of the geopolitical one, and it is composed of all the history, all the lives, all the memories and sorrows and hopes that have swirled between the Sea Islands and the Appalachians, a rich inheritance indeed. I was drawn into the spell of this place. It was no easy task to select the thirty-six stories that make up *Inheritance*, and I am still haunted by many that, with reluctance, I could not include.

Much as I was tempted to include certain entries because they represented an unexpected angle of vision, or gave an inside glimpse of a little known corner of South Carolinian life, I am too much the writer, too much the exacting coach of emerging writers, too much the rigorous critic, to settle for anything other than the highest quality as the standard for selection (except, that is, for the disappointing fact that some of the finest stories were disqualified because no writer could be represented more than once.) I was a strong dissenting opinion on this issue, and by way of compensation I urge readers to buy, beg, or borrow any book or magazine containing work by Ron Rash, Cecile Hanna Goding, Rebecca Parke, or Cynthia Boiter. They are exceptional writers whose stories have been prizewinners more than once over the years of the contest. Nevertheless, since I was in the enviable position, as judge, of having an embarrassment of riches from which to choose, the *Inheritance* you now hold in your hands (in spite of the excluded stellar stories) is to be treasured.

This anthology demonstrates that the short story is alive and well, no matter how often one is told that mainstream publishers prefer novels, that short story collections receive minimal review space, that publishers do not promote them, that they do not sell. The short story is seen by many as a Cinderella in the house of prose fiction, a genre waiting for a prince or a fairy godmother to turn it into a novel so that it can escape from the kitchen and gain admittance to the literary ball. Recently, however, increasing numbers of critics and literary theorists have noted what short story writers have always known: that the genre is not a rehearsal for a novel, but a fundamentally different—and indeed, a more demanding—form. Since I write both short stories and novels, and since I teach fiction workshops in both genres, I am in a position to comment.

Trying to articulate the essence of the difference is not, of course, a new thing. Poe, writing on Hawthorne, insisted that the "single effect" of the short story was the crux of the matter, and indeed, in such stories as Patricia Benton's "The Egg People" or David Burt's "Paperboy" or Phillip Gardner's "Wrecker," every detail bears down upon one poignant flash of revelation. *The truth is complicated*, begins the narrator of "Wrecker." *I don't mean knowing it. Knowing it isn't so hard, sometimes. But getting it told can be next to impossible.*

Charles May, the leading contemporary literary theorist on the short story, sees the genre as a modern expression of something ancient and primal. He finds the origin of this compact epiphanic form back in ritual and ceremony, in the ancient and universal enactments of mystery, of sacrament, of rites of passage. The last lines of Rebecca Parke's astonishing story, "Stuck," mapping the moment of passing from life to death in a hospital bed, and on to the life beyond, illustrate this:

> Lady Woman was singing to me this time…She didn't show me no visions.
>
> No, I didn't even see the dancing pigs that come to you when the nurse give you that shot to keep the new baby's coming from tearing you asunder. Didn't see no burning bush, no heavenly light, no long white-haired white man having his way.
>
> Saw only the little crack of light under the door, the little call bell's red spot shining, and Lady Woman unhooking my arm from the ceiling, undoing that sugar line from my arm, singing, "Follow me. Got to get you free." I thought we was headed for the highway, until we made our first step into mid-air.

Frank O'Connor, in *The Lonely Voice*, saw the novel as a social animal, a chronicle of the society in which it was embedded, while the short story, he argued, articulated the single voice, the cry in the dark, the isolated life. In his view, the short story is distinguished by its "intense awareness of human loneliness" and certainly such a view pertains to this anthology, which one might easily have called *All the Lonely People.*

But of course, all these sad and isolated voices *are* contemporary society. It is for this reason that feminist and African-American and post-colonial critics have seen the short story as the genre *par excellence* which has brought the subtext of the social order to the surface and has given its subvocal layers a hearing. To listen in on the stories in *Inheritance* is like having your sound system pick up a hundred disembodied cell phone conversations, splinters of all the intimate secrets that swirl about you, fragments of all the submerged and repressed and silenced voices crossing and criss-crossing paths.

Can you grasp what you are doing? White families aren't bothered because white families keep out. Has it occurred to you that we'll be shot? It is the intense voice of a husband to his wife. They are living in Africa. *You mean to be heroic... you are Southern. But it doesn't matter. What matters is, you are a mother. You are not called to be heroic. I cannot allow your heroism.* (Rosa Shand: "A Garden with a Mango Tree")

I'll tell you another thing, to show you that old people are creatures of habit... You watch and see if this fellow's glasses aren't in his left shoulder coat pocket. The poor souls take them off just before walking into the lake. I don't see what they're saving them for... Nobody wants to wear a dead man's glasses. (David Tillinghast: "The Swimmer")

...rolled him up on the tracks knowing that about two in the morning a train always comes along... Deputies first didn't

know what it was, couldn't find the head, but Judy recognized John by his boots…Never did find the head. (S. Paul Rice: "Junnie, the Coin, and Grandpa Dickens")

First, try understanding that we've got a laundry in here. The crazies over on Bull Street soil themselves and their sheets pretty regularly…I put in five years on the sheets, forty hours a week…I was on a first name basis with excrement, understand …(Robert Poole: "Break")

There are complex stories of interracial friendships and poignant accounts of people who sit by the beds of elderly parents who no longer recognize them. There are accounts of people stunned by divorce, or by a child custody case, or by a diagnosis of terminal illness. But the most haunting refrain, which recurs over and over in a minor and melancholy key, is the chorus of sad wise children, stoic and adult before their time. So many have to fend for themselves, defend themselves from violence, take care of the adults who are supposed to take care of them. The lucky ones have other children to cling to.

> When Uncle Zeke came home from work the whole house would fill up with sorrow. The smell of it would get into our clothes, cling to our skin, and we could even taste it in the water…
> He would accuse Aunt Leah of nasty woman acts and then all five of us kids would have to wrap ourselves around Aunt Leah's body, our fingers holding tight, tight to each other's arms. We would hold our breath and squeeze our eyes shut, bracing ourselves waiting for the blows…(Nichole Potts: "Dealing with Uncle Zeke")

In these stories is embedded the kind of hope that is hard won. Not a single child settles for the role of victim. They fight back, they look after alcoholic parents, they escape, they live by a dark and resilient humor. They are survivors. They have no choice.

Except in a sitcom, says the narrator of Lori Wyndham Jolly's "Objects in Mirror are Closer than they Appear," *two more perfect children you'll never find. Marcia and Peter Brady, that's us. If Carol Brady wants to marry a bank teller only twelve years older than me, we don't complain.*

From "Burnt Beans" by Sandy Lang Quick: *When the Oldsmobile got low on gas, we drove home and I got Momma to lie down on the couch. Her high heels dropped to the floor and she sipped on the last of the whiskey. By about 2:00 she was asleep with the TV on. I went to my room to do my homework.*

Neglect breeds a fierce determination in the orphaned cousin taken into the household of Uncle Zeke and Aunt Leah.

> "That's all that's left? Oh, Lord God."
> "Woman, you shut your mouth about my money."
> I would press my face against the cool door and imagine the sound of Aunt Leah's hand slapping his face. But Aunt Leah was not that type of woman, not the type of woman I wanted to be.

Not at all the type of woman that the narrator shows every sign of becoming in a final act of redemptive defiance:

> Uncle Zeke's getting off time was around 5 o'clock. I took the lead pipe from beneath Aunt Leah's bed and decided to meet him at the liquor store…
> When Uncle Zeke came out with a bunch of men and a brown bag, I stepped directly in front of him and looked him dead in the eye. "I come for the rent money…"
> I stuck my hand out and stared him in the eye. "The rent money and we need things besides," and then I heard myself say, "It's what a man ought to do."

What remains with the reader is the sheer insistence on hope. All the sad children and all the lonely people spy it out and seize hold of it, no matter how fleeting, no matter, even, when the possibility of happiness is merely glimpsed in a rear-view mirror, an echo of something already gone. The forlorn brother and sister, uprooted from school and friends at the insistence of their negligent mother's young boyfriend, share such a moment as they speed down the interstate to Florida.

> We pass a trailer park; on the side of the road a young girl, ten or eleven years old, is supporting her little brother on an adult-sized bike. His feet barely reach the pedals and she is balancing the frame as she runs alongside…
>
> I look back at them in the mirror as they shrink into the distance. Both of them are laughing, their hair blowing in the Mustang's windy wake. They don't seem too worried about losing control or falling, or about the darkening sky. (from "Objects in Mirror are Closer than they Appear")

In the ironic juxtaposition of ending and title, the delicate optimism of that balancing act—a glimpse of happiness gone that may nevertheless be closer than it appears—lies the true core of South Carolina's inheritance: a tough and redemptive hope for a bright future.

My Father Like a River

One November afternoon my father watched from a sandbar as my brother fought for his life in a river that, like my father's life, was moving in the wrong direction. Minutes seemed to pass as I watched my brother surface and disappear, tumble and spin away from us as my father did nothing, though surely it was only moments before he roused himself, stumbled and splashed downstream to salvage a part of his shattered life. For this was the autumn my father's brief ascent into the white-collar world had fizzled like some cheap Fourth of July firework. He was thirty-five years old, a man with a wife, four children and no job.

"I can't believe he fired me," my father had said a month earlier when he sat down at the dinner table. He sounded puzzled—no bitterness or fear in his voice, not yet. My mother and I, even my nine-year-old younger brother, let our roast beef and mashed potatoes lay untouched on our plates. The twins in their high chairs continued to eat. As did my father, with a fierce relish as if he believed his plate might be snatched away at any moment.

"Maybe he will reconsider, realize the mistake he's making," my mother said.

"No," my father said, swallowing a forkful of potatoes as he refused my mother's morsel of hope. "He's been setting this up for weeks. I just refused to see it coming. He's wanting to show he's in charge, not his daddy-in-law's ghost. He didn't even offer me my old job back."

My father shoved his chair back from the table, his plate bare.

"I wish Mr. Hamrick had left me in the weave room," he said and walked out the front door. Through the dining room window we could see his silhouette in the yard, the flare of his lighter as he lit a cigarette. He stood at the edge of the cul-de-sac as if on a cliff as he surveyed the rows of brick houses that lined both sides of the subdivision's street, houses new as our own, as heavily mortgaged.

"You all need to eat," my mother told my brother and me.

"It's cold," my brother said.

"Eat it anyway," my mother said sharply. "Your father worked hard to pay for this food. The least you can do is eat it." She lifted a forkful of roast beef to her mouth with a grim determination. My brother cried softly but followed my mother's example, as did I. We ate with heads bowed and in silence, our supper a communion not of remembrance but of anticipation, a first taste of what a suddenly uncertain future might hold.

We had moved to the subdivision eighteen months earlier, the first home in three generations someone in my father's family had owned. His parents and grandparents had lived in the mill village, as had we before my father had impressed Mr. Hamrick, the mill owner, as management material.

"A man doesn't have to have a college degree to wear a tie," Mr. Hamrick had said at the mill's Christmas party when he announced the third and final promotion that had taken my father from weaver to shift supervisor to management. "Hard work and experience are more important than some piece of rolled-up paper."

Mr. Hamrick had waved us up to the podium to join our father. He had kissed my mother on the cheek and shaken hands with my brother and me. "You boys should be proud of your daddy," Mr. Hamrick had said.

But Mr. Hamrick's philosophy was not shared by his son-in-law, and when Mr. Hamrick died one morning of a heart attack my father's rise became a free fall.

He started looking for work the following morning and found a job by afternoon. Clyde Harmon, a contractor my father had known since they had been in first grade together, added my father to a crew repainting the junior high. Clyde was five months behind on the job, so his offer was a pragmatic act of kindness, tempered further by his making it clear my father's employment would only last the four weeks or so it took to complete the job.

And so my father returned to a school he had attended two decades earlier, climbing a ladder to prove how far he had fallen economically. Instead of a white shirt and tie, he worked in white coveralls smudged and crusty with dried paint. His co-workers were two brothers, one twenty and one eighteen. Each Friday when Clyde Harmon took a thick roll of ten-dollar bills from his pocket, my father placed two fewer in his wallet than his co-workers. He had never painted before, so he learned from men half his age the discipline of staring at walls day after day.

For that month my father was a looming presence in my life—in hallways when I changed classes, up on his ladder as adolescents moiled under him as if he were some creature treed and held at bay, or peering into my class-rooms as he painted window frames.

That I pretended to ignore him was only natural for a fourteen-year-old, for at that age a parent's mere presence is a source of embarrassment, but I'm sure my father be-lieved my downcast eyes were caused as much by my shame at his descent as adolescent quirkiness. He was as uncom-fortable as I when we saw each other during the school day, our acknowledgement of one another a quick turning away of eyes.

In the middle of my father's month-long career as a painter, Turner Realty raised a *For Sale* sign on our lawn like a flag of surrender. Almost every evening strangers snooped and poked around and sometimes under our house while my father searched via phone or car for a permanent job, a less expensive house for when we sold ours. We ate on paper plates and quickly, our suppers a tense huddle of silence. Someone was always coming or my father always leaving, sometimes my mother with him if house hunting. They would strap the twins in the back seat and leave my brother and me to let in the realtor and her latest entourage.

By November the realtor had made her sale and we had moved into a small wooden house in the mill village where my father had grown up. Unlike his parents, my father would, if he kept up the mortgage payments, own his house, but how could he not sense that he was back where he had started eighteen years ago. With the help of relatives we made the move in a weekend.

My father still had not found a permanent job, and the work at the junior high was almost done—the inside painting, the trim work. Now it was odds and ends, poles and doors. On the Friday afternoon of my father's last day, I came out for recess and saw him in the distance climbing the water tower ladder, a paint bucket and brush grasped in one hand, gripping the metal rungs with the other. Except for the faded black letters that proclaimed our school's name, the water tower was white, white as the clouds on this bright early-fall afternoon, a crispness in the air signaling colder weather to come. As my father rose higher it seemed he might ascend into the clouds themselves, but then he stopped, halfway between the ground and the sky, and dipped his brush in the paint.

I watched him raise the brush, follow the faded letters, his arm moving above and then out to his side as if semaphoring. The letters slowly brightened into blackness, my father filling in each letter's outline like a first-grader learning the alphabet, his message already determined by the pattern.

It was my mother's idea for us to go fishing the following day. Perhaps she thought it might take my father's mind off our uncertain future for a few hours, give him a chance to spend some time with his sons, something he'd had little time for in the last month. She filled a picnic basket with sandwiches and cokes and found an old quilt for us to eat on. My father gathered the rods and reels and rusty tackle box from the cellar while my brother and I shoveled up earthworms in the backyard.

It took an hour of driving curvy two-lane roads to get to the upper corner of Watauga County where the New River flowed into Virginia. My seventh grade history teacher claimed the New the second oldest river in the world, only the Nile being older, but what amazed me was the river's ability to flow north instead of south, as though the river had found a way to defy the laws of gravity.

When we entered the gorge the road was no longer paved. We bumped and jolted down to the river, passing leaf-stripped trees gray and skeletal. People had lived in this gorge years ago before the government bought the land. They had raised crops and homes and families, but now all that remained was an occasional chimney crumbling above a collapse of rotten wood and rusty tin.

The state of North Carolina stocked rainbow trout under the bridge where we parked, and these fish along with an occasional knottyhead and snag were what my brother and I had caught on previous trips. My father usually fished with worms as well, but this day as he rigged up our Zebco rods and reels he tied a Rapala plug to his line instead of a size ten hook. There were smallmouth bass in the New, some reaching four or five pounds, and a few brown trout even bigger. Perhaps my father believed a trophy smallmouth or brown might signal a change of luck in his life.

As with most fishing trips we took, he had little opportunity to find out, for almost every time he moved a ways up or downstream my brother and I would bring him back with a bird's nest in our reel, a hook caught on a rock or drowned log.

My father was usually a patient man in such situations, but on this afternoon his face darkened each time he lay down his rod and traversed the rocky bank to untangle a line or wade into the river to free a hook. The few casts he made brought nothing but his lure back to shore. The day was warm for November, but we were deep in the gorge. By three o'clock the sun was falling behind mountains, the air chilly.

My brother complained he was cold and wanted to go home, and though I said nothing I was ready as well. The fishing had been slow, three small rainbows in four hours. We were bored, the bait unchecked as it lay on the stream's bottom, so my father was now free to move up and down the shore, fishing with a fixed concentration I had never seen before as he made long, looping casts toward the far bank, changed the speed of the retrieve, even adding a sinker to the line in hopes the right depth might make a difference, might bring forth the miracle a big fish always is.

"I'm going to the car," my brother whined. He picked his rod up off the rocks and reeled for a few moments before the line tightened and the rod bowed. "I'm hung up, dad," he yelled to my father, who had waded out onto a sandbar fifty feet downstream.

"Unsnag it yourself, dammit," my father said.

My brother hesitated, waited for my father to say or do something else, for he had always warned us not to enter the river without him close by. But the river's wide presence had our father's full attention. My brother placed his hand on the taut line, followed it into the swift current. He was up to his knees when he lost his footing and floundered downstream into deeper water.

When I yelled my father looked up to see his son appearing and disappearing in a current that shoved him toward and then past the sandbar. I ran towards my father, towards my brother, shouting at my father to do something. I was close enough to see his eyes, and in that moment I believed he would let my brother drown. Then he started

running too, tripping and bloodying his knee in the rocky
shallows before flailing into the deeper current, tumbled
and spun downstream himself as he closed the gap between
my brother and himself. He caught my brother, and lost him
as a drop-off pulled the riverbed out from under their feet.

Twenty yards further downstream he collared my
brother again. They had been pushed closer to shore, the
water shallow now. My father lifted my brother to his feet,
held him there as they both gasped and sputtered for
breath. I watched my father's hand as it slowly reached back
and touched an empty pocket. I had followed my father
into the water, and as my father dragged my brother toward
the bank I held onto my brother as well. At that moment I
feared my father might change his mind and loosen his grip,
let the river have its way with his son, perhaps with himself.

We came onto shore like survivors of a shipwreck, each
of us dripping and shivering. My father carried my brother
to the car, stripped off my brother's clothes and then mine
and wrapped us in the quilt. He placed us in the front seat,
cranked up the engine and turned the heater on high.
"When you and your brother get warm, cut off the engine,"
he told me.

He walked the shoreline an hour, his eyes searching the
shallows, occasionally wading into the river to get a better
look. The last light faded and soon he moved in the dark.
My brother had fallen asleep, his head on my shoulder. I
watched my father until I could no longer see him. Then
I too closed my eyes. I had seen enough for one day.

We lived close to the bone that winter, and the week's
pay the river snatched from us must have been a festering
memory to my parents each time they sat down at the
kitchen table to decide which bills to pay, which not to. It
was January before my father got a full-time job at Shuford
Mill fifty miles away in Hickory. We moved for the second
time in five months. My father was again in the weave
room, where he had started out at eighteen. Though he
would work at Shuford Mill for thirty years, he'd never wear

a tie or make half the salary he'd brought home those two years he was a manager. No one ever told him again that hard work and experience meant more than a rolled-up piece of paper.

We make our own choices on how we remember our parents. I remember my father on a November afternoon, as he stood mid-stream on a sandbar as if marooned. I remember how he watched his son sweep past him. What he felt at that moment, what he didn't feel, I will not, as I did at fourteen, presume to know. Instead, I will remember how he found something worth holding onto in that wrong-flowing current that carried all of our lives.

Ron Rash is the author of four books: The Night the New Jesus Fell to Earth, Eureka Mill, Among the Believers, *and* Casualties. *He lives in Clemson.*

Peter Fennell

ROPES

Fifth grade when I first knew him. The fastest white boy ever seen. Hands like glue. All I did was lean back and sling it high and deep, spiral it up so it flying like a bird, and he took care of the rest. Run below it, everybody else chasing hard, still they falling back. Over the middle? He didn't care. Go screaming across the field, feet sliding up dust, dive if he had to. Come up with a mouthful of dirt. In a crowd? You'd say, no sir. Too many hands, elbows, people in his face. But listen. He got a finger on the ball and it was his, wasn't nobody taking it away. I thrown it too high before, too hard. Gave up looking. But there he goes. Up, up, up. Arms growing for the sky. Hands reaching back. Death grip. It's his. I say this: that boy could do anything.

Twice a day we had a game. It ain't fair, both us on the same team. Even those sixth grade chumps couldn't hang. It was touchdown after touchdown, like the National Football League. I chased him down the field every time, putting on moves like he did. Shake this way, shake that. Run past everybody, all them rolling their eyes and wondering where he went. There he always was, laughing past the end of the field. I'd jump on top of him, squeeze my arms around his neck, and sling his skinny self to the ground. When I let him go he'd get up smiling that cornbread smile, holding the ball like a loaf of bread. Spin it, I'd say. Make it dance. He knew what to do. He'd put the ball near the ground, flip his wrist. Now the ball's standing up in the dirt, twirling like a top. We jived around in circles, the ball in the middle. I'd say, Robby, you the man. You are the man. Can't nobody catch like you.

Those games never lasted long enough. The bell rang and everybody started heading in. So we drug ourselves in too.

School over, I walked home. Why we need a car? I lived right there, in those apartments could be seen from the playground. Sometime my mama came, sometime not. Robby's family had a car. More than one. His mama came for him everyday, like clockwork in her blue car. Lots of times they cruised by me, driving slow near the school. Robby'd roll down his window and lean outside, his face still dirty from diving in the dirt, teeth white like chalk. He stretched out his arms and say, Hit me. I lean back and throw, watch that invisible ball run from my hand, go spinning all the way to that blue car rolling down the street. At just the right time, Robby reached out his hands out far and, bingo, he pulled it in. He'd yell, Yonder goes the best quarterback in this town. I'd yell back, You just making me look good. Then before the car got to the corner I'd watch his mama's arm come over and jerk him back in.

Sixth grade came and what do you think? More of the same. We was men among boys. They tried to split us up. But none of that. Give that other team the ball first. Let them take more players. It don't matter. I throw it over you, around you, through your legs. Robby will tip it in the air just to fool you. But no. The ball, it ain't touching the ground. Sixth grade, my arm felt loose and fast. The ball left my hand singing, a tight line cutting the air in two, a rope from me to Robby. I'd spot it way out front, lead Robby so far you'd say only a black man can run that far that fast. But there Robby came every time to meet that spot.

That year it was still touchdown after touchdown. More running up and down the field. More jiving and grooving around that spinning ball. More all that, but still the same

Robby. Still the same me.

Time for seventh grade. They shipped everybody to a new school. So no more football at recess. We traded that in for uniforms. Helmets. Practice. Coaches trying to kill us. Just let me throw. Let Robby catch. That's all those coaches need to know. But they don't like that. They got set ideas. There's other quarterbacks, other receivers, teams from other schools that must be beat. I stayed on the sideline. Robby too. Next year, that would be our year.

After practice, there his mama came. In that car. There goes Robby getting in. They took a different way home. I still walked. It ain't that far.

Next year came and yeah I was the quarterback. First day of practice I seen Robby jetting down the field. Here I was ready to throw. But the coaches say, Stop. You must give the ball to Warren here. Hand it to Warren and let him run. That's how we'll beat those other teams. We don't throw the ball unless we have to.

Well, we need to throw, Coach. I believe we got to.

But the coaches said, Team. We're a team. There's no I's here. We play as one and do what's best for the team.

So I gave the ball to Warren and let him run. And he was fast. He was strong. People tried to tackle him, but they slid off like he was taking off his shirt. One man, he wasn't bringing Warren down. It took three or four. And they were sorry they did.

Robby was being Robby, running fast as ever down the field, his eyes back at me, his arm waving. Hoping I'd throw. Finally to Robby the coaches say, Stop. What are you doing? You see that man right there? That's your man. You block him. You don't run past him down the field. Your man's the one making the tackle. Now try again.

Robby wasn't a blocker. Never was. He was a receiver. A runner. He had wings. He was best out in the open, sailing down the field. Next play, what you think happened? Robby got pushed aside and his man was one of them who tackled Warren. The coaches yelled, Robby on this team,

the receivers block. If a receiver wants to play, he has
to block.

Game time and it was my first as the quarterback. My
arm, it never lift higher than my shoulder. I couldn't put
it high no more. It was only good for handing the ball to
Warren. He ran and ran, then ran some more. Robby sat
on his helmet and watched it all.

After the game Robby's mama say, You have to try
harder. You don't try hard enough. Robby don't answer.
They went to the parking lot and drove away in the blue car.

Another practice. The coaches yelled at Robby, If you
don't want to give this team your all, you don't need to be
here. Robby took off his helmet and slammed it to the
ground. It bounced and rolled in the dirt. Robby ran from
the field and was gone.

Football was over for Robby. He gave it up. Just like
that.

The next day I say to him, Why you quitting, Rob?
He say, I don't need that team. I say, What about passes,
man, the ropes I used to throw? You used to catch?

He say, That's in the past. Stop living in it.

I say, Go ahead then. Quit. I don't care.

It got to be I almost forgot about him. He went to his
side of the school. I went to mine.

Eleventh grade now and it's a Friday. Game day. I'm
wearing my jersey. Number eleven. But I ain't thinking
about that. Something happened. There's talk. A buzz here
you can feel. We're going to take over the school, they say.
Somebody has to pay.

I read the newspaper. But they say the newspaper's
a lie. There's two stories. Story one you can read in the
newspaper. A man, a black man, died while walking down
a county dirt road. Run over by a car. Hit and run. The
sheriff's investigating, and would anyone with information
please come forward. That's it. Story two's the talk you
hear. It say that, yeah, a black man's dead. But no, it wasn't

no hit and run. Story two say this man had a white girl-friend. Story two say he was tied to the back of a car with a rope, was dragged down the dirt road for three miles. Left for dead with his clothes scraped off, parts of him rubbed down so bad he'd been skinned. If you ain't believing this, hear the rest of story two. Something's missing from the black man's body. The sheriff knows this, but that man ain't telling.

We'll stand up for our fallen brother, they say.

But I don't know this black man. I don't know nobody who knows this man. He's dead but he ain't my brother.

Today the halls move like sand. They filled with noise, talk. None of it make sense, no word can be made out above this buzz. Then I realize somebody's talking to me. It's Warren. He wears a jersey too. He say, Pick one. Just pick one. When you pass in the hall, slide over to their side. Then swing your elbow out and, bam, they'll go down. They'll know we mean what we say.

I ask him what they have to do with it. He say, Who? I ask him again what these people have to do with this black man who's dead. He say, Nothing, but that's their bad luck. I tell Warren I'm taking no part in this. And I ain't worried about him. I know Warren's all talk.

All day I hear stories of fights. But I don't see any. I hear the cops were called to haul somebody away. But show me the police cars. One time I see people running down the hall and out the doors. Fight. Fight, they shout. Like they always do. Everybody here has seen that before.

But I know some of it must be true when a man comes on the loudspeaker. He say, All this needs to stop now or we'll cancel school for the rest of the day. Some people clap at this. And if you think that's funny, the man say, we'll cancel the game tonight too.

It don't stop. The next time I see Warren his jersey's pulled out from his pants. He drags his leg behind him but he ain't hurt. He's strutting. Cooling. I ask him what's wrong with him. I told you, he say. I told you. They know what we talking about now.

I say, You forget we got a game tonight?

He say, I don't care about no game.

We end up walking the same way down the hall.
A couple of other dudes join up with us. Nobody carrying
books, except me. Nobody worried about school no more
today. I shouldn't be part of this crowd. A quarterback
should be smart, but I keep walking with Warren and his
fool friends.

Who you think this trouble found? The first person we
see who's different from us, the first one in this part of the
hall who shouldn't be. Who comes walking back here,
pretending he ain't scared?

Robby is scared. He's heard the talk. He feels the buzz.
But he ain't no more smarter than me. He's all alone back
here, asking for this trouble Warren's carrying. He's up
close against the wall, carrying one or two books under his
arm. Looking straight ahead, not at us. Then his eyes glance
my way. Pick me out from all the others. And just as quick
they go back down. Nothing else. Not a smile. Not a nod.
Who is he? Acting like he ain't knowing who I am. Warren,
like he warned me he would, slides over to Robby's side.
I don't stop him, don't even try. He opens his hand and
whams Robby in the shoulder. Robby flies against the wall
and drops his books.

What's your problem? Robby say.

I'll show you my problem, Warren say. He goes at Robby
with his elbow high-raised, his fingers ball up tight.

The math here, it don't add up. Four of us, one of him.
Still Robby's keeping up his act. Now he's buying time by
backing up, but he's winding his wiry body into a coil like
he's getting ready to spring it all over Warren.

Other people see something's going on, so they come
pushing behind and make a crowd.

Robby should remember what he is: a runner.

Warren steps closer, like he's ready to jump. I step in,
say, Wait, Warren. This white boy's mine. I'll take care of

him. Outside. I'll take this white boy outside.

Robby say, I'm not going outside with you.

I say, Yeah you are.

Double doors at the end of the hall. Not too far. I bend my knees and bury my shoulder in his stomach. I wrap my arms around his back and now I'm pushing him. Best I can. He swings his fists down to hit me on the back, but I hardly feel them.

Warren and them, they follow behind us. They say, Yeah, yeah. Now you'll see, white boy.

I get Robby to the door, shove us though. Outside I give Robby one big push, then grab the handle and slam the door in Warren's face.

Now run, I say to Robby. And I take off past him without waiting. Robby don't move.

But then the doors bust open. They're coming through. That gets him moving. He takes off and now he's right behind me and we're flying across the grass in the front of the school, him a few steps behind but catching up. I ain't too slow myself. But Robby hasn't lost a step. Warren and those boys chase us, but we stretch away. Robby leaps over a bush. He sidesteps a concrete pillar. He stiff-arms a metal trashcan. He jukes this way, then that. Warren and them, they never had a chance. I look back and see him stopped and standing by the flagpole. He raises his hand and throws it down in a way that say, *Forget them.*

Robby and me run more, go around a corner and stop. We're breathing hard. Laughing. Bending over to catch our breath.

The parking lot's in front of us. School ain't over. But will be soon enough. After we steal back our wind, Robby say, Let's get out of here. He walks away toward the lot and I follow behind to see how far he'll go.

I ask him where he's going. He say, I don't know. We walk past rows of cars. We step on gravel, crushed soda cans, tiny pieces of glass under our feet. We step past another row and there it is. That blue car. A hand-me-down from his mama, more dirty, more beat-up than it used to be. Now Robby's to drive. Get in, Robby say.

I stand there and watch him open the door and sit on the seat. A bell rings behind me at the school.

I walk around to the side of Robby's car. I climb in.

Peter Fennell grew up in Chester and received a Bachelor of Science degree in Mechanical Engineering from Clemson University. He is currently an engineer for a water utility in Mount Pleasant, where he lives with his wife, Gina, and their daughter and son. He is at work on his first novel.

Patricia Benton

THE EGG PEOPLE

The rose and willows and grass were pretty, but the best thing summer did for our place was grow the corn so high you couldn't see Pappa's chicken houses. During the winter a couple years ago Pappa had built a little white frame house for the egg people to live in and it was just over our property line, so next spring Daddy set out a hedge row to block it out, too, but the red tips hadn't had time to grow much. Pappa had given Daddy two acres on a corner of his small farm, and Daddy had built a home for him and Mama and Mary Sue and me.

There was a big screened-in window over our kitchen sink and every day when my big sister Mary Sue and I did the dishes, we didn't mind our own business like Mama kept telling us to. The house was small and far enough away for us to see their front yard and their back yard at the same time. And since they hardly ever closed a curtain, some-times we watched them at night. "Becky, you and Mary Sue mind your own business now. I'm getting tired of telling you that," Mama said.

They were always hicks. All of 'em. "As long as Pappa won't pay them enough to live on, all he's ever going to get is trash. And *they're* not going to stay." Mama said that over and over. Pappa had thought the house might keep 'em longer. They stayed longer, but it still wasn't very long, only a few months.

There was something about poor people that interested me. Everybody that moved in seemed to have a brother or sister or some relative or another living with them. I sure never wanted any of my family tagging along with me after I got married. Being poor must do something to you.

The Reynolds had moved in during the spring. They were a young couple with an eight months old baby. Martha and Frank were dumb and ugly and they had her sister living with them to take care of the baby. Glynis was super dumb, but she was pretty. I kept wanting to look at her.

The reason I say they're dumb is one time I was walking alongside the chicken house and I stopped to say hi, and they were all three there, along with the baby who was lying down on a stroller laid back, and flies were crawling all over the baby's bottle and then they picked up the bottle and put it in its mouth, and I gagged and gagged, but they just smiled at the pretty baby. Mama said the baby was probably used to the germs is why it didn't get sick.

You didn't have to see 'em to know they were hicks. You could tell by listening. In the evenings their voices floated in the windows—country as you please. We never knew "I Saw the Light" could sound like that. Mary Sue and I knew just about every verse to every hymn they sang, so sometimes while she was washing and I was drying and putting away, we'd crank up and throw a twang in our voices and sing out the window right along with 'em. Till Mama made us stop.

Mama never wanted us to have anything to do with any trash—including irritate 'em—but after school was out for the summer, sometimes I'd be helping Pappa grade the eggs so I could get some money, and Martha would be in the egg house, too, watching so she could learn more. She said she liked to learn things, if she wouldn't be in the way. My cousin Andy had been there earlier, visiting on the farm for a few weeks, and working in the egg house, and he and I had gotten to be kissing cousins, but now he was gone and Papa decided it was easier to have someone else helping than for us to go back to doing it ourselves. So he asked Martha.

I told Pappa how dumb Martha was, told him how I thought it would be better to invite Andy back for the rest of the summer, but Pappa didn't think that was a good idea. He said Martha was the smartest help he'd ever hired, and before long he was letting her candle the eggs. I saw that she did all right on that, never broke an egg or anything, and even I broke eggs sometimes. Some nights just the three of us, Pappa, Martha and I, would be in the egg house. I'd pick up the heavy wire baskets of washed eggs for Martha and keep boxes ready for Pappa, and Martha would pick up an egg at a time from the wire baskets and put it on top of the light and look at the inside shadow of the yolk, candling the eggs, and weighing 'em, and then Pappa would put 'em in cartons and I'd pack the cartons in boxes to take to the Red and White.

Martha was always happy about working in the egg house. She'd clean herself up nights before she came down. It wasn't part of the regular job he'd hired 'em for, and Pappa said he'd pay her extra if she'd help. It was part of Frank's job to wash the eggs down in the baskets with a hose after he'd gathered them, and he said after he'd done that he was tired nights and he'd rather watch TV, the old one we donated to the house they lived in. Martha had her hair pulled back in a ponytail tied with a ribbon and her face was shiny from soap and she started putting on lipstick, and she wore a fresh dress that hung long in the front the way all her dresses hung low in the front because of the way she stood. She didn't seem to be as shy at night in the dim light of the egg house and away from Frank, but she still didn't talk to you unless you spoke first.

Pappa teased her. Pappa teased people he liked. "Martha, you're not stealing my chickens are you? I think I've got some missing."

She laughed and looked up at him. "No, sir, Mr. Kinard. We ain't stealing your chickens. We ain't going to do nothing s'gonna make *you* mad."

"Just thought I'd make sure. You know, the last people just loaded up a trunk full and took off one night. Stole everything else they could pull loose too, didn't they, Becky?"

"Yes, sir. They sure did."

"Well, we poor people, but our Mamas taught us to try to be good people, Mr. Kinard. We planning on staying long as you'll have us."

"Well, good, Martha. I'm mighty glad to hear that."

"You just don't know, Mr. Kinard. I'm tired of moving. And we got it good here, with the house and all. Glynis, she likes it here good as me and Frank. So many pretty places for her to walk. Her mind's slow, but she likes pretty things and she likes to walk. Walks in the woods. All over."

When she said that, I knew Martha was thinking Glynis just walked in the evening after she was through picking up eggs and could take care of the baby herself, but I saw Glynis walking around with that baby on her hip in the daytime. Couple times I saw her on the dirt road, sometimes headed toward Mr. Glover's store, sometimes headed toward home. Her with that baby straddling her hip, just wandering around.

Some packing sheds were pretty close to the house, so when the tomatoes started coming in, I lied about my age and got a job grading tomatoes. So did Mary Sue. Hundreds of people worked there in the summer. Mostly the girls graded and the boys loaded the crates into the trains and tractor-trailer trucks. You had to be careful not to get run over, there were so many trucks on the highways and in the parking lot and backed up to the shed. I never could figure out where all those trucks came from.

Once during break Mary Sue and I walked down to Mr. Glover's store to get an RC and when we were coming back up the steps to the tomato shed, we looked over and there was Glynis just as big as you please, sitting up in one of those18-wheelers. Her hair looked pretty out of her ponytail and hanging over her shoulders and she wore red lipstick. She was smiling and it dawned on me I never had seen her smile before, except at the baby. And I never saw her wear lipstick before, either. I figured she'd sneaked Martha's.

"I don't care if she is a moron—she's got enough sense to know right from wrong." Mama said, and she told Pappa.

That night we were working in the egg house and Pappa was going to tease Martha. "I hear Glynis is getting herself some boyfriends, Martha."

"What are you talking about, Mr. Kinard? Glynis ain't got no boyfriends. She don't even talk to nobody but me and Frank." Martha kept watching the eggs she was putting on the light. "Look, this here's another one with a double yolk."

"Well, then, how come Becky and Mary Sue claim to see her sitting up in a big truck over to the packing shed?"

Martha looked at me kinda stupid like and then lowered her head and grew shy again. "I reckon I'll have to ask her about that."

I felt an ache in my chest and I looked at Martha and she looked like she was hurting and I looked at Pappa and it looked like he was troubled 'cause he had said something that disturbed Martha.

"Tell you what, Martha," he said. "I been thinking I'd build you a porch to sit on out in front of your house. How would you like that?"

"I reckon that would be real nice, Mr. Kinard. Thank you." She looked up and smiled at him, but then she didn't say anything else and she didn't look up anymore.

Martha and Frank talked to Glynis that night. I heard fussing and crying. I went into the kitchen and turned off the light, but I couldn't see anything in their little house.

Next day, I saw Glynis, with her hair down again, wandering around the trucks over at the packing shed like she was trying to find somebody. Some men walked over to her and she started laughing, but the machines started up and I had to get back to work grading.

Day after that, I was home fixing myself some lunch and I looked out the window and saw Glynis leaning out a window, trying to put the baby on the ground. It would have to drop some, so she pulled it back in and then climbed out without it and took off. I figured I'd better go tell Martha.

Martha started crying and Frank put his arm around her. "I nailed the damn doors shut," he said, and tears came in his eyes and Martha cried harder.

Glynis didn't come home that night and nobody knew where she was for about a week. Pappa heard that she'd been taken in by Old Lady Jakes, a baggy old whore Mary Sue and Mama and I couldn't see how anybody could stand to touch. Soon as Pappa heard where she was, he went by to get her. He knew Martha and Frank were bad ashamed and he was figuring if he could get Glynis to come with him, maybe they wouldn't have to know where she'd been. But she wouldn't come.

Soon as Daddy got home from work, he and Pappa and Frank took off for Old Lady Jakes' place. They brought Glynis back.

Sometime during the night the Reynolds cranked up their old Chevy and pulled out, loaded down with everything they owned and nothing more. They left a note on the kitchen table for Pappa, but he already knew they'd be leaving, and he was mighty sorry.

Next morning Mama started in again about trash never staying long enough to make moving them in worthwhile. But I don't think it had anything to do with being trash this time.

Patricia Benton, a Charleston native now living in Hilton Head, has won numerous short fiction competitions and received an award from the South Carolina Press Association for feature writing. Her novel, Traveling Shoes, *was a finalist in the PEN/Faulkner Awards. She is currently working on a book-length true-crime story.*

Rebecca T. Godwin

Visiting Hour

Hey, Mama.

I come in and you're sitting there in that chair over by the window as usual. As usual, I come over to you by that chair and you do not look up at me or blink your eyes or in any way at all let me know you know I'm here.

Hey, Mama.

But now you start to rock and I get the comb off your bedside table because your hair's all tangled, just sitting. It's funny, how all you do is just sit here and look out this window, Mama, and sometimes I guess you must lie in the bed, but that's it. That's all you do and still your hair.

Don't rock right now, Mama; let me comb your hair.

I like combing it. It's still thick, though the top is thinned some, and I see your scalp shining through, pink and a little scaly. Like cradle cap. Like I had, Mama. Remember you used to say how that had embarrassed you somehow, made you feel like an unfit mother, and you'd scrub it and scrub it, till my little scalp would be sore. And still it wouldn't go away.

Your hair's so pretty. Silvery and a little wavy. I like the way it makes this turn right here by your ear.

Don't rock, Mama. Not while I'm doing your hair.

I remember Daddy used to trace that wave with his finger sometimes. I don't think he ever knew I was looking. I don't think he ever really knew even that he was doing it.

It was like he'd be thinking of something else, but he'd reach over and let his finger go down that little curve of your hair. Not like he was touching you, Mama. More like he was touching himself.

The light's coming right in on you, isn't it? Right in your eyes. I can fix that. Look at these blinds. Mama, just covered with dust. I'm going to have to talk to them about this. They need to keep this place up.

I pull up the small folding chair, right up close to you, facing you. Your eyes are still so blue, Mama, it's startling. They seem so clear. You know what I wish? I wish I could get in there, behind them, and see what you see. I need that. To know what you see.

I hate how you pick so at your hands. Pluck on the skin of them, nervously, unceasing. They're red—you've been at it some this morning, I guess. Mama, don't do that.

I put my hands on yours and hold them still and still you try to move them and I try to hold them gently and I stroke the top one and you stop. I see your fingernails are so long. So long, Mama. I'm going to file those down for you, okay? So they won't be so sharp. Maybe you won't hurt yourself.

The room's all quiet now—just your steady breathing and my own and your clock and this file.

Should I take that clock out? Does it bother you, the ticking? Does it matter to you, really, what time it is? I'm sorry. Maybe it does have meaning still. I don't know, see? I just don't know.

There, your hands look so nice now. I remember how you used to say they were your best feature. You were always too modest, Mama. You'd hold them up, bare but for your gold wedding band, slender, long fingers gracefully relaxed, and you'd say: When everything else is gone, I'll still have these hands. You'd say: They're my best feature, sweetie.

They really *were* pretty. And I remember when they started getting stiff and when your knuckles got bent like this and I remember that you didn't say much about it, but

I know that you cried the day you couldn't get your ring over the knuckle. You gave it to me, and I wear it now for luck, since the other gold band I had didn't turn out to be so lucky. And every now and again I feel a twinge of something in *my* fingers. It feels almost familiar; something's coming.

You are rocking again, and now you start to hum and it's tuneless but underneath it has its own distinct melody somehow and to me it's sweet. You used to hum to me, remember? I know you did it when I was a baby, but even after that, when I was six or seven. I remember that we'd sit on the rocker out on the porch in the evening right before my bedtime and you'd rock me, slow and quiet, like you're rocking now. You'd rock me, and I'd feel like nothing in the world could touch me then. So safe. And then you'd hum. Not like you are now. But I can still hear enough of it in this new voice to recognize the old. I'd close my eyes and lay my head against your softness and breathe in your smell and listen to your sweet, sweet voice.

Ah, God. That was a long time ago, wasn't it. And yet it just came back to me that instant so clearly. Does that ever happen to you? Are you sometimes thinking of things like that and all of a sudden you really seem to be back in that time? See, that's what happened, just now. I remembered how it felt when you were still my mama.

Look here, turn around here and look at me. Think. Do you remember that time I fell out of the tree and they thought I'd ruptured my spleen and you held me and told me not to cry, that everything would be all right? Well, you lied, Mama. It's not. It's not all right at all. And you don't even know.

You stop humming and I get up and throw the nail file across the room and go to your bedside table and throw the clock down and the glass breaks and the alarm goes off and I grab the picture of you and Daddy and me off the table and I throw it on top of the clock and the glass on that breaks and a little piece of the clock bounces against the wall. And I'm waiting for someone to come because I've made a lot of noise here and the alarm is still going off, but then it stops and no one comes and you have stopped rocking and humming.

I'm sorry, Mama. My voice is very quiet in this very quiet room. And I am. I'm so sorry. And I come over to you and sit back down again. You look at me, and maybe you see me this time. And maybe not. I don't know, see. I touch your face with my hand and your skin is very, very soft.

I clean up the mess I've made and I go to the desk and tell them about your room, that it needs some attention, and then I go back. I mean to say goodbye, to tell you that I'll be in tomorrow or next week or sometime, but I look at your back, still straight, and your head, still proud, and I can't say the words. I mean, what's the use, you know? But I have to say something. So I say, Thank you, Mama. And I don't know if I mean it or not.

Bye, Mama.

I walk down the long corridor and step outside just as Laney pulls up in front, finished with her errands and ready to give me a ride home.

"Hey, Mama," she says, voice all crackling bright. "How's Gramma?" And the sun on her light hair is enough to break your heart.

"Fine," I say. Just fine.

Rebecca T. Godwin has written two novels, Private Parts *(Longstreet, 1992) and* Keeper of the House *(St. Martin's, 1994); her fiction has appeared in* Paris Review *and elsewhere; she received a 1994-95 NEA fellowship in literature. A graduate of Coastal Carolina and Middlebury Colleges, she currently works at Bennington College.*

Laura Lance

THE SOUNDS OF FALLING BOMBS

Someone once told me that it would be like being hit upside the head with a two-by-four. When the Bomb came, everything would happen so quickly we'd never hear it coming, much less, find a safe place to hide. Of course, growing up in a town that manufactured plutonium for nuclear bombs, I was always privy to such worst-case scenario speculations. From scientists to mill workers, from fathers to daughters, and from the very young to the very old, we all made predictions about falling bombs.

People nowadays rarely talk about bombs dropping on our once-small southern town, but there was a time—during and after the Cuban Missile Crisis—when no back-yard barbecue was complete without such talk. This was the heyday of the bomb shelter. Back then, a well-outfitted family fallout shelter was the benchmark by which to measure the Joneses. Converting basements and carving underground caverns from backyard lots became the raison d'être of many fathers as they crafted a legacy of survival for their loved ones. Some of them wove their plans in secrecy; others openly boasted about the luxuries they'd prepared for subterranean life. All of them, no doubt, shared the same nightmare: the specter of screaming air sirens, the visions of brave sons in Dr. Dentons and sleepy wives and daughters, dressed in long white gowns, hurrying to the safety of The Door.

Despite the ominous purpose of these shelters, their arrival was cause for revelry among some families. The Dorns, for instance, who lived across the street from my best friend, Fay Lynn, conducted neighborhood tours of their shelter—a converted basement—complete with a generator, a television, a radio, a jillion games and a bed for their dog, Rudolph. The Dorns' shelter set the standard for excellence. The Jenkinses, on the other hand, had a secret shelter. My sometimes-friend, Chrissy Jenkins, once whispered to me, "Don't tell," as she peeled back the corner of their dining room rug to reveal a wooden trap door with a slot cut out for the handle. "There's not enough room down there for anyone but our family. That's why Daddy keeps a gun." She pulled the door open, and the two of us just sat there in awe, savoring the forbidden safety of that dark, secret room.

My family didn't have a fallout shelter, but Fay Lynn's did. Theirs was a small, no-frills shelter, a single room buried inside the ground beside their clothesline, which contained little more than a wallful of canned goods, six bedrolls and a deck of playing cards. While everyone else was weaving their plans, Fay Lynn and I—being the eight-year old pioneers that we were—wove ours. When the air sirens sounded, I would run the mile-long dirt road to her house, and she would beg her parents to let me spend the night, and they would say yes, just like they always did.

We spent the first week after the shelter's inauguration rehearsing our escape plan, which amounted to little more than sneaking down the metal ladder into that dark cavern, and opening the sacred deck of cards so that we could play "Go Fish."

Like most childhood pastimes, our shelter days were short-lived because, during that summer—which I will always remember as the summer of the fallout shelter—the world around us was unfolding faster that we could take it in, beginning with the two mimosa trees that bloomed like magic beside the fallout shelter. We spent our earliest June hours climbing those trees and waving like monkeys at our parents below, settling, at times, into long spells of silence as we watched the hummingbirds whirl and chatter among the pink clouds of mimosa blossoms. Other days, we played in the green clovered shade beneath the trees, looking for four-leafed clovers, eating baloney sandwiches, and—when our parents weren't watching—slapping honey bees dead with our bare hands. We stayed, perhaps, long enough for all the blooms to fall—raining, as they did, like fairy gowns from the sky. Then we moved on.

Beyond the mimosa trees and the silver-gray splinters of Fay Lynn's backyard fence, there were a million other kingdoms to explore—whole worlds contained within the pastures, woods, trees and barns of our town—all of them existing solely for our pleasure. We took them in without fear because we knew from birth, without ever being told, that our lives were held within an invisible safety net, a net that was tended and watched over by our parents, our neighbors, and every benevolent stranger we had yet to meet. We were, it seemed, impervious to harm.

The dividing line between Fay Lynn's neighborhood and the rest of the world was only a half-block away and was marked by a collapsed, easily-scaled wire fence that encompassed a wide patch of frog-and-bird-chirped swamp. Spread beyond this was an immense field of bright green grass, banked in hillsides of blue bachelor buttons. Some days, we picked bouquets of the flowers and took them to Mrs. Burnette down the street, whose husband had recently died. Other days, we rolled down the hills as careless as puppies before we moved on to the nearby pastures to visit the brown horses and white ponies who happily accepted the apples and fistfuls of grass we brought to them. Over time, we earned their trust enough to sneak an occasional, barebacked ride around their pen. In the near distance, there were dusty, red-dirt roads lined in mammoth magnolia trees, whose long, gracious arms nearly touched the ground. We had our favorites for climbing, where we could oversee

the whole town: the spired church steeple with its scattering
of pigeons, the potbelly of a green water tower with its
smatterings of teenage graffiti, and trees as far as the eye
could see, each of them waiting to be climbed. If there is
such a thing as perfection, that summer was surely it.

So we barely noticed, mid-summer, when the bomb
shelter sprung a tiny leak, then another, and another of
those small insidious drips that fell faster that her parents
could patch them. I don't remember how that summer
ended, but I do remember autumn's arrival, because it
came especially fast that year and lives, still, like a collage
in my memory, its colors layered in their inevitable order:
summer's bright blues and greens overlaid with tarnished
shades of gold, rust and brown. Mrs. Burnette died that
September. Her death brought an unsettling silence to
the neighborhood. No one would say what happened, only
that she died of sadness.

It struck me as odd—as wrong, actually—that life
should go on as usual after her death, but it did anyway.
That Halloween, Fay Lynn and I dressed up as gypsies,
and we dared each other to go trick-or-treating at Sephus
White's place—a large, ramshackle, Victorian beast of a
house. As far as we knew, Sephus White never left his house
and was never seen, except when he banged on the windows to scare away the kids who were always sneaking into
his yard to pull the large iron ring on his hitching post, an
act which was known to cast spells on children.

Our Halloween plan was to brave the steps to his dilapi-
dated, gingerbread porch—something no one else had ever
done—and then we would ring the doorbell, like it was the
most natural thing in the world to be doing. From there,
we would improvise, according to what Sephus White did,
although our secret hope was to make friends with him and
possibly gain entrance to his legendary house. His doorstep
was to be our last stop of the night. The porch was dark
when we arrived, and, despite our bravery and our persis-
tent doorbell ringing, it stayed dark: Sephus White declined

our dare.

And as Fay Lynn and I returned down his long driveway, a dark, graveled passage, shrouded in ancient oaks and over-grown privet, we bragged about our extraordinary courage. I'm sure, however, that she felt just as relieved as I, that we'd averted an encounter with that pale wraith of a man. We didn't hear the rustle in the bushes behind us, the footsteps raced across the gravel, until it was too late. There were three of them—three grown men who ambushed us, banging our heads around like they were tetherballs, all for two sacks of candy. We were lucky. It could have been much worse. I learned that the following spring, although I never told anyone how.

Life went on. Safety nets that never existed unraveled, and I relegated ideas like perfect summers to the past. In time, even the bomb shelters became obsolete, although, to this day, they all still exist in one form or another. Some of them are concealed beneath webbed roots and corroded metal doors, their vent pipes reduced to mere bird perches, encrusted with thirty-odd years worth of rust and bird droppings. Other shelters were converted back into base-ments, which now serve as home gyms, play rooms and offices.

Long before any of this happened, the leak in Fay Lynn's backyard bomb shelter got even bigger, and the lock on the door became obscured by a thick fist of crab grass. Fay Lynn and I found the key one summer day, a couple of months after her parents' divorce. It took all of our strength to break the seal of rust and roots that held the door clamped shut. When we saw how high the water had risen, we immediately began making plans for a secret swimming pool, but something stopped us. We began to see other things in that water—bloated, blue-ticked corpses of bedrolls, bobbling lifelessly in a sea of swollen, rusty cans, their usefulness long-forgotten.

I felt a deep shudder pass through me as I looked into that water. There was something terrible there, something that defied mere words. I didn't try to tell this to Fay Lynn; I didn't have to. We both saw them, drifting in the gathering clouds' reflection: the ghosts in long white gowns, their safety long-since abandoned for the uncertainty of things that fall without sound.

A child of the South, Laura Lance often draws from her native Aiken for her fiction. She is currently working with an agent on her novel, September Songs, *set in a place like Aiken.*

David J. Burt

The Paperboy

She was watching me. I just knew it. Up there, past the gray shadows on her porch, just behind those pulled drapes: She was looking out at me.

I could feel it.

There was no movement. No sound. No indication of life from inside her unlit house at 5:30 a.m.

But when I reached over the fence to set her *Morning News* on the inside lower rail, I felt she was watching me. Or was I just dreaming?

It was the first of June, the first day of summer vacation, and my first day alone throwing C-152, my first paper route.

Me, just turned seventeen, the first of five carriers to arrive at the paper drop, Bill's Gulf Station. Then digging through the mound of bundles for my three: the head bundle with 28 papers, marked "C-152" in red crayon, and two unmarked bundles of 50 papers each. Then neatly tucking the papers into my two new *Morning News* paper bags. Then walking the two blocks to where my route began on McKinney Avenue, where I would cut back and forth across the street delivering my papers.

So there I was: 127 papers still to throw…but I had started imagining things at my first customer's house. Or had I?

I crossed McKinney toward my next delivery but glanced back toward her porch, still shrouded in the morning's darkness. What had Jimmy Chambers told me about her three days before when he was teaching me the route?

His words echoed: "First house. On corner. Widow Lady: never seen her, since she pays in advance by mail to the office. Wants the paper right here inside the gate. Not on the porch. Just inside the gate, whatever the weather."

The Widow Lady, Jimmy had said. I wondered if she lives by herself there in that beat-up, wooden one-story with a waist-high picket fence around the unmowed yard.

Like the house, that fence must have been painted white once. Now the paint was just mostly weathered down to the natural wood. The Widow Lady's fence: just kinda leaning there, held up by its own pickets, enclosing a yard full of tall dandelion weeds.

Even the gate had pulled loose from its top hinge and was tilted crooked toward the house. Yet that was where she wanted the paper: inside that falling-apart picket gate, on the bottom rail.

Squinting back at the house, I knew that it wasn't my imagination. I knew, just darn dead-solid knew for certain, that she was awake and staring out at me at 5:30.

At home, I checked my Collection Book. Just like Jimmy told me. Written in his own handwriting: Alma Tomlinson, 4300 McKinney Ave. PIA: 6 mo.

Every day after that, I could feel her presence but could never see her. She was up there, ever waiting and watching, ever unmoving and still. But waiting for what? Or watching at what? I couldn't figure it. It wasn't like she had to be up, like I did. But she was awake: a silent sentinel to the dawn's faint streaking.

This wondering about her finally got to me after a few weeks. So I tucked a note inside her folded paper: "Mrs. Tomlinson, I'm your new paperboy, David Stewart. Do you want me to throw your paper up by the door?"

The next morning, I found a gray envelope on the bottom rail where I set her paper.

Her reply was scrawled across the bottom of my note. I strained to read it in the semi-darkness. "No. Where you put it is fine."

"No…that's *not* fine," I mumbled.

It wasn't fine because I really wanted to throw her paper up there into the shadows from out here beyond the fence. Wanted to hear it smack against her house in the morning's stillness. Wanted maybe to startle her as she peered out at me. Wanted maybe to disturb her a little bit like she was me.

I could have done it, too. Because I had just about learned to control my throws. I could toss a *Morning News* porchward with a sidearm flick so that it would break in a soft curve from left to right and land flush where the screen door opened. So my good customers could reach their papers without having to step outside.

Or I could zing it hard and straight from the sidewalk so it hit with a loud wap to rattle the screen doors of the houses that let their dogs run loose.

Those darned dogs! Their sudden, fierce guttural growling from out of the quiet darkness always scared me. And shattered my morning's peace. Sometimes a snarling dog would rush out from the bushes at me, and I had to defend myself with my only weapons: my paper bags and papers.

Then I would fly a paper up at that house with a hard right to left curve so it would slam in just behind where the screen door opened. So they would have to walk way out onto the porch in their pajamas to fetch it.

And I made all those throws with the paper hand-folded cleanly and tightly, with the headlines tucked inside so they wouldn't get scuffed or torn.

Oh, I would slap that paper over my knee to fasten the fold securely and then just let it sail! I knew that it would never come loose in mid-flight and float sections all around the yard like Jimmy's used to. Well, almost never.

And that was the way a paper carrier did it: hand-folded

neatly, without using rubberbands, like the young kids did. Except for Sundays, when the paper went to 130 pages and needed to have a rubberband and had to be carried almost right up to the porch before underhand tossing it.

All the porches, except Mrs. Tomlinson's. Just set her Sunday paper inside the gate, where she wanted it.

No sweet sight of her weekday paper's curving arch cutting though the faint morning light into dark recesses of her porch. Nope. She had to be different. I had to drop her paper out by the sidewalk.

That's the way mornings went out there for the next six months as I built up to four bundles: 162 customers. Quiet. Nothing out of the ordinary. At least until December.

The money was pretty tight at home, so in December I took over Sal Levatino's route, C-143. It ran parallel to mine, but two blocks to the east, and only had 84 customers. I figured to deliver Sal's route first, since it started right there at Bill's Gulf and had fewer papers. Just loop through the short route and then back to pick up C-152's papers.

Well, that was the plan. But on the third day of throwing it that way, as I reached over her tilted gate, I found another gray envelope with a note on gray stationery and a stubby pencil inside.

She wrote: "Why are you late with my paper? Alma Tomlinson."

I penciled below her lines: "Added another route. Throw it first."

The next day, on that same gray stationery, her reply was penned beneath mine: "David, I need my paper by 5:45. Alma Tomlinson."

Now that really got my attention. Not "Would you?" or "Could you?" or "Please." Just "I need my paper by 5:45."

The next day, after I threw C-143's first two blocks up to the white two-story on Justin Avenue, I crossed over two blocks on Lauren Lane to McKinney to deliver her paper. By 5:45.

I don't know why I did this for her, and it bothered me,

just like her watching bothered me. Why did she *need* her paper at that time? Why was I doing this for someone I didn't even know?

But I did ask Mr. Miller about her that morning, when I stopped for donuts at his store. Miller's Grocery had been there for about 30 years, and Miller knew everybody in the neighborhood, except for all the renters in the new three-story apartments on Knox Street. And he made the best donuts in town.

"Oh, yeah, the Widow Tomlinson," Miller said softly, as he passed me my usual two glazed, "...she used to teach at Fitzhugh School...Then married a doctor and had two boys. But them and Doc Tomlinson was killed in a car wreck out by the lake. Her a widow at age 40..." He paused to hand me a free chocolate-filled.

He shook his head. "I dunno. It like to have made her give up on life. She just shut herself up in that house. Never goes out at all. Phones in her grocery orders once a week. I used to set the bags over her fence myself after work. Did that for about nine...maybe...10 years. Paulie Jr.'s been dropping 'em off for the last seven or eight. She mails in her bill...Just give up on life, I reckon."

Well, hearing that helped a bit. Three weeks later I picked out a Christmas card for her. One with a manger with shepherds around a crib. Inside, a Christmas message: "May the peace of Christ be in you." I signed the card, "Merry Christmas, Mrs. Tomlinson, David Stewart."

The day before Christmas I put that card in her paper and set it on the bottom rail inside the gate. Then, working quickly in the December cold and darkness, I unscrewed the gate's broken hinge and replaced it with a new one. The gate rested straight and in line with the fence. All this before 5:45, too.

The next morning, Christmas, was overcast, dark, cold, and drizzly wet. At Mrs. Tomlinson's sidewalk, as I pushed her paper into a clear cellophane rain bag, I thought I heard a noise.

From up on the porch, the screen had creaked. Then it swung slowly outward. Toward me.

In the darkness, a shadow emerged from behind the screen and moved out onto the porch. As it started down three wooden steps and out toward the fence, it took a shape, a definition, and then the human form of Mrs. Alma Tomlinson cloaked in a dark blue raincoat. Her head was uncovered, and her silver-white hair, pulled straight back into a perfect bun, seemed to radiate light as it glistened in the rain.

She walked erectly across the yard and came so close up to the fence that I could see her blue eyes, their gaze direct and penetrating.

She offered her open right hand to me. To accept the *Morning News* which I still held. As she took the paper, she extended her left hand with a white envelope in it.

She nodded once as I took the envelope, then turned and walked slowly to the steps, and dissolved again into the shadow by the door. Then even the shadow was gone, as the screen door creaked softly behind her.

Under the street light at the corner, I opened the envelope there in the rain. Her message: "David, thank you for fixing my gate. Alma." Beneath her name she added: "And here's for delivering my paper where I want it by 5:45."

I pulled out three worn one-dollar bills. I folded these and put them securely inside my wallet. To keep.

Then, because I knew that I would never see her again, I placed Alma Tomlinson carefully inside my mind: the haunting image of the silver-haired woman intensely alone. Yet calm, centered, almost serene.

And I went back to delivering my papers.

David Burt teaches English at Francis Marion University in Florence. He is a two-time winner of the South Carolina Fiction Project and has written and directed two award-winning video-documentaries.

Cynthia Boiter

THE PROPOSAL

It was so cold sitting in the pick-up truck that I just about couldn't feel my toes anymore. My teeth had gone past chattering to jumping, so I clenched my jaw tight and that set my whole head to trembling, just like those tired old brown leaves clinging to the scrub oaks outside my momma and daddy's house. Just like me they were hanging there, shaking, wanting to let go, but afraid to fall.

It was quiet under those November stars, with the wind barely whistling through the doors of the truck and the tree limbs coughing as they pushed and tugged at each other above us. It was too cold for crickets. Next thing I knew, Avery reached over with that big old arm of his and slid me across the cracked vinyl seat of his truck to where our thighs almost touched and the gearshift banged hard against my knee. He didn't mean it to hurt. With my knee still smarting and the back of my legs burning from the cold of the seat, he gave me a kiss. At first, it scared me like I don't know what. It was a lot rougher than I'd always thought a kiss would be. Pretty soon though, my mouth softened up and it got easy and nice and I could feel myself start melting away. Before I knew it, I found myself kissing that man back, and me, who never in my life kissed a soul what wasn't in my family, well, I was feeling fine. But my head was full.

It was really going to happen and I was going to let it. It was just like being born all over again. The world was about to turn on over and be sweet because, I, Mary Anne Lane, was about to become Mrs. Avery Watson and any minute now I would walk right into that house right there and tell my momma and daddy that it was so. Nothing else in the world mattered. All the sack-cloth dresses and knotty rubber bands I'd worn in my hair—they didn't mean a thing. Always being last to bathe my body in a tub of dirty, lukewarm, been-used water didn't matter at all. I didn't even care about not going to the Sweethearts Dance, even though the boys had picked me as a senior class contestant. Who knows, I just might've won, if I'd a had a dress that amounted to something and Daddy'd let me out the door. But none of that mattered. The world was new and fresh, and I was never gonna sweep a dirt yard again in my life.

I felt like I could breathe.

Avery got out on his side of the truck and stood there for what seemed like forever before he came around to get me. When he opened the door and put his hands around my waist to lift me off the seat, it must have been a month before my feet ever touched the ground. He made me feel dainty and precious, like Doris Day. He was Prince Charming and I was Cinderella and that 1949 black Ford pick-up was my pumpkin carriage. I didn't even mind that Momma had left her spit jar on the front porch steps. We just walked over it like it was a bug on a log. And, when the door to the house didn't want to open because the rain swelled it up so, Avery leaned his big shoulder against the stubborn wood and pushed, and slew that dragon right then and there. He was strong.

The heat from the wood stove parched dry our faces as soon as we got inside, and there wasn't a lamp lit in the house. But I could hear Doreen and Peggy giggling in the other room. They weren't asleep, but they were playing like it so Daddy wouldn't fuss and Momma wouldn't cry. Little pockets of sage and pepper and turkey smells still hung in the corners of the kitchen. Momma had left a plate on the table with slices of fried fatback, baked sweet potatoes, greasy with lard, and two pieces of cornbread on it. Avery saw it, once't our eyes got used to the dark, and reached over and grabbed himself a piece of bread. I didn't want to say anything, but I knew Momma and Daddy would both a'thought that was too familiar of him to be doing.

Momma had only seen him three or four times before. One Sunday afternoon he was waiting on our front porch when we walked up from church. I could see him sitting there from way on down the road, a long time before he saw us a'coming. He'd brought me a handful of petunias he'd picked from his granny's yard and for Momma, he'd brought a sack full of scuppernongs that grew down by Tobe's Lake.

"How do, Mr. Lane, sir," he'd said, reaching for Daddy's hand.

"Miz Lane," he said, holding out the sack.

We sat on the steps and watched ants crawl in and out of hickory nuts while, in the house, Daddy slept in his chair with the batting hanging out of it, and Momma and the girls fixed Sunday dinner. I kept waiting on them to call me in to come do my share, but they let us alone pretty much. Except Doreen and Peggy kept peeking out the window and making kissy noises. When I heard Momma's chipped blue plates bang down on the table and the chicken stop sizzling on the stove, I told him it was time for me to go in.

He stood there in the yard, whistling and fidgeting, with one foot on the stoop and the other planted firm in the clay, while I ran a pint mason jar full of water for the flowers. Momma looked at me over the pan of green beans she was dumping into a bowl and said through her teeth, "Was you wanting that boy to eat Sunday dinner with us?"

"No, Momma," I whispered, dried clay clinging to the back of my throat. "He's just a boy." I started putting the biscuits on a platter, burning my fingers with every one, and dropping them so the flour from the tops flew like mist in the air.

I didn't dare look out the window to see if he was still

there, but when I heard Doreen say, "There he goes,"
I glanced over once. He was walking up the road with his
hands stuffed down in his pockets, kicking stones every
step of the way. It was funny the way the sight of him made
me feel. Not entirely good. He could just as well have eaten
with us. Would've been glad to have eaten with us. Momma
would've been glad to have him, mostly 'cause Daddy
would've had to behave. But I reckon I felt a little pleased,
too, not to let him in. And a little bit scared, to see him
walk up the road by himself, not knowing for sure whether
he'd walk back down it again or not.

Another time, we had all rode in to Greer to get tobacco
for Daddy, and buttons for some dresses Momma was
making. There he was. Lord, he looked fine, walking across
the street with a paper bag in his left hand and a Coca-Cola
in his right. He had on this pale green summer shirt with
blue stitching along the collar, and his sleeves were rolled
up high on his arms. He had a pack of cigarettes, Lucky
Strikes, tucked in his pocket next to a blue fountain pen,
the same color as the stitching on his shirt. The same color
as his eyes. My heart about stuck to the back of my chest
and I could feel the heat crawl up my neck toward my face.
My ears burnt red. I was scared to death Daddy was going
to see, and I didn't know what he'd do if he did.

But it was Momma who saw. She looked at me, then she
looked at Avery, then she looked back at me for a long time.
I couldn't read her face, to save my life. Then she sent me
back into the remnant shop with a nickel for a spool of
white thread and, when I got back, Daddy was talking to
some men about a tractor and Avery was nowhere in sight.

Five months later, there we stood in my momma's
kitchen, him eating cornbread and me feeling like it was
Christmas morning and afraid to look under the tree.
There might be a bag of nuts, or there might be a pair of
socks. But there hadn't ever been no tin doll under the
tree for me.

I lit the lamp on the table and the room took on a glow.

Momma's gingham curtains, bleached almost to pink, fluttered as the heat moved through the house. Light bounced off the wire of the pie safe and made it sparkle like silver threads. The deep green glasses set on the shelf above the icebox caught the same light, like emeralds, and I swear, they glowed, too. I poured Avery a cup of buttermilk and he turned it up and drank it without a breath. I quick wiped out the cup, dried it on a towel, and put it away.

"Well," he finally said, taking in a breath and looking at me all matter-of-fact. "Let's do it."

The faucet dripped into a worn black pool in the bottom of Momma's cast iron sink. Four, five, six times. "What we gonna do?" I finally said and tossed my chin up like I wasn't sure what he was talking about.

"Well," he said again, looking out the window over the sink into pitch darkness that went on and on. "You think you're gonna be able to spend the rest of your life with me, or not?"

I had to blink the tears out of my eyes right then and there. See, my momma loved me and she showed it, whenever she could. But my daddy didn't give a flip for none of us, and most of the time he didn't seem to care much about Momma neither. All I knew of a daddy, or a husband, was fussing and drinking and sleeping and, one time, he told me that if I didn't have a good head of hair, I'd be ugly as a bird.

So here's this good-lookin' man, with a decent job at the mill, and a bought-and-paid-for truck, reaching under the hair laying on my shoulder and holding the back of my neck with the softest, sweetest hand, next to my momma's, I'd ever known. His nails were clean, and his skin was smooth, and he smelled like something other than gin or sweat. Puddled in his eyes were two little pools of tears shining scared in the light of the lamp and, Lord have mercy, I'd've been a fool not to have loved him, too.

But I was no fool.

I knew good and well that every man who ever walked

either beat his wife or he didn't. As far as I knew then, drunkenness was as much a way of life as visiting the cemetery come the first Sunday of the month, and eating new potatoes in May. Still, I was a girl and girls don't want to bother with worries like that. Even though they was what kept me most company when I lay in my bed at night.

The girls had gotten quiet, Daddy was snoring, and the faucet still dripped.

It could be, I caught myself thinking. I moved closer so I could stand by him on the rag rug, still wet from supper dishes. Looking down, I could make out pieces of aprons and overalls and baby dresses woven into it, and little whiffs of ammonia floated up from our feet. Maybe a man could make a living and eat his wife's biscuits and not raise the first hand to her. I'd heard that kind of talk—from the preacher and some of the girls at school. It might be that money could be in the bank, and flowers grow in the yard, and blessings be said before a meal. Drinking might be nothing more than a little something out of a jar on a cold dove field. I caught myself thinking.

The first few drops of rain plinked down on Momma and Daddy's tin roof and I took in the smell of washed dust as it drifted up from the cracks in the floor.

It could be so.

But not even forty-five years ago, young as I was and as much as I'd'a given anything to, never would I have ventured a wish or a prayer of how good it really could be. That nightfall could bring whispers not to wake the babies, and touching feet, when it was too hot to curl up in bed. Wrinkled hands, rubbing knots out of stooped old, garden-weary shoulders. Flowers on my kitchen table. And looks from blue eyes that could go so deep into my soul they'd draw up fists full of memories and sore places and sweetness so fine it'd bring a lump to my throat in the middle of the day—and even now as I remember his face, gone these many years. Never would I have guessed. That was the kind of thing only angels could tell.

By then, the rain was pouring a steady song on the roof. I felt light in my limbs, like my elbows could float and pick me up off the world. So, I took hold of his hand and let go of whatever breath I had left of my own, and we walked into the little hall where Momma kept her ironing board set up. Cases of empty Coke bottles were stacked on the floor. With the third knuckle of his middle finger on the hand I wasn't holding, Avery tapped three times on Momma and Daddy's bedroom door.

"Mr. Lane, can I have a word with you, sir?"

My toes were still numb.

Cynthia Boiter is a freelance writer whose essays and non-fiction have appeared in such publications as Southern Living, Woman's Day, Family Circle, Parenting *and* Bride's*. She lives in Chapin with her husband and two daughters.*

MIDWIFERY

Near midnight, Joshua wanted to know when his
mother was coming home.

"Go back to sleep," David said. "She'll be here soon."

"Why don't you sleep?" Joshua asked.

"Josh, where's your pajama top?" David left his seat
by the window and crossed the living room. He touched
the boy's shoulder. "It's too cool to run around here half
naked."

"They're all dirty." He stared toward the floor.

David tried to think of something to say. He looked
down and saw Joshua's pink feet. The boy was watching
his toes as they stretched and wiggled.

"You go put on one of my T-shirts," David said, guiding
the boy to the door. Joshua sighed. "Go on, now."

David waited by the door until he heard him crawl into
bed. He wondered about Joshua, about what the boy felt.
Joshua, Connie's son by her first marriage, was a quiet
child. He rarely questioned his mother and David, although
he seemed to know when they were ridiculous. If an eight-
year-old kid never complains, does that mean that he's
perfectly balanced?

An acidic pain cut across David's stomach. A glass of
milk might soothe the burning. The wine in the refrigerator
door caught his eye. Connie bought that bottle last week,
the day after she came home from the midwives' confer-

ence. It was the only alcohol that had sat in that refrigerator since they'd been married.

She'd said a glass with their meals couldn't hurt anything. In a week and a half, she'd drunk three quarters of the bottle. That wasn't so much. But David was afraid if he started, he'd return to his old habits—the wild binges that could last for two or three days. Maybe he should tell her that, instead of making those quiet, self-righteous refusals. He closed the refrigerator.

After 3,000 miles of hitchhiking, David had been halted by a lone nail. One rusty nail through his treadless tennis shoe and he was stuck. While the last driver coaxed him back in the car, then sped him to the clinic, David never guessed that he'd live in Fulton for the next four years.

The doctor, a large man with white hair and red-rimmed eyes, sponged the foot with warm water. After he'd cleansed the wound, he probed for damage. He didn't appear concerned about the blood that spattered his smock.

"I'll probably have to owe you for this," David said from his bed. "I'm about broke."

The doctor stayed bent over the foot, working his fingers around the wound. "Where you from?"

"Washington State. I've been traveling for a few weeks."

He began to wrap David's foot with a huge bandage. "You a student?"

"I quit college last year. My last job was picking apples in Yakima. When that ran out, I started thumbing. The rides were good, so I decided to keep moving, for a while, anyway."

"Maybe this is a sign for you, son." The doctor clasped the bandage and stood up. He stared directly at David. "I didn't get to be a doctor by moving around. I had to focus on something. You're not going to be any good to anybody, even yourself, till you can do that." He tapped David's shoulder. "You pay me when you earn some money."

David hesitated.

"Just check at the front desk." The doctor smiled. "If Connie gives you any trouble, you tell her you've got to stay off that foot a while. That her dad says you're looking for a job in the meantime."

David limped around Fulton, deciding what to do, while he waited for the foot to heal. After x-rays, the doctor found a buried speck of the nail. He reopened the wound and excised the problem. By the time David was mobile, Connie had helped him line up work as a brick mason's helper.

David didn't remember walking out to the porch. He wondered how long he'd stared at the stars. If the toilet hadn't flushed, maybe he'd have fallen asleep. Joshua usually didn't have trouble sleeping, didn't often get up in the middle of the night. David hoped the boy would go straight back to bed.

The empty asphalt at the end of the driveway held David's attention, even after he started for the door. Not long after they'd met, Connie had urged him to become a Christian. She revealed her past "sins"—two abortions. They were before Joshua, before her first marriage, when she was still in high school. Her father, one of the few doctors in town, performed the operation without help— they'd wanted no one else to know. Three weeks later, he repeated the procedure. She'd been pregnant with twins.

Her argument was as consistent as her friendship, and, after several months, he felt himself weakening. On a spring night, when they were naming stars and constellations, he agreed to convert. Then they married.

Three years later, he couldn't understand why she'd bring up those abortions again. They'd been praying to have children. Then she went to that conference, met the midwife who made her feel guilty about her abortions.

"She asked me if I'd named my aborted babies," Connie had whispered. "She said that until I named them I was avoiding the issue, that I wasn't dealing with my grief."

"That was ten years ago," David told her. "What good

can it possibly do to go back to that? Sometimes you have to forget."

"But I can't forget. That's just it. This woman says you can never forget until you deal with it."

"So deal with it. If you think naming them will help, let's do it now."

"You don't understand. She found the father, and they named their baby together. That's how it has to be done."

"You're right. I don't understand. I raise Josh as my own son, you tell me I'm his father. I can help you name your babies."

"That's different."

The conversations ended with no resolution but their both being upset. Several days of that and she wore him down. Go, do it then, he told her. Deal with your grief.

About 4 a.m. David cupped his hands against the window and peered out. The porch light revealed the scattered gravel in the driveway. The trees formed a black wall.

She could have left, done her naming or whatever she needed to do, without telling him she was going to do that. But no, she wouldn't do that. She didn't only need David's knowledge, she needed his consent.

The midwife told her the naming was an emotional experience. Connie had said that only once. He should have asked what that was supposed to mean. Was the midwife a married woman now? Was the lost-and-found father a high school boyfriend?

Brock Lehman. He spun around the mountain roads, this year driving a red Triumph. He was single, worked in his father's restaurant on the lake when he wasn't at Appalachian Mountain for ski season. Good old Brock. Sounds like Good Old Boy. Good old Brock the Good Old Boy. How long does it take to name a baby?

David needed another glass of milk, but he had the

wine in his hand as soon as he opened the refrigerator. The tapered bottle had a nice, frictionless feel. Its cool glass felt good against his forehead. She'd drunk only a few small glasses. He wasn't going to start.

Over three years neither of them had touched alcohol or drugs. All their food was natural. They strove to live on a spiritual plane. The religion was one thing, but there was also Joshua. David had thought they were setting an example for the boy, creating a healthy environment for him. Then one day the wine was in the refrigerator. Never in the house before, but David had to bring up the subject.

"Oh, a little drink with meals doesn't hurt anything," Connie answered. "Jesus drank that much."

"But I thought we weren't going to drink."

"We might have to rethink some of our beliefs. We should never let ourselves become rigid."

David understood now that she had been changing for months, maybe since her father had died. The pattern was similar to the Constance-Connie thing. When he'd met her, she was telling everyone to call her by her Christian name, Constance. Over time, she got tired of reminding people of the change, then gave up. David bet he was the last person to use the name Constance. He bet Brock never used it at all.

Five birthings in the last three months. She lived with the expectant parents, sometimes for days, waiting for the delivery. Joshua seemed a little more dependent on David after each of Connie's absences. And each time she returned, David felt a little less of her had come home.

Several months ago they were making love more than ever. They talked about having their own baby, and they made love more. Then something twisted. She didn't get pregnant. Something happened in the relationship, and they weren't making love so much. Then less and less. But talk about babies never stopped. It's her business. The baby business. Comes after monkey business. David was getting punchy, but dawn was close.

What else did they put in her head at that conference? Her only lively conversations lately were about how she had to see Brock Lehman. David thought if he said okay, she'd find something else to talk about. That was a gamble. Maybe now she'd have nothing to say. Or they could talk about Brock—his styled hair and designer clothes and singles' lifestyle and money to burn and everything they'd left out of their lives. That was who she was convinced should help her name her aborted babies. Who she had to visit at his apartment where they could be alone to select two good names.

Joshua wanted to know where Connie was. His eggs sat untouched.

"She had an emergency birthing."

"The phone never rang," Josh said.

"Now how would you know that?" David asked. "You weren't awake the whole..."

Josh stared, hair mussed, dark patches under red eyes. He seemed ready to fall asleep at the table. David realized that he and the boy looked alike.

"Let's get ready for church," David said.

Josh came back in a tie and dress shirt. Every piece of clothing he wore, David had selected for him. They got their last haircuts together, same as always.

"How do I look, Dad?"

Like a miniature of me. The gravel crunched, and they went out to meet her. She stopped short of the porch, her mouth almost a smile, then quickly expressionless.

They looked at each other a minute. Suddenly she brightened. "Want to know what the names are? Celeste and Brock."

"Did you have an emotional experience?" David didn't know how he had let himself say that. He'd sworn he wouldn't.

She looked at him like he was odd. "What are you and

Josh doing up this early?"

"You forgot it's Saturday. We're going to church."

"Now? The only service this early is the foot-washing."

"Can I have the car keys?"

"You can't take my son to a foot-washing. That service is for adults."

"I'm his father," David said. "And he knows more than you think."

"You didn't tell him…"

Josh was already in the front seat. David backed the car gently down the driveway, gripped the steering wheel to steady himself. He looked in the rear view mirror: She stared, unmoved from where she handed over the keys, disappearing as they disappeared.

Andrew Poliakoff is a full-time lawyer in Spartanburg. He received his Bachelor and Law degrees from the University of South Carolina and a Master of Fine Arts degree in creative writing from the University of Oregon. He taught English at the University of South Carolina at Spartanburg, then Converse College. He has been published in Emrys Journal, Touchstone, *and was a winner of the* Washington Fiction Project.

Wesley Moore

Airwaves

In the moonless night this trailer goes nowhere, resting on concrete blocks in a rural lot. There are two live oaks but no grass; the dog, a shepherd, sleeps in the dust. Across the road, in dead cornstalks, crickets buzz.

Over the hum, in bed with her mother, Bobbi hears the occasional swish of a truck or car sucking the night away. She listens intently for the beginning of the sound; hope and dread swelling as it approaches...

Daddy?

But it passes roaring, then whispers into oblivion, an 18-wheeler rushing down the road.

Bobbi's been looking at clocks all day. The big hand and the little hand. You couldn't catch them, but they moved, and so did the day. The road and field got yellow and glowed down slowly into night. The screen stamped her nose as she leaned against it, but none of the cars was her daddy.

That whirring must be the clock, its light blocked by Mama, bumpy like a mountain with the sheet stretched over her. This new clock makes the softest of sounds, but shhhhhhhhhh, swoooOOOOOshhhhhhhhhhhhh... swoooOOOOOOshhhhhhhhhhhh...swooOOOOOshhhhhhhhhhhh...

Rice steaming...the fan churning...Mama slicing an overripe tomato...Daddy not drinking beer while he listens to the Atlanta Braves on the radio...

~ 64 ~

A car door slam jerks her awake and the bed creaks as Mama gets up, breathing hard. Light stabs through the open door, then it is dark again.

Loud clunks, up the metal steps, no knock on the door, but herky-jerky rattling—it's Daddy—his voice growling, but too slow, like he's forgotten how to talk. And Mama starts in on him, like she always does, but Bobbi wishes that Mama wouldn't, that they all would go to sleep and in the morning everything would be all right; everything forgotten, Daddy smiling and rubbing her hair with the palm of his hand.

She puts the pillow over her head then her hands over her ears. It makes Daddy sound like that Merle Haggard tape that got ate up. She doesn't want to hear, but lets up a little on palms pressing down.

"Bobbi," she hears Mama say, "what about Bobbi?"

"Lockhair, lockhair…" Daddy starts saying, but she can't make out the words and presses her palms down hard again.

It makes an ocean sound, as if she's pressing seashells to her ears. She remembers long ago last summer, a trip to the beach, a happy time, her daddy lying beside her, Mama on the other side. Her daddy didn't wear a shirt, and she could look at his Valentines. One on his arm says "Wanda + Wayne." But there's one on his chest right over where his real heart is, saying Bobbi: B-o-b-b-i, Bobbi.

The dark of tightly closed eyes beneath a pillow blanches slightly and shuts down dark again. The door latches, and she senses Mama looming over her.

"Take that pillow off your head, honey," she says between sniffles. "You gonna suffocate yourself."

"Is Daddy all right?"

"Your daddy's sick in the head. I'm sick and tired of putting up with it. I ain't putting up with it much longer."

The radio in the living room blasts on. Daddy turns it up and down, up and down, up and down.

"What are you doing, Wayne?" Mama hollers, "What

are you doing that for, Wayne?"

The nice man's smooth voice wobbles when Daddy twists the knob, then music like they play up at K-Mart goes LOUD-soft, LOUD-soft, till Daddy shifts the dial, stopping on a country station, then the volume whips whoop-woo, whoop-woo, whoop-woo.

The bed is quaking with Mama's crying. Bobbi puts her hand on Mama's high hip, whispering in her ear. Mama's nightgown is wet, and her bare skin feels loose. Bobbi begins to stroke her beauty-parlor-stiff hair, saying over and over, "Don't cry, Mama; don't you cry."

But sleep is dragging Bobbi away like undertow. The radio waves are rocking her; her daddy's rocking her. He's not smushed-up dead on the highway somewhere No-sir-ree, tomorrow afternoon he'll be as sweet as pie and swear to God he'll never do it again, and maybe even drive her up to K-Mart to buy her something pretty.

"Don't cry, Mama," she says. "Don't you cry no more."

A two-time Fiction Project winner, Wesley has also been published in
The New Southern Literary Messenger, The Upwith Herald, *and* From
the Green Horseshoe: Poems of James Dickey's Students. *He teaches
at Porter-Gaud School and lives on Folly Beach with his wife, Judy Birdsong,
and their two sons.*

Lori Wyndham Jolly

OBJECTS IN MIRROR ARE CLOSER THAN THEY APPEAR

Maybe what distracted me was the desire to stuff the GameBoy up my brother Logan's nose if he didn't start talking to me. Maybe it was my getting wrapped up in the lyrics of a Tom Petty and the Heartbreakers album. Maybe it was the magnificent scenery on I-95. Probably it was trying not to scream and to neatly consume a Dove Bar at the same time, in July, in my mother's boyfriend's Mustang convertible.

The CD I'm playing is *Southern Accents*. I'm wishing Brad—isn't that the perfect gigolo name, Brad?—would let me put the car's top down. Even though Mom and Brad are riding two cars ahead, he'll notice if I change anything on the Mustang in any way. I would really like to crank up the bass on this CD player; I turn the sound up a little instead. I can always turn it down before we stop. Logan slips the GameBoy headphones out of his ears and wrinkles his face at Tom Petty. "Moldies," Logan says. 1985, the date of this album, is old to him.

"It's your age, moron," I tell him, polishing the last molecule of dark chocolate off the wrapper and putting the paper into Brad's little wussy litter bag that hangs off the cigarette lighter.

We have slipped back three cars and a semi now. For several minutes, I lose sight of the Mercedes entirely. Soon we'll leave the interstate for our hotel; Brad will want his car back, and I will have to give up the sensation of driving 75 miles per hour. On a curve, I can still see the Mercedes ahead, a boxy maroon shape. It looks slow, but Brad says it can bury this car. The Mercedes engine is big and powerful. Brad says the Germans know how to build things with no mistakes. I wonder about Brad's opinion of Hitler. Probably some kind of buddy feeling. That Mercedes was paid for with Dad's life insurance benefit; Brad persuaded Mom it was an investment. Dad's insurance policy is also why we're moving to Florida and leaving Virginia, where I grew up, where all my friends are.

Logan sighs, tucking the GameBoy into his backpack at last. Low batteries, probably. I'm surprised he doesn't have one of those things where you can plug it
into the cigarette lighter.

I'm signaling to pass a Holly F arms truck and looking back to make sure the passing lane is clear. Behind us, a classic car that looks like *Christine* speeds up. There's an intense-looking crew-cut guy driving—probably can't stand someone to pass him, the jerk. After he passes us and the chicken truck, I change lanes. I check the rearview as I pass the semi, and then I check the wing mirrors. In the passenger side mirror, I see that Logan's face, pressed against the glass on his side, is streaked with tears.

I open my mouth, but up ahead the Mercedes is signaling, and there's no time. I look frantically around for the instructions Brad wrote for me on a Hardee's napkin, but it's probably balled up somewhere on the floor. Anyway I can just tail Brad. Horsepower or no horsepower, he's too paranoid to speed through some redneck town. We take an exit that says ALLENVILLE ALABASTER IVY and get off on a woodsy state road. Almost immediately there are potholes. There is no other traffic on the road; Brad seems to be going about 50 miles an hour. I can relax. No problem keeping up.

In my peripheral vision, Logan is wiping his eyes on the sleeve of his Levi's jacket. I have no idea what to say, but he speaks first, trying to keep his voice steady.

"Kim, you ever miss Dad?"

I slow up a little, hit Cruise Control. "You know we fought a lot." I glance at him; he nods. His eyes are still red. "It made me feel guilty when he died, you know? Like I didn't love him enough—so he got taken away."

"You still feel that way?" Logan asks. He is looking out the window at the swamp. I am having trouble looking at him too.

There's almost no quaver in my voice. "Well, let's put it this way—have you heard me argue with Mom about anything lately?"

I'm not exaggerating. I haven't. He hasn't either. Except on a sitcom, two more perfect children you'll never find. Marcia and Peter Brady, that's us. If Carol Brady wants to marry a bank teller only twelve years older than me, we don't complain. I had a zany farewell slumber party for my little friends; Logan labeled boxes of stuff to be unpacked "Kitchen" and "Den" and "Garage." I served the movers coffee. I pulled out all our photo albums that Brad had slipped into the trash and I hid them in two moving cartons marked "Kim's Underwear."

And now I'm driving the Mustang and keeping the two of us out of the grownups' hair. And I haven't burnt holes in the seat with the cigarette lighter or ripped off the rear-view mirror or scratched four-letter words on the spoiler with a pocketknife. And I am trying to keep Logan's head likewise together.

"Look, hon," I say to him, "we're screwed. We can pitch a fit if we want to, but it's too late. Mom is going to marry Brad whether we like it or not. We're going to Florida, like it or not. All we'll accomplish by fighting it is making sure she'll never listen to us again. You know I'm right."

He nods, but his bottom lip is all puckered out, and he looks about five years old. It would probably make me mad, except I feel the same way.

I continue, "We're an exclusive club: people in our

family who know that Brad is a jerk. Sometime we probably will have to fight him. Something really important is going to come up, where we have to convince Mom we're right, and…"

"Mom marrying an idiot isn't important? Moving isn't…"

"What I mean, is, Mom won't trust us at all if we act like whiny brats, Logan. She'll think we're just being stupid kids. You want Brad to be the only person she listens to?"

I know I'm right. I want to major in psychology when I go to college. Only thing is, being right doesn't make me—or Logan—feel any better. I lay my hand on his shoulder, which is so tense it feels almost skeletal. He is staring out at the pines again. Fine.

At that moment, Brad's CD changer slips in the next CD, Jimmy Buffett's *Songs You Know By Heart*. "Cheeseburger in Paradise" blares out, so silly that we both break out laughing. I snort through my nose, which makes us laugh even harder. "I'm hungry," Logan says, grinning. I feel better. He joins me to sing the ordering part, "I like mine with lettuce and tomato, Heinz 57 and French fried potatoes…" We used to sing most of that album along with Dad. Oddly it doesn't make me feel sad. It feels comforting, like a team song, maybe. Even if we look like idiots.

Up ahead, I can see the Mercedes signaling a left turn, pulling up in front of a white frame restaurant that obviously started life as a farmhouse. It doesn't look like the kind of restaurant Brad likes; it probably won't have a no-smoking section or take traveler's checks. The hand-painted sign says Benny Bee's Barbecue.

"Dang," Logan says, still smiling a little. "I really wanted that cheeseburger." I am smiling too. I like the Coca-Cola sign nailed onto the porch and the blue-painted shutters and the picnic tables under the trees. I'm willing to bet there's a jukebox in there.

I turn the CD player down, then switch it off as I park near the Mercedes. As I'm reaching under the seat for my purse, I also find the directions to the hotel. Logan draws in his breath sharply and I straighten to see where he is looking. A young couple, a black man wearing Bugle Boys and a Hootie T-shirt, and an Oriental woman in a loose, flowered dress, are getting out of the Mercedes. It has South Carolina, not Virginia, plates. In short, it is not Mom's car. The couple walks up the steps and the man pauses to adjust the tilt of the Coca-Cola sign.

"I'm still hungry," Logan says.

"Ah hah," I say to Logan.

He says, "What you were saying about being whiny brats—do you think that might also apply to getting sidetracked in Hick City in the precious Mustang? As far as us looking stupid?"

I nod. I can feel my ears getting pink. Wise big sister.

A chirruping sound comes from the back seat: Brad's cellular phone. Logan picks it up, unfolds it and answers. "Oh, hey, Mom." He grins at me. "Kim had to go. Girls gotta pee every ten miles!"

I sock him in the thigh, and he wags a finger: ah-ah-ah.

"Oh, yeah, Mom, she's coming back. Here she is." He opens, then slams his door, hands me the phone.

"Hey, Mama," I say, giving Logan a dirty look.

"Is everything all right?" Mom says, her voice crackling a little. I wonder if we are almost out of range.

"Oh, sure." I look over at Logan, who's making a pitiful face. *I'm hungry*, he mouths. "Mom, there's a burger place on this exit. Would it be okay if we went ahead and ate there? Logan says he's starving."

There is a long silence. Brad says something, I'm not sure what. "Hold on," Mom says shortly, and my heart sinks. Brad won't stand the Mustang out of sight this long. Brad says something else, but Mom's hand is squeaking over the mouthpiece and I can't hear. I bite my lip. If she says no, I don't know how much longer I can be Marcia Brady. I hear Mom say distinctly, "Well, I trust her, Brad. Now you trust *me*."

Her voice gets louder. "Kim? That's fine, honey. You have the directions to the hotel? And enough money?"

I say yes.

She tells me to be careful and hangs up. As I flip the phone shut, I can feel my pulse beginning to slow again. I let out a big lungful of air as I say to Logan, "That was dirty." He smiles. "Do you think they have cheeseburgers?"

They do. They have cheeseburgers and a jukebox, and the furniture is metal dinette sets with checkered table-cloths. Logan orders his cheeseburger medium rare with mustard and an onion slice. I order mine with the lettuce and tomato and I put Heinz 57 on it. We manage not to break out laughing again.

After I get my directions straight, we head further down the state highway, which the cashier said curves back to meet the Interstate again. On the way, Logan pulls his GameBoy back out and plugs in new batteries and a Tetris cartridge. I smile, shake my head, and press Play on the CD player again.

We pass a trailer park; on the side of the road a young girl, ten or eleven years old, is supporting her little brother on an adult-sized bike. His feet barely reach the pedals as she runs alongside. He pumps his fists in the air like Rocky as they gain speed.

I look back at them in the mirror as they shrink into the distance. Both of them are laughing, their hair blowing in the Mustang's windy wake. They don't seem too worried about losing control or falling or about the darkening sky.

Logan looks up. "Whyn't you play that Buffett CD again?"

I smile and reach for the dash. I think it's time to fold down the top.

Lori Wyndham Jolly is a graduate of Furman University and an expatriate Southerner now living in the United Kingdom. She dedicated this story to her parents, who gave her that rarest gift, a happy childhood.

Kent Nelson

A Clear Territory

Alene had not been able to leave until after work, and by the time she got south of Tucson a few miles, the sun was already low over the mountains and the heat was ebbing.

Carl did not necessarily expect her. His invitation, as usual, put the burden on her. "Look," he'd said, "if you want to come out to the cabin on Friday, I'll be there." He'd given her directions.

She had no trouble finding the "T" at the intersection of dirt roads in the foothills east of the interstate. After that, she was to go 7.2 miles on County Road 38—clear enough—but vandals had obliterated the road sign with bullets.

The terrain did not give her much to go on. The hills were serrated rocks, cactus, and brushy arroyos, and in both directions from the T, the road disappeared into dry sand creeks that descended toward the river and the interstate behind her. If Carl had only said north or south, but he hadn't.

So she chose by flipping an imaginary coin. What could happen? At worst, she thought, she'd have to drive 14.4 extra miles.

Three and two-tenths: she kept track on the odometer.

The road traversed a ravine, then another, still running parallel to the river below. Creosote and paloverde filled the sandy streambeds, and higher up were bajadas—gentle slopes accreted from the erosion of the mountains.

She was uncomfortable in this arid country: the shadows of saguaros and ocotillos, the dark facets of rocks made her uneasy. She was used to the wooded hills and seascapes around Boston.

Carl was different from the men she'd known in the East. Even after six months, she barely knew him. He was gentle, quiet when he spoke, and he never forced her into anything she didn't want to do. But he knew her story. After eight years of marriage, her husband announced one night he was in love with someone else.

She'd moved to Tucson because it was far away, and gradually, pain had dissipated into bitterness. Carl had once said something curious: "Nothing is worse than being scared."

The gravel road zigzagged up a steep grade, and from the rocky outcroppings near the track, she picked out the shapes of a decrepit man, a cathedral with a broken spire, a headless bird in flight. Already the freeway seemed miles ago.

The dust drawn up behind the car was golden now in the pale light, the dead grass honey-colored. The mountains above her drifted in and out of shades of black and pink.

"You're welcome to stay the night," Carl had said one night, months ago, when she'd given him a ride home. "But you don't have to."

She'd laughed at his manner. "So it doesn't matter to you?"

"That's not what I said." He held her hand, but at the same time looked away from her out the side window of the car.

"I understand," she told him. "You want me to choose."

"I want you to be peaceful," he said.

Five and eight-tenths miles. She was not peaceful now. At the top of the hairpin curves, a plateau opened out for a mile or so, and the road wound through sparse junipers. In the heat of the day, nothing moved, but when darkness started, the land came alive.

Every animal had its own definable territory, Carl said, whether in grasses, in saguaros, or in the bushy draws. At night they were safe. Deer emerged from the creek bottoms to forage on the hillsides. Owls came from their secret roosts to hunt for mice.

The cabin was his, Carl said. That was his place, the place he felt most like himself.

She coasted down into a deep arroyo, then accelerated on the upslope and gathered speed. For a moment near the tip, the road vanished beyond the rise of the hill, then reappeared suddenly in the middle of the curve. She skidded on loose gravel and bounced hard upon a rock.

The tire blew instantly, loose rubber thumping against the rim. "Hell!" she said aloud. She braked quickly, but could not hold the car, and it slid off sideways into the ditch.

She found a flashlight in the glove compartment, waited a moment to calm herself, then got out and stood on the side of the road. Even if she could have changed the flat, she was not certain she could extricate the car. And where was Carl? Damn his vagueness. Was he on this road or miles away?

She had never been so conscious of the slide toward darkness. The mountains were gray now, and the sky seemed to fall away from her, as though receding each minute into deeper blue. Color faded as light squeezed out of the day. The yellow grasses turned ochre, green junipers black. Stars came out. She saw no headlights, no lights of houses.

The heat had eased further, and a cool wind blew off the mountain. Of course there were limitations: darkness was one, the road another. She could not venture cross-country dressed as she was, even with a light. She checked the odometer: 2 miles to go, a little less. Having come this far, she might as well see whether Carl was here.

She sprayed the beam of her flashlight back and forth

across the road, listened to her own footsteps snap on the gravel. What bothered her most in that country was that life was defined by lack. Water was scarce. There was no margin for error. When there was no rain, the ocotillo rolled its leaves. Animals roamed the darkness because it was cooler; they did not waste energy. They adapted.

She had suffered, yes, but that was not the same as carving a niche. She was careless, indulgent, detached. She had that luxury. In what place was she most like herself? What a strange phrase! Carl was a good man and gentle, but what had he ever made her do?

She stopped still, aware of a movement ahead of her, and she shined the light carefully over the tan strip of gravel. A snake moved slightly, its body defined more by languid gesture than by its differentiation from the ground. She moved forward two steps, three. As a girl, she'd always run from snakes and had screamed once when she had touched one. So it surprised her now that she crept forward in a tucked position, trying to hold the light steady in her shaking hand.

She might have walked around the snake—it could not be far now if the cabin were there—or she could have turned back. Instead, she crouched down. The snake coiled itself into a tight mass and lifted its head, its rattle blurring beside its yellow eyes.

She had heard of mesmerizing animals with light. Hunters spotlighted deer, and she had seen rabbits paralyzed by headlights upon the highway. But she did not know whether it would work on a snake. The wedge shaped head swayed slightly as she crept closer. How far could it strike? She kept the light steady.

Five feet, four, closer still by inches. The body was a beautiful pattern of black diamond lace. She could see the vertical black slits in the yellow eyes, the black and red tongue lapping the air.

She circled on her hands and knees, and the snake followed the light, moving only its head. Alene slid along slowly, slowly, inches at a time. Her arms ached from holding the light, but she was not shaking now.

She felt a calm take hold of her, a kind of silence. When she reached the other side of the circle, she began to back away, slowly still. She stood up and moved backward a few steps, then turned away.

She walked quickly for a few minutes, then stopped to catch her breath and shut off the light. Without a moon, the ridges of the mountains were nearly inseparable from the sky. She smiled to herself, feeling the space and the quiet, and she lifted her arms into the darkness to let the breeze cool her body.

Kent Nelson has published three novels, four collections of short fiction and more than ninety stories in America's best literary magazines. His novel, Language in the Blood, *won the Edward Abbey Prize for Ecofiction. Other awards include two NEA grants, five PEN awards, and the Nelson Algren Prize. He lives in Colorado.*

Anne Creed

Voice of the Dog-God

Every time I walk to the fence the dogs bark and jump up against it, like there's some kind of magnetic force that lofts them upward with a tremendous racket whenever anybody passes by. My daughter home from college for the summer walks back and forth and back and forth in front of them, just to see them levitate. Sometimes she makes strange, soft dog noises to them from our den window to get them to bark. At first they are quiet, listening for the voice of the dog-god. Then they howl in praise and adoration, building into a frenzy of competition for favors that never come. Jackie, my daughter, laughs, then is moved to pity.

She does not have to live with them year round. They are not nice dogs. And they are miserable, so their only entertainment is to cause others misery. These dogs are half-starved mutts my sorry neighbor collects, probably to make me mad.

He collects dogs and runs his stereo to drown out their noise. Sometimes I can hear him playing his ridiculous country music. And the worst thing is, I think he's had enough of them, too, so he's poisoning the dogs and trying to blame it on me.

So even though I have forty people coming for my daughter's debutante luncheon this afternoon—out on our back porch and around the pool, even though I told her the dogs would run us all inside—I can't do a thing about the dogs. Except hope that he is poisoning them and it will take effect before one o'clock.

Jackie calls me inside. "Mama, you got to quit staring at those dogs. Don't make eye contact. They'll be barking all afternoon."

"My staring's got nothing to do with it," I say. "They bark all night when I'm trying to get my eyes closed. I was checking to see if they'd been poisoned."

Jackie looks at me funny. I know she thinks I'd poison them, too. And me the former president of the SPCA.

"The caterers want to know where to put all the ice."

"In the deep freeze," I say. Where do they think it goes? In the bathtub?

The dogs go into an uproar every time the caterers— two pudgy women, a scrawny young man and the three waiters they've brought along—go out to their truck. I turn on Mozart's *Requiem* and blast it all.

Last night she asked me if I would cash in a CD set aside for her college education so she could go to Greece for the summer and be a shepherd. I think she was serious.

She has two years of college left, for goodness' sakes. And what does she know of sheep, living in a place where the weather gets hung up around the 100-degree mark for days at a time? The only sheep in the whole state are in an air-conditioned exhibit at the zoo. Who'd look out for her, with the wolves and the whatever coming to eat the sheep and finding her. I don't like anything about the idea, including the boy who gave it to her.

The house looks particularly nice with flowers in every room. Raymond would say it looks like somebody died, but he is in Mwandi with a group from the church on a medical mission, so I can have flowers wherever I want. He is a physician and does these trips every few years. He'll be back in ten days. I used to go with him.

Right when we get to the Agnus Dei, I get a tap on the shoulder. It is the blond pudgy caterer.

"The man next door says your music is upsetting his dogs," she screams into my ear. She looks very unhappy, as though she does not cater to Mozart. I will have to turn him off, I can see. How strange it must be to drive around town feeding the same people over and over again, but feeding them at different people's houses.

Even though the debutante balls aren't until Christmas, there are about two parties a week all summer honoring this or that girl. The same people go to all of them, just wearing different clothes. Most people try to outdo each other. Last week, there was a casino party down on the docks and a murder mystery party at the Victorian mansion that's also a funeral home. The mortuary received a body late in the evening, giving all the girls the creeps, until it turned out it was one of the dads playing a joke.

The caterer is getting flustered, I can tell. She's run out of places to put stuff and is shoveling my pile of mail that's collected on the kitchen counter into a drawer. She thinks I don't see her.

The food is in big bowls and trays all over the kitchen table and the counters. Pickled shrimp and Vidalia onions, a wheel of Brie covered in brown sugar and almonds that will be caramelized before serving, hearts of palm with Gorgon-zola piped in swirls down the center, Belgian endive stuffed with lobster mousse, smoked turkey cream wrapped in romaine, marinated vegetables, quail for grilling, wild rice and chocolate pecan pies and lemon pies. We'll be having Bloody Marys and Mimosas first, then wine with lunch. I hope I get a chance to eat.

Jackie comes in from the back yard. "Mama, you're not wearing that, are you?"

I have on my red-checked shirtwaist, the one that makes me feel like a colorized June Cleaver. How must I ordinarily look, that she thinks I would wear this thing for company?

"What would you like me to wear?"

"Your blue outfit you got at Snooty Hootie's."

I look like an aging hooker, or somebody from Texas with new money, in that get-up. But it is her party. And maybe if I wear what she wants, she will try to get along about that Greece thing.

We've bought a new outfit for her for this party. A pink linen sundress that shows off her pretty back and shoulders.

"Mrs. Lunce? Mrs. Lunce?"

It is one of the caterers. They can't seem to do anything themselves.

"What is it?"

"There isn't enough room in your freezer for the ice and the sorbet. Our contract said you would provide us storage space."

"I'll take care of it, Mama," Jackie says, going toward the laundry room where the deep freeze sits. "You go get dressed."

So I do. She's much better at organization than I am.

There isn't much reason to get dressed up. I've known most of these people since I came here 25 years ago after marrying Raymond; I looked better then and that's how I hope they're seeing me. I try to do the same for them.

I can see my horses through the window. How much better it would be to be riding one now, trotting through the woods with Jackie. Showing her fox squirrels you never see in the suburbs, and scaring up some white-tailed deer who'd scare our horses even more. But she's seen all that now. Now she's wanting sheep. And worse.

There is a frenzy outside in the dog world. Maybe the poison is taking effect, or maybe they are cannibalizing each other. I hope whatever it is, they are finished by one o'clock.

"Mama, those dogs must have been starved," Jackie says as she plops down on my bed.

"They're like some people; they always look hungry," I say, thinking of her boyfriend.

"They're not starved now!" she says. "I gave them all of Daddy's moose meat."

There were at least 300 pounds of moose meat in the deep freezer from Raymond's trip to Alaska a couple of years ago. He believes in eating what he kills, but since we never have much of a taste for game, it usually sits in the freezer until it's inedible. We even had a rattlesnake in there once. Might be there still. But even so, I'm not sure feeding Bullwinkle to the dogs is a good idea.

"We need to get the meat back," I say. "If those dogs are getting poisoned, everyone will think it is us."

"They're not getting poisoned," Jackie says. She does not know about poisons, how you can't tell they're there.

I look out the window. The neighbor's dogs are dragging moose meat all over their yard. It looks like hyenas after a kill. Maybe something Raymond is seeing in Africa. I hope my neighbor isn't poisoning them. I will report him to animal control on Monday. It is time for this to end. But right now, it is almost time for our guests.

The dogs are strangely quiet, with only an occasional yelp, when I top off the water in each table's centerpiece. Jackie has chosen yellow, peach and white. The florist has left a white gardenia for Jackie's shiny, dark hair. With fifteen minutes until the guests arrive, I light the votives in the floating arrangements of roses, daisies and freesias and set them loose in the pool. It seemed silly to get candles for the daytime when I ordered them, but the day has turned out to be a little overcast with a nice breeze. The flowers drift around the pool like they have somewhere to go.

I hate giving this party, but hope it is good enough.

Jackie has changed and signals to me from the doorway. I bring her the gardenia and help her pin it in her hair. It is heavy, and wants to point downwards. She is the most beautiful thing I have ever seen.

The other mothers and daughters arrive; some look like sisters. Money buys many versions of happiness. I wonder if

I should be envious. I wonder if something is wrong with me that I am not. If it means I am tired of life.

Jackie steers the first group of guests to the back porch and then disappears. I, too, would like to leave for a moment to catch my breath.

"Well, Freddie Lunce, do you remember me?" I look at the woman who has grabbed my arms and kissed my cheek. She is tall with a dark tan, green eyes and hair the same blond as half the women here. "I'm Suzy Curtis—used to be Suzy Davis—from Nangaree! Finally, somebody here in Providence I know from way back."

I hear myself squeal in delight, and wonder how I manage it. I don't have any idea who she is, or how she ended up at my party.

"Suzy," I gush. "It's been too, too long!" I hug her back, catching a whiff of her Opium perfume and feeling her stiff linen and lace sleeve under my hand. Even her fabrics make me tired. I look to see if she is with one of the girls; maybe then I can place her. But all the mothers and daughters are mingling. "Can I get you anything to drink?"

She squeezes my hand and I squeeze hers back. "It is just SO GOOD to see you!" she exclaims. "You look wonderful."

Mindy Banks walks by with her daughter, Sally. "Mindy," I say, "Do you know Suzy?"

I pass Suzy off in this way. Mindy would have done it to me.

The dogs aren't barking. Even with all of these strange people in my yard, they are quiet. I can see them lying around the neighbor's yard. I feel a surge of panic that I must get this party over with and check on the dogs.

Surely he wasn't really poisoning his own dogs. But I had seen him take hamburger meat, wrap it around something, and toss it to the dogs. They fought over it, and the next day the big black one, the one who had run away from the group eating something like he had won out, was dead.

My neighbor left the dead dog in the yard until the following day, then put it in a garbage bag and slung it into the Herbie Curbie.

As a joke, I told Raymond I poisoned the dog. For a moment, I could tell he believed me. For a moment, even I thought it was true.

Raymond helped build the Mwandi hospital, with money, labor and love. I went with him the next year, thinking I could help, even though I'm not a nurse. Maybe an extra pair of hands would be useful.

We worked side by side, and I was useful. There were four visiting American doctors, plus the one local one and several nurses. People came from villages a day's walk away, bringing their sick relatives, their children. The simplest medicine is a miracle in the jungle.

I worked with the pregnant women, giving them vitamins so their babies would be healthy. I told them I took these vitamins and that these pills would do many wonderful things. Raymond said that their diets were probably better than ours.

On Sunday, their preacher thanked God for blessing them with so much. And he didn't mean us; he meant the river. Through a translator, we heard: "Whatever we need, God sends. We have fish. We have water. We have sun, and music." A look around the crowded church showed me they knew he spoke the truth.

The next morning a woman and her daughter came to see us, bringing gifts. We had two chairs, so the mother and I sat and smiled and gestured at each other in what had to pass for a language. Her daughter, who must have been around eight, climbed off and on her mother's lap, and was fascinated by my hair, which was long then, hanging in a braid down my back. I let her stand behind my chair and play with it, which was a little strange because she would pull it hard enough so that my head would tilt up toward the ceiling. I was relieved when she grew tired of this game and I could focus my eyes on her mother without suddenly being interrupted with a view of the ceiling. I didn't know that she had picked up my bottle of sleeping pills. I didn't know that she thought they would make her hair grow long and shiny.

Raymond and Dr. Preston were able to save her, but it was a horrible couple of days.

Someone else can hand out vitamins. I never went back.

As soon as the dessert dishes were removed from the tables, it began to rain. A light spitting at first, just to tease people into thinking they didn't need to hurry. Then a deluge that chased them all into the house, where they stopped just long enough to leave.

The rain roused the dogs, too. I am relieved, but suffering from a little post-party remorse.

"Are you sorry we didn't have a dance for you down at the club?" I ask Jackie as we nibble on leftovers and watch the rain erode the ice sculpture—a leaping salmon—we abandoned down by the pool.

"Everybody has a dance," she says. I am worried that she feels left out until she adds, "Boring."

"But it would have been nice if your father were here," I say, wondering why I can't let it go.

"Not for him. He hates parties."

"For you, we could have talked him into going."

Jackie shrugs. "Mom, it was a great luncheon. That's all the attention I want. Now can I go to Greece?"

"When you graduate."

"Mom, it's a summer job. Tending sheep."

When I don't say anything she goes inside. I stay on the porch and count my neighbor's dogs. There are eleven of them. Either scratching fleas or trying to find a way out of the rain.

She comes back in her bathing suit and heads to the

pool. I'm glad it's not thundering, so we don't have to haggle about that.

Several of the dogs run to the fence barking at Jackie. All my pity is gone.

I am very much afraid, and very much alone, with my daughter sulking in the pool and my husband healing others in Africa. Even these people who bore me, the party guests, provided some comfort.

I will swim with Jackie. It doesn't take long to get suited up; I sit on the edge and dangle my feet in the water.

"This feels good. Even the rain," I say.

"The flowers are nice. We should always have floating arrangements," she says.

Good, I think. We are speaking. "We should always have party leftovers."

"It was a nice party," she says. "Thanks."

I start to ask her who Suzy Curtis is. If she's somebody I'm really supposed to know. But I don't care if I know her or not. She is gone. Good riddance.

I start to ask her if we should call her dad. But that's just to fill the silence between us.

I start to ask her questions I know the answer to, just to hear her talk.

She begins to swim lazy laps, the kind you do when you've had two Mimosas and a heavy lunch. I slip into the water and bend my knees so that the water licks at the bottom of my ears. The rain drips off my nose. I point my bottom lip up, aiming my breath, and blow the drops off.

If she does not go to Greece this summer, she will still be gone. She grows out of my arms, into the world.

I hear the splash of her strokes and feel a few drops as she swims by. Or is that the rain?

Maybe I should offer to go with her to Greece. To take her on a trip. But it is not sheep or Greek countryside that calls her.

I dive under and swim to the side of the pool. Hovering

next to the cool blue tiles patterned with yellow seahorses,
I listen to my voice letting out soft, high-pitched dog howls.
I hear the sound of dog collars shaking. I softly yowl again,
and wait.

They answer, the mournful cry of the pack.

Anne Creed is a two-time winner of the South Carolina Fiction Project and was awarded the South Carolina Arts Commission's Fellowship in Fiction for 1996-97. Her fiction has been published nationally and her plays have been produced in both Carolinas and Off-off Broadway. She received her Master's in Fine Arts from Vermont College and now freelances from her home in Hopkins.

Robert W. Heaton

A Close and Holy Darkness

Even as a child, David would sit alone for hours meticulously copying stories from books in long hand, word by word. When he finished or when he was satisfied with the length of his transcription, he would copy the title and put his name down as author. David had always wanted to be a writer. Many years later, when he finally started writing his own stories, he found himself curiously bereft of ideas. A good story could be written about anything, he theorized, from the most mundane and inconsequential to the most dramatic and traumatic. But when he sat down to put pen to paper, the only stories he could devise were filled with death, murder, and violence.

He first noticed the lump on his arm on Sunday, but he consciously chose not to think about it. Health problems were the last thing David wanted to consider on this end-of-summer, September day when the heat bore down on him like a physical weight and the humidity made the air feel like warm Jell-O.

The lump was on the soft underbelly of his forearm about halfway between his elbow and his wrist. It felt like a soft pearl anchored to something just under the skin. It would slip around like a bed of quicksilver to avoid direct pressure, but it was not painful unless he pressed on it.

On Monday, he phoned a doctor's office and told the nurse about his lump. Yes, he had insurance. Yes, he had just noticed it. No, it was not growing. No, it was not painful. No, it was not discolored. No, he had not been losing weight. No, he had never had cancer. And so on and so on. When he got off the phone, he lay down, resting his head on the arm of his sofa, and closed his eyes.

David pressed the lump on his arm between two fingers, stood up, and walked to a window. On the street below, pedestrians streamed by in an endless procession. Even if he did not know it was Monday, he could tell that it was by the expressions on the faces he saw walking by. And it was only faces that he saw, not people. Each of them was in their own world, their own bubble, apart and removed from everyone else around them. One of them could catch fire and no one would notice unless they got singed walking by. He squeezed the lump on his arm and returned to his desk.

David was not close to any of his coworkers. Though he had worked there for eight years, they did not understand his humor, his politics, or his view of life. Nor did he understand theirs. His doctor's appointment was scheduled for Wednesday morning. He did not tell anyone about his lump. Nor did he tell them that he was going to see a doctor. Among these people whom he had known for most of a decade, he felt as isolated and alone as the pedestrians he saw walking by on the street below.

He found comfort in solitude. He had lived alone in his college dormitory and, after graduating, moved into a one-room basement apartment just off campus where he lived while performing his alternative service as a conscientious objector. He enjoyed company, but never longed for companionship. When he went out to clubs and bars, he went alone, and he watched the partygoers and drunks like he would watch a theatrical performance. David thought of himself as a harmless voyeur. At times he felt he was watching his life pass him by, but was powerless to do anything about it. He was not sad, but could not honestly say that he was happy either.

David was ten minutes early for his doctor's appointment. After completing the appropriate and necessary forms to the staff's satisfaction, he waited patiently for one hour and ten minutes. Then, he was led back to an examining room where a nurse took his blood pressure and temperature. Twenty minutes later, the doctor walked in holding David's file. The doctor was a short man, about sixty years old, with a full head of hair that was reddish and disheveled. The skin on his face was pink, and wrinkled in a way that suggested he had lived all his life in the city. He looked Irish.

As they talked, the doctor examined David's arm and probed his lump. He felt under his arms, listened to his chest, and looked at his throat. When the doctor fell silent and started recording notes in David's file, he started to worry for the first time. A few minutes later, the doctor stood up and exited the room as abruptly as he had entered it. The nurse who had led David to the examining room soon returned bringing with her a package wrapped in green cloth and a tray with a hypodermic and needle, gauze bandages, several packages of suture, and a few other items.

The nurse, who looked too young to be giving anyone orders, directed David to remove his T-shirt. She then positioned him on his back on the examination table, silently attached a metal extension arm to the table, and proceeded to tape his arm to that metal extension. Then, she left the room.

David was cold and immediately noticed itches all over his body. He closed his eyes and listened to the quietly blasphemous copies of Sixties rock hits. They seemed to be concentrating on the Rolling Stones. He wondered if one of them had died. David was middle-aged now. He might as well get used to the daily indignities that seem to fall disproportionately on the old and infirm. The spotlight above him, which should have been trained on his arm, was pointed directly at his face. It did not bother him as long as his eyes were shut, but he did not want to keep them closed. He wanted to look around the sterile, cold steel room. He wanted to memorize it. His nose itched. A lushly orchestrated "Jumpin Jack Flash" played slowly, quietly on the radio.

When the doctor and nurse finally got down to the business of cutting, David was relaxed again. He had closed his eyes and nearly had dozed off. The injection of Novocain stung, burned, and then he felt nothing. He was not one to watch himself being injected and cut open, so, for the duration of the procedure, David either closed his eyes or counted the tiles in the ceiling

As he listened to the metallic surgical tools clicking against each other, he could only wonder what was happening. When he felt the skin pulling near the crook of his elbow he surmised that the doctor must be sewing up his wound. Then, he heard the unmistakable sound of tape tearing and he knew that the doctor had finished and that his arm was being bandaged.

He turned his head and looked at his arm. It was neatly bandaged, though he could see a few patches of blood around the edge. On the floor was a bucket filled with sponges and bandages stained red, pink and orange by his blood and the disinfectant used to prepare his arm for surgery. The doctor was grim faced. On the stainless steel counter behind him, David saw what he assumed to be his lump in a small glass jar filled with a clear pink fluid.

The doctor told David that he did not like what he had seen. He was sending David's lump to a pathologist for analysis and the pathologist's report should be back in about twenty-four hours. The doctor promised to phone David with the results as soon as the report came back.

On the walk home, David thought about what the doctor had said. He had not liked the look of David's lump. David wondered why. It looked innocuous enough in its little glass jar. Was that sad looking, little piece of torn, bloodied flesh the genesis of his undoing, he wondered. Was that his killer? He stopped for a moment to clean his glasses. The trees looked greener, the sunlight yellower, and the sky bluer than he remembered.

When David got home, he phoned the office to inform them that he would not be in for the remainder of the week. Then, he sat at his typewriter and stared at the screaming whiteness of the blank sheet of paper facing him. His arm was beginning to hurt now. He looked down at the bandage. Blood was starting to soak through it. Perhaps he should write about his surgery, about his own red badge of courage. He felt for his lump, but it was not there. His prodding fingers caused a dull ache to throb in his arm.

He remembered the pain medication the doctor had given him. He had only been home for fifteen minutes, but it seemed like hours. David walked to the kitchen for a glass of water. The clock in his bedroom ticked so loudly that he could hear it across two rooms. He opened the refrigerator for some ice.

He saw the five beers sitting on the bottom shelf and, for a moment, considered picking one up. They had been there for three months, two weeks and five days. He had bought a twelve pack on the first Friday in June and downed seven of them right away. David knew that if those beers were not in the refrigerator, he would never have been able to stop drinking. He knew they were there and each day that he did not touch them was a small victory, a quiet achievement he could take pride in.

When he was young, David would drink himself into blackness and write the most insipid, unintelligible drivel imaginable. He would awaken in the middle of the night wishing he were someone else. For the past five years, he drank only on weekends. There was an occasional bottle of wine, but no hard liquor. Once or twice a year, he would let his consumption get ahead of him and wake up with a hangover. It was nothing like the old days when his hangovers were as regular as the rising sun.

With his more temperate lifestyle came the sinking feeling that he had been consumed by middle age. Now, he would awaken in the night worrying about aches and pains in his midsection. He would lie awake staring at shadows on the ceiling wondering what would happen if he suffered a stroke or heart attack. These were the worst times for him. He judged his life a failure and questioned his ability to stop drinking even if he wanted to.

On Monday morning, he woke up in disgust. After showering and making himself a bagel and coffee, he resolved that this would be the last morning he would obsess about the myriad mysteries of his aging body. He was not an alcoholic. He knew that. And he would not commit himself to teetotalling, but he would stop drinking for a month or two to let his body rest. Since that day, he had felt better about himself. He had even started writing again, but his stories still drifted in the direction of murder and mayhem.

David let the refrigerator door close and sat down at his kitchen table. He stared vacantly at the door he had just closed for several minutes. "I am Sam. Sam I am," he said. "I do not like green eggs and ham." Then, the pain in his arm snapped him out of his reverie. He walked to the sink, filled his glass with water and took his pain medication. Though it was still light outside, he went to bed and slept all night long.

When David's clock alarmed at 7:00 a.m., he was already awake. He usually hopped right out of bed and showered, but this morning he decided to sleep in. The traffic noises outside sounded oddly musical. He listened to his neighbors greet one another in the hallway and felt, even in his silence, that he was part of a huge symphony. David had never been a true neighbor to anyone, but he knew them all, even if they did not know him. He could recognize their individual voices flowing in and out of a larger musical context outside his window and outside his door.

For a moment, he questioned his sanity. Maybe my lump is cancerous, and it has metastasized to my brain, he wondered, but, just as quickly, the thought left his consciousness and the street music continued. David desperately wanted to put his thoughts in writing or in musical form (if only he could). His art would live even if he did not. Thoughts and feelings were flowing uncontrollably through his mind. Some were pleasant and some were not, but they all begged for expression and recognition. David was surprised at how calmly he accepted his impotence or, at least, his incompetence in this area. He wanted to say some words to "the close and holy darkness." He wanted to pray but did not know how.

He was growing older now and had stopped fighting the battles of the young. His submission, albeit gentle, had been a drawn-out affair and only now did he understand the depth of his acquiescence to time. It was a battle everyone lost and only the young were foolish enough to fight. The sadness he felt was liberating.

Art was for the young. They search for it, study it from difference angles, in different lighting. They "ooh" and "aah" over it. They analyze it and debate it with friends. He no longer attended art openings or went to galleries. Over the past couple of years, David had been drawn to music, especially classical music.

Music is for the old. It can be brought into their home and enjoyed in the solitude of a living room or bedroom. There is no need to pontificate or extrapolate. It is a solitary, introspective pleasure which is beyond words. It is enjoyed for its emotional resonance, not as a conversational dynamic.

Tears rolled down David's cheek. Perhaps his lump would kill him. He did not know and did not want to. For the first time, he was feeling like a part of a whole, not a separate, isolated and lonely individual. He did not want to die, but, if he did, the world would go on spinning. Nothing would change. He thought of his writing. David had lived his life at one remove from reality. Just as an overzealous photographer regards life as a series of images rather than a flow of experience. David observed the world around him the way a playgoer looks at a stage.

The wound on David's arm was throbbing now. He had been touching it and feeling it all morning. Blood was beginning to show through—a crusty, brownish blotch at the wrist end of the bandage. He sat quietly listening to Brahms's Fourth Symphony. He looked down at his arm, at the bandage with the small brown patch of dried blood. From where he sat, he could watch the people walking by on the street below. He wondered if the woman in the green, ruffled blouse knew about the quarter-sized grease stain on the rear of her skirt. He wondered why the impeccably dressed gentleman with the stylishly trimmed salt and pepper hair had not gotten the middle button replaced on his Armani jacket. There were so many sad faces. A few looked frightened and a few of the people appeared to be genuinely happy.

When the first side of the Brahms' symphony ended, David did not want to leave the window to turn it over. He wanted to remain where he was, to continue to embrace the pedestrians below with his eyes. He wanted to go outside and touch the strangers who walked past his windows. He wanted to hold them and make them glad.

As he walked toward his stereo, his telephone rang loudly. His clock read 4:38 p.m. It must be his doctor phoning with the pathologist's report. The ringing of the phone jolted him for a moment. He stared at the telephone feeling both frightened and angry. Would the doctor tell him he was going to live or die? Could he return to his old comfortable life and return to work or would this be the beginning of an endless procession of clinics and hospitals where he would fight small painful skirmishes and grand, inglorious wars with an unseen enemy until he was too weak to battle any longer?

David still had his hand on his bandaged arm. His lump had assumed a sort of life. It had evolved into a kind of transforming essence. God-like it had breathed a life into David's spirit that he had never known. As the phone continued to ring, David valiantly stood his ground moving neither in the direction of the stereo, the telephone, nor the window. He did not want to talk to his doctor. He did not want to know. He wanted the telephone to stop ringing before he moved again, as if fearful the doctor could somehow hear him moving around his apartment through the unanswered telephone.

When, at last, the ringing had stopped, David forced himself to move again. He turned his recording of Brahms' Fourth over to the second side. Then, he walked to his refrigerator and got himself a beer. As he settled back into his window seat to watch the people below, he realized that he had never tasted a beer that felt as good going down. Nevertheless, he drank only one. Then, he lay down on his sofa and he went to sleep.

Robert W. Heaton was born and raised in Anderson and graduated from Emory University in 1971. After graduating, he lived in Atlanta, New York City, and Berkeley, California, until 1985, when he returned to South Carolina. He currently works as a disability examiner and lives in Anderson with his wife and daughter.

Thomas L. Johnson

Nocturne on a Winter's Night

I

Marmac Hotel, Midnight, Friday, January 16.
Beginning of a Two-Day Pass

Tonight Rachmaninoff played Columbia.

If someone were to say to me in a few weeks or months or years that the great Russian pianist and composer had actually come to give a recital in South Carolina, I would scarcely believe it. But I know it's true. I heard him with my own ears tonight, although it is already like a dream.

Lieutenant Delano, Sergeant Trotter and I got back to Fort Jackson from the nightmare of our Army detail in town at the Genillats' a little before 6:30 this evening. My weekend pass started at 7, by 7:30 I had checked into the Marmac, and at 8:30 I was seated in a packed Township Auditorium with thousands of others from all over the state who had come to hear the Maestro, ready to forget for a while the day and the week and the past month.

The fireworks began when Mr. R., after making his way in a measured, austere manner to the piano at center stage, opened the evening unexpectedly with a rendition of "The Star Spangled Banner"—playing it as only Rachmaninoff could have, those initial bass notes descending heavily and deliberately, and then reversed, resounding like the dramatic opening of one of his concertos. When he finished, the audience, already on its feet, broke into wild applause. It is safe to say that none of us ever heard the national anthem played like this, each note struck like the clear, strong tone of a giant bell. It was a tolling that everyone obviously felt, living as we are only a few weeks this side of Pearl Harbor.

I wonder what Mr. and Mrs. Genillat would have thought and felt if they could have heard it. What were they doing the moment it was played? What were they doing now, in the first few minutes of this second day in what for them is a new age?

With scarcely a second for the audience to sit down again, Mr. R. launched into his first programmed piece of the evening, a Liszt transcription of Bach's "Prelude and Fugue in A Minor," which established the sense of the night: liquid mathematics, suspension upon suspension, resolutions made only after all doubt and confusion had been played out, and then not made easily, but haltingly and deliberately.

Bach, the man of faith, had all those children. Did he ever lose one, or outlive any of them?

II

The next big piece Mr. R. played was Beethoven's "Sonata Appassionata," which some no doubt thought was the peak of the evening. Others complained that the last movement was a romp-through. But I liked the Maestro's insistence on not sentimentalizing the work.

Sitting in the first box to the right of the stage were some of the Fort Jackson brass and their ladies. I recognized Major Gen. and Mrs. J. P. Marley, Col. and Mrs. George Shea and Lt. and Mrs. Earl Kindig. Their places in that box allowed them to see Rachmaninoff's face better than I could, but his hands not at all.

I wonder which of them first received the message for the Genillats, and which of them have children.

III

Two works by Schubert, the "Impromptu in A Flat Minor" and a Liszt paraphrase of the "The Trout," ended the first half of the program. The "Impromptu" was nocturnal in feeling. Could it have been written after 1823? "The Trout," lilting as it is, represents but an interim lyric in the life of a composer who died young, unmarried and childless, but also of a man who would set Heine to music: "What life takes away, music restores."

Early this evening—it would have been sometime between 5:30 and 5:45—I wanted to say something to the father who stood in the entrance hall of his home, the afternoon paper crumpled in one hand, and wished to embrace or at least hold the hand of his gray-haired wife, who, called in from the kitchen where she had been preparing dinner, stood next to him, wiping her hands on a towel, her eyes growing larger and larger as she looked at the three of us standing just inside her front door in our Army uniforms and began to listen as Lt. Delano read the contents of the communication in the brown envelope and realized what she was hearing. If nothing else, I should like to have offered them tickets to tonight's Rachmaninoff recital at the Township.

IV

Mr. R. began the second half of his program with three works by Chopin: two mazurkas and a nocturne.

It was the nocturne, "Nocturne in D Flat Major," that constituted the climax of the evening for me. It was the single most exciting and unforgettable number in the recital: a concentrated, relentless expression of nerve and feeling and will. It began with a single high note soaring aloft for a minute—almost in slow motion, like an eagle in flight—and then it multiplied, developed, expanded, only to fall and shatter, but then to rise again, Phoenix-like, toward another life of its own. This piece was six minutes of sheer grace, an incredible mixture of simplicity and complexity, of plaintive melody and drilled rhythm which caught up everything we had been through today, in these weeks, in a lifetime. Chopin, this sickly, childless, spoiled dandy of a composer, had also discovered in the face of his own mortality what needed to be said and how to say it.

V

The Maestro next played three pieces of his own composing. The first two, "Humoresque" and "Daisies," could have come out of Gershwin's Charleston, redolent as they were of Southern street scene and lullaby. During the rendition of "Daisies" all I could think of were these unseasonably mild days we're having right now and the only lines by Henry Timrod that stick with me from school:

> Methinks that I behold,
> Lifting her bloody daisies up to God,
> Spring kneeling on the sod.

His "Oriental Sketch" began with the pounding drive of a railroad locomotive. Perhaps he's ridden the Orient Express and played recitals in Tokyo, Shanghai and Manila.

VI

Rachmaninoff is an old man with the face of a child in which the wrinkles are thus strangely incongruous. He wears his hair like a soldier's, close-cropped upon his head. In pictures I've seen of him, his hands look huge, suitable for carrying children and doing the work of a peasant. From where I sat tonight I could not tell whether or not they really are all that large.

But I know he's carried children. He married his first cousin and had two daughters. He did not pause at the beginning of tonight's recital to find his granddaughter, Sophie Wolkonsky, and nod to her, as I have read is often his custom when she is with him on these tours. She had not come with him on this one.

Mr. R's last two scheduled works were by another piano prodigy and showman whose presence had already permeated the recital tonight through paraphrase and transcription.

Rachmaninoff had begun and now ended his program with Liszt. The first of the two pieces in this section was the "Sonetto del Petrarca in A Flat Major." Petrarch, who declared that love was the crowning grace of humanity; Petrarch, who said that where we are is of no moment, but what we are doing there; it is not the place that ennobles the person, but the person the place. Mr. R. played his final number, Liszt's "Rhapsody No. 2," like a madman, as if he had conserved and then focused much of his energy expressly for the playing of these extended variations on the dance of life and death, as if his hands had been made for this elaboration of Hungarian peasant music shaped by Liszt, another man who had had two daughters—and a son. Liszt's son: Whatever had become of Liszt's son?

Just seven hours ago—an eternity—as Sgt. Trotter and I stood at attention at diagonals three feet behind Lt. Delano, we listened as he, stiffly erect and in the special cadence of his deep machine-like Army monotone, delivered the message to Mr. and Mrs. Genillat:

The Secretary of War desires to express his deep regret that your son, Darden E. Genillat, was killed in action in defense of his country in the Philippine Islands, January 2, 1942.

After Lt. Delano placed the communiqué back in the brown envelope, stepped forward one pace and handed it to Mr. Genillat and then stepped back, the three of us saluted, executed a smart about-face and in single file left their home without another word. The gentle shutting of the door behind us in the first few moments of the darkness of the night stabbed the place behind my eyes where all is clearly seen and heard.

I am an enlisted man. My hair is close-cropped upon my head. Today I have done the work of a peasant. Until the moment I saluted, my large hands hung loosely at my sides. I made music only in my head.

Along with my fellow soldiers, I mutely confronted these innocent souls with the news of the death of their only son, turned on my heels and left, without a hand or personal word extended in sympathy or compassion, honoring the military protocol of the dignity of silence.

In today's paper, in an article heralding the Maestro's coming to Columbia, he was quoted as saying that music should bring relief: It should rehabilitate people's minds and souls...It must reveal the emotions of the heart.

My pass is up Sunday evening. On Monday I shall mix those words in well with my spit and polish, as I stand by to go out again next week as a silent messenger of death. When I go I shall remember that on January 16 Sergei Rachmaninoff played Columbia and in my heart and head shall listen to his music in the night.

Thomas L. Johnson has been associated with the University of South Carolina for more than twenty-five years as an archivist and English instructor. A True Likeness (1986), a book he co-edited on the work of Columbia photographer Richard Roberts, won a Southern Regional Council Lillian Smith Award. A prize-winning poet, he serves as an honorary life member of the board of governors of the South Carolina Academy of Authors.

Burnt Beans

"Right here, right now Elizabeth Ann, you come look at this."

"What, Momma?" I said, walking into the den and wiping my hands on the dish towel.

She was standing up pointing at the television. "This man on TV's talking about a girl in Fayetteville who had a terrible stomach ache. She was on the commode and the next thing she knew, a baby fell from her into the water."

They had a picture of this girl on the news. She couldn't have been much older than me, maybe fourteen or so, all smiling and holding a baby. The announcer was telling how the girl didn't even know she was eight months pregnant, and wasn't sure how she got to be carrying a baby in the first place.

"You know that's not the truth," I said. "She's just telling that story to save herself."

"Now why would you say that? This is *the news*. Those reporters just tell what comes to pass." Momma sat back down on the couch to see more TV.

"Oh please," I said and went back in the kitchen to finish the dishes. That girl on TV had to know she was pregnant. Your body wouldn't keep that kind of a secret from you. She just had herself in a pickle and didn't know what to do when the pickle fell out of the jar. And all that smiling and acting like she didn't know how she got that way. Maybe she'll say she got pregnant from sitting on a toilet at the mall. Or she'll cry and say she got taken advantage of when she was drunk one night.

"'Wheel' is coming on, Elizabeth Ann. Why don't you come in here and watch with me?"

"Can't. I got some more dishes."

"Ooh, you should hurry. Vanna's got one of them shiny dresses on."

I was scrubbing the last and worst pot—the one with the pork and beans burnt thick and black on the bottom and the sides—when I heard Daddy drive up in this truck. You can always hear it from inside the house because of the creaking of the shocks when he drives right over the front walk in the yard. He likes to park close to the door.

I pulled out the stopper to let the water drain and left the bean pot to soak, since it would wash up better that way later. "Buy a vowel, mister," Momma was telling some guy on "Wheel" when I passed her on my way to my room. That's where I go most evenings. Lots of time I lock the door, sit Indian-style on my bed, and cut words and pictures out of magazines. I scotch tape what I cut out onto note-book paper—"vibrations," "When he asks you out?" and "pretty face" are some of the words I've been clipping. When I get enough to fill a page, I'll make a little poster to put on the wall.

They were starting again, in the den.

"What the hell do you mean, why am I late?" Daddy hollered.

"Stop yelling, I can't hear my show."

I turned on the clock radio by my bed. There's a program called "Love Lines" that I like to listen to on weeknights. The guy has this whispery kind of voice and he's real encouraging about love. If I had a phone in here, I'd call him—like all those other girls do—and make a dedication. That girl on TV, the one who says she didn't know she was pregnant, she probably liked all these slow songs and listened to them when she lay down with the guys. She knew exactly what she was doing.

I wouldn't be like that. If I heard a slow song and was with my boyfriend, we'd just dance or kiss or something. I wouldn't end up pregnant. My Daddy would kill me. And even if he didn't, like if he was dead or had run away from me and Momma before I had my baby, what kind of a life could I give some poor, crying kid?

"I have not been sitting here all day. Just look in the kitchen, I cooked your dinner and did your dishes." Momma was yelling louder than the radio. I wanted to drown them out, but I didn't want to turn the music up too loud and get them madder.

"Give me back my glass," Momma yelled.

It's easy to see why some girls have babies. They just want somebody to love them. I understand, because I would like someone to hug me and to love me—to really love me. Momma does, but not very well, and I think Daddy does. He's just too mean to know it.

Sometimes when Daddy gets paid, he puts on Old Spice and takes us out to eat and for ice cream in cones. And every week or two Momma will ask if she can braid my hair while she's watching TV. It feels good to have her hands in my hair, and she's careful not to pull too tight.

I don't have a boyfriend right now. Actually, I've never had a real one. One who says, "This is my girlfriend..." or "Me and my girlfriend..." But I'm good at softball, and the boys' games are right after ours on the same field, so I know that some of them watch me. I want one to see me and to like me and to want to hold hands on the bus. The ride is so long every day, and we sit three to a seat. It would be nice to spend that time holding hands and talking.

I heard a pot slam on the stove, and stopped cutting out the words "hot date" from my magazine.

"These beans are burnt," Daddy hollered. "Elizabeth Ann could cook better than you."

Damn, I thought if I dumped the burnt beans in a clean pan, he wouldn't be able to tell. I mean it wasn't the really bad ones I dumped, it was the ones that hadn't gotten stuck to the sides.

My friend Robin had a baby. It was last year and she wore sweatpants and slept a lot in the afternoons and on weekends so her Mom wouldn't figure it out. Robin was pretty fat, so she could hide it. Anyway, when the baby came she couldn't give it up like she said she was going to. It was so tiny. "Tiny and warm," Robin said, "and it looks at me, right into me." I held that baby one day. It made me feel like humming. I did hum, but the baby heard me and could tell I wasn't Robin and started crying.

Daddy banged on the door. "What are you doing in there? Your Momma burnt my supper and I told her you could cook one better."

I didn't open the door. I knew he was just saying that to get Momma upset. He didn't really want me to cook for him. Those two—I told Momma once they should divorce. Well, I asked her if she ever thought they would, but she said their lives were too tied together to unwind.

I was right. Daddy didn't stay by my door very long. The rest of the night I heard the TV, and Daddy changing from channel to channel, but not much more yelling. At least nothing serious. Not like that time he punched the wall. Momma bought a picture frame to hang and cover up the dent in the drywall. She put my school picture inside. I'm smiling in it and I have on the yellow halter. I look pretty good.

"Nighty night, Elizabeth Ann," Momma said after she tapped my door. She always says that, last thing, ever since I can remember.

When I heard their bedroom shut, I went to the kitchen. Soaking in the dishpan was two of those short, heavy glasses that say Jack Daniels on the side. Daddy got them in a set last Christmas. The bean pan was soaking too. I stuck my hand in the water. It had got cold and lost its soapiness, but I washed the glasses and scrubbed the pan anyway. There wasn't much else I could do.

The next morning Momma was crying when I left for school. Her mascara was filling her wrinkles with gray and black. She's got wrinkles from the sun, not age. I kissed her before I left. Daddy was already gone.

There's parts of school that I like and parts I don't. My homeroom teacher is pretty and once her husband walked in with purple flowers. He was tall and had thick, dark hair. His clothes were pressed and he looked like he smelled like a new book. We all clapped when he handed her the vase. My teacher smiled the rest of the morning.

In art class we've been doing sculptures. You can make anything you want. I take the cold clay and turn it into bodies—bony, naked ones curled up to do forward rolls, and fat ones stretched out on their backs, grinning at the sun. The boy next to me has been trying to make a skateboard for a week, but the clay wheels keep falling off. Today I offered to help him and he let me for a minute, but when my hand accidentally touched his, he pulled it back. I don't know if he meant to do that, but it made me look at the clay that was thick under my fingernails and drying my skin to an elephant color. I looked down at my jeans that were too tight and too short, and at my tennis shoes with their cracked, dirty leather. My hands started to shake and I knew I wouldn't be able to get the slippery wheel on the skateboard. I told the boy I had to go to the bathroom and I planned to stay there until the bell rang for changing classes.

That's where I was when Momma came to my school. Pinetree Middle School is no big place, so after the office secretary came to the art room and didn't see me, she and Momma went straight to the girls' room. I was scrubbing the clay from my hands when they walked in.

"Momma?" I said. I'd seen her at school before, but not here in the tiled girls' room in front of "Ms. Todd's English class sucks!" and "Rachel loves Bill" and all the other stupid stuff written on the walls.

Momma was wearing a dress and high-heeled shoes like

she was going to church. She took a couple steps toward me, teetering a little.

"Elizabeth Ann, you need to get your things," she said slowly, and like she had marshmallows in her mouth. "Your father left a note. Says he's leaving. That piece a shit, after the home I've made for him…"

Everything smelled like clay and hairspray and pee. I thought I might faint. The office secretary was looking back and forth between the two of us. "Momma, stop," I said.

"I'm not going to let him leave with some whore. It'll be you and me, Elizabeth Ann. We'll be the ones going off, making something happen. We could drive to California. Get me on a game show. I'd win."

The secretary moved closer to me and patted my back. I took a deep breath. "But I have school, and my sculptures aren't dry enough to carry." I wanted to calm Momma down, to get her away from the secretary so we could work this out.

Momma swung her arm up to point at me, which made her lose her balance just for a second. "You and me, we can do this. We're a team, Elizabeth Ann, you know that." She opened a stall door and went inside. I could hear her unroll some toilet paper and blow her nose. Then she said, "This lady here—from the office—she tells me you'll need to go to your locker. Why don't you do that while I tinkle and I'll meet you at the car? I'm parked out front."

The secretary was small, except for her helmet of curly hair, and smelled like cigarettes. She put her arm around me and we walked out of the bathroom.

Momma had filled the trunk with clothes from my closet and her closet. Our pillows and blankets and bathroom stuff were in the back seat. I got inside and Momma put her finger to her lips. She was listening to the radio and wanted me to hear. People were calling in to whistle the "Andy Griffith" show song. Whoever could do it best would win dinner for two at a steakhouse.

"Hon, we need to get a car phone. That'll be the first thing," Momma said and we drove out on Route 48 in her blue Oldsmobile with the velvety seats. She was whistling.

"Where's Daddy's note?'

"Elizabeth Ann, you're so silly. Can you imagine your lazy father taking time to write me?" She was laughing. "I just said that because that nosy little secretary, she didn't want me to take my own daughter out of school."

A bottle, almost empty, rolled across the floorboard and hit my foot. "Momma did you drink that today?"

"Some today. Some last night."

I noticed her lipstick. I don't think she was wearing it in the girls room. It was orange and it was drawn too far above her lip on the right side. Her mascara was thick and her cheeks were swollen like pink sponges.

"Momma we got to go home."

"Well we ain't. We're getting out of here, like I told you."

"We got to. I left my diary there and I need it. I use it every day."

"You'll just have to start a new one. We'll go by the store and get you one so you can start over, one with all blank pages."

I thought a minute, while she kept whistling. Even with the orange lipstick she looked beautiful just then, driving with her hands high on the wheel. Her back was straight and her yellow hair was floating above her blue dress like the sun in the sky. "Okay, let's go get another diary," I said. "Do you have money?"

Momma pushed her black vinyl pocketbook toward me. I felt through chewing gum, matches, and lipsticks. From the bottom I pulled out her billfold and opened it on my lap. We were at a stop sign and Momma was watching me. I counted out three one-dollar bills including one that had been torn and taped. She bit down on her orange bottom lip.

When the Oldsmobile got low on gas, we drove home.

I got Momma to lie down on the couch. Her high heels dropped to the floor as she sipped on the last of the whiskey, and by about 2:00 she was asleep with the TV on. I went to my room to do my homework—there was going to be a history test. I started to think about Daddy, and I couldn't concentrate.

He would be finishing up at some house right now. Probably spent the day putting in a big bathroom for somebody's wife or adding on a nursery for some family needing room for their next baby. It's a real hopeful thing when people put additions on their houses. They want another place to go to be with each other. And my Daddy makes those places.

I went with him once. It was a brick house, ranch-style, with lots of grass and a couple of pear trees. The wife who lived there, she and her three kids were having a picnic on the lawn and watching my Daddy's crew pound nails and saw 2 x 4s. They were building a family room. I was only about eight and the sawdust was making me cough so the lady asked me to come sit on the blanket with her. Her kids were smaller than me. Two were rolling in the grass and one was asleep with his head on her lap.

When I remember that day I think about how sunny it was and how she gave me some sweet lemonade and later I fell asleep too. The lady was singing real soft and once I felt her finger brushing the sawdust off my cheek.

Around 4:30 I got up from studying and went to the kitchen to make macaroni and cheese casserole with a can of tuna mixed in. When I was sprinkling the breadcrumbs on top I heard Momma laughing. She was in the den on the couch, and the TV was turned up, loud.

Sandy Lang Quick grew up in Surfside Beach and makes her home in Mount Pleasant. A two-time winner of the South Carolina Fiction Project, she has also had short stories published in Contents Magazine *and the* Lowcountry Heritage Society Anthology. *Besides writing, her art includes design and photography.*

S. Paul Rice

Junnie, the Coin, and Grandpa Dickens

Junnie watched the red moon shrug off oak trees and make itself silver as it hung higher and higher. By the time its full face rose above the top of her window, her eyelids sank lower and lower, until the moon and the window had no reality at all, none at least until the train whistle went jagged in her sleep.

Footsteps cluttered the house, and rustling voices brought her out of a dream of scattered mirrors and into a world of the now-high moon and the mystery of a two-in-the-morning knock on the front door.

Junnie's daddy and granddaddy were up and in their boots; no one thinks much about a moon when there's early morning trouble, and being knocked out of sleep is never a good thing, at least not in Harris County. At the back door, a crewman from the railroad, a man well-smoked and well-oiled, swung a kerosene lantern in and out of the light from the kitchen door; she could hear an edge of animal panic, a sound she knew in the squeal of pigs when a cold blade stuck something warm and important.

"Junnie, you get back in your room!"

The railroad ran across the back line of her daddy's land, and big engines pulled the world past Junnie's eyes. One great black belcher, number 36, she had named "Grandpa Dickens" because the machine seemed as old and big as the devil. Grandpa Dickens hauled the late, late run out of the woods and back into the woods beyond; Grandpa Dickens was a night engine, too black and fiery for sunlight, out of place in daytime, a hellworm roaming the iron roads, feasting on flesh and darkness.

Sometimes Junnie made a little profit putting coins on the track for the big iron wheels to flatten, something she always did at night to keep the Hearne boys from making off with them. A boy once gave her fifty cents for a silver quarter flattened by the train. She had drilled a hole in it, and the boy wore it on a red string around his neck. Train money has magic; it is almost as powerful as the silver dollars used to close a dead man's eyes.

The night the train man came, earlier, just as oaks began to show up dark against the reddening sun, Junnie had taken a wonderful coin to the track, a new fifty-cent piece she earned cleaning out the smoke-house. "Silver for smoke, silver for smoke," she sang aloud as she looked for the best place to lay the money, up the tracks, maybe, away from the road, out of Willard Hearne's way. Junnie prayed for everything, and she prayed for the flattening of the half-dollar. Let the train hit it right; let the silver be safe from thieves; let it land where I can find it.

Junnie went back to her room, but opened the window screen and slipped out into the night, hiding behind the shrubbery. From the waxy dark behind the boxwoods she could hear most of what the train man was saying, that he needed to use the phone, that the engine had run over a man lying on the tracks, that it took a quarter mile to stop the train. Her daddy and granddaddy brought the old truck around, and soon the three men loaded up and were off into the dark. The silver coin was a bright spot in her mind as sleep filled the room, and the dead man was no matter until Saturday morning when the red dirt road was important with deputies and community folks on foot.

That morning Junnie got a story from the neighbor girl who heard it from a cousin's husband.

Man was John Lucas, bad to gamble, been locked up many a time, always in trouble, trouble in jail too, sometimes howled all night in jail, howled about his dead dog, about a little child his ladyfriend said wasn't his but he knew was, probably howled because there wasn't any booze in jail. John been gambling with friends in the shack down by Blue Judy's, John called Willie Daniel a bad name, no I can't say what in front of a child, anyway, Willie shot John, loaded him on a piece of tin and dragged him down the hill, rolled him up on the tracks knowing that about two in the morning a train always comes along, tried to make it seem like an accident. Deputies first didn't know who it was, couldn't find the head, but Judy recognized John by his boots and deputies finally found the piece of John had the bullet hole in it. Started checking around, Willie's story didn't work, finally hauled him in. Never did find the head.

For Junnie this was grown-up business; her main concern was for the silver coin, that somebody picking around in John Lucas's pieces would find it. The deputies weren't letting anybody near the area, so all day the neighborhood gathered in small bundles at saw horses the deputies had set across the road.

By afternoon the possibility of lost magic burned a hole in Junnie's patience. She was a girl who had little respect for signs and lines and barricades, a girl who turned to trees and creeks, to hawks and owls looking for her own sense of right. So she went down across the back of their land, crossed the track around the big curve, then went up the bank on the side away from the barricade. Nobody would ever see her. Except for old Dee Hearne who had done the same thing.

"Junnie, you better get back to your house!"

Hearne stammered over the crossties and ballast rocks steadied by a hickory walking stick. He paused a couple of times and turned over pieces of John Lucas with brass tip of the stick.

"He was a light-skinned man judging from the looks of

this," said Hearne.

Junnie ran/slid down the bank and hid in a clump of sumac until Dee Hearne got tired of his poking. Looking out she could see the old man starting down the path toward home. The girl slipped out of the green thicket. Climbing back up the steep bank fifty or so feet from where she slid down, she felt a cold gravity in the briars. Parting a clump of blackberry vines she looked down deep into the hazy eyes of John Lucas.

Beside the head was a flattened silver half, full of more magic that Junnie could have hoped for. Running for home, she could imagine the fire of Grandpa Dickens, the train noise among the pieces of the shot man, the dogs dragging the head; she could see the silver coin flipping, flipping, high up in the dark, catching the light of the moon, becoming a moon itself. A head in the briars, magic in the money—the very thought made tides in Junnie's blood.

S. Paul Rice is Professor of English at Coastal Carolina University. He is the principal in S. Paul Rice Appraisals, a firm specializing in art and antiques appraisals. He has a doctoral degree from the Catholic University of America and a Master of Fine Arts in creative writing from the University of Arkansas.

Rosa Shand

A Garden with a Mango Tree

Till the hail stopped—she had that time to think. Alec wouldn't come till the hail stopped.

Bang. . . .Crack. . . . Bang . . . Bang . . . Crack. Crack crack crack crack crack crack crack. It was battering the roof. She stood still in the middle of the room.

Anna was thin. With the long hair plait she wore, thick and light-colored, people in Africa stared at her. Now her body swayed. A child butted her. Another child shrieked and yanked her blouse. One more buried in her skirt. Her hand, automatic, patted heads. Her voice, automatic, said "Okay okay okay." She didn't notice who was yelping. She didn't pick a child up. She didn't move her eyes, which were vaguely focused out the window. She kept on standing in the middle of the Lego set and fiddle sticks and pink and yellow pop-beads and picture books scotch-taped together. She didn't think about the noise. Hail was common. The ssekibobo's visit she thought about. Alec's reaction—Alec was her husband—she thought about.

The ssekibobo had just left. He had not sat down. He'd barely stepped inside. The man was heavyset and clear-featured. He spoke with an Oxford English accent and normally he moved as if he glided. This time he entered jerkily. His fingers twined and intertwined. The sight made Anna hate the scheme of things so when he said, "Will you take the baby?" she said "Of course of course." His fear dropped. He rushed at explanations, cut them off, reached out to her.

The baby was the grandson of the king. This baby would have been Kabaka of Buganda because the routed kabaka had no son. The coup against Buganda, Obote's coup, started yesterday. Obote's soldiers burned the palace. The kabaka vanished. News was rumor news. No one could move after dark. You saw smoke from the direction of the village. You heard gun volleys. Rumor said whoever hid a member of the royal family would be shot.

She had to do something. The children should know before the ssekibobo brought the baby. The thought makes her look down, feel their kafuffle, see Will's mangy half-scalped head where he got scissors at himself, see Sophie's scabby turned-up nose, see Amy's diapers hanging round her knees. Tears were muddying down Amy's cheek. Sophie was sucking her finger with her elbow poking out. The tiny ball of her other hand was pinching at her dress.

Anna was afraid. She pressed her children's heads against her thigh. She shouted over the barrage of cracks: "See it bouncing? Isn't that funny?" Little bodies scrambled up the sofa, leaned over the back, pointed out the window. She screamed at them: "I have a surprise for you." She was drowned out but she didn't notice. She was thinking she would have to move Amy into Sophie's room. She would have to get Leah to say the new baby was her baby or some hanger-on of hers. She would have to tell people something, maybe that they thought they should keep Leah's baby since Leah's room was cramped.

Wilfred Kabuka-Musoke—that was the ssekibobo's actual name—had come in secret. The ssekibobo was up near the king in the Buganda roll of honor. He was the baby's other grandfather and he was chief of the district she and Alec lived in and taught in. The ssekibobo had gone to Amherst as well as to Eton and he didn't hate Americans. Currently it was the fashion to despise Americans: Americans had bombed West Nile to root out Congolese communist Simbas and the country had spun up in an anti-American frenzy but the ssekibobo had ignored the atmosphere and welcomed them.

She tried again. She shouted: "You are going to have a baby brother." Will was four and the dignified oldest child even if his brown straight hair poked out in a moth-eaten fashion. Will turned around and for a minute he looked puzzled. Then he screamed, "I want a BIG brother."

She shouted back at him, "This is a baby brother and that's what you get and you have to promise me you won't tell anybody..." Will couldn't hear and wasn't trying to. He was licking Amy's arm where Amy'd smeared her marmite. Anna heard what nonsense she was mouthing and her words trailed off and her mind slipped back: she had to tell Alec. Alec wasn't happy with her lately. She was more interested, he pronounced, in digging up mattresses for Cyprian and hauling roofs for Sylvester and scrounging medicine for Leah than in spending time with her husband. Her misguided Southernness, he added, meant she couldn't stand up for herself, meant she couldn't remind anybody that she had a few other obligations, like children and a husband and a teaching job.

That was Alec's interpretation. He didn't have it right. She wasn't happy spending her time hauling scrappy roofs and sorry mattresses. She'd majored in art history. Yes she'd come to teach in Africa but it was Alec with the big idea they stay. Not that she'd objected. To get back and forth to Africa you had to go through London and Paris and Rome and Athens and Cairo with maybe a sidetrip to Venice where the Morandi painting with the tall red bottle was. But once in Africa she'd blossomed with children and that kind of productivity didn't give her Alec's status or an office with a door to lock. She was slotted as approachable, and in spite of her wanting to read about Morandi it seemed ornery to come to Uganda and hide. So she did what people stuck under her nose. That was that. Only Alec wasn't happy about that.

This new disruption should not be a shock. Over coffee she and Alec had tried to figure what they were doing in Africa. They thought it had to do with escaping suburbia, taking risks. So they expected malaria, amoebic dysentery, bilharzia, cobras, mambas, tsetse flies, scorpions, thieves, outhouses, worms, jiggers, slimy water. They hadn't expected born-again Christians and they hadn't expected this, but it was here. And Alec would recognize it. She shouldn't make so much of it. She would simply, offhandedly, slip it in their talk that she—not he, she—was keeping Wilfred's grandson. She'd kept other people's children and anyway Alec would not remember who the grandson was because he didn't pay attention to children and what difference could it make to him if she had three children or four children.

Bang bang . . . crack . . . . bang . . . . . . crack. Quiet. She looked outside. Hush was more ominous than bangs. Alec would be home now hail had stopped. The ground was white and silent as snow, all but the circle under the mango tree. For a minute Will and Amy and Sophie stared. Then Amy fell off the sofa and all of them tumbled out across the porch and squatted at the hail's edge. They poked fingers at it. They squealed. They tested bare feet on lumps of ice. They acted like it was fire. Amy tried to catch hold of a lump. It slipped. It kept slipping. She got one ball in her tiny fist and brought it in the house. She opened her palm to show her mother. The lump was gone. Her palm was wet. She cried, twisted round and round to find it. Sophie watched an ibis in the bougainvillea.

Alec came in. Anna was squatting on the floor. Amy was between her legs, tangled in her skirt. The skirt was wet.

Anna stared up at her husband. He was very tall with dark brown hair. He had a goatee and bushy eyebrows and sharp thin features. He wore glasses. He looked even taller from the angle she was in. Perhaps she had an odd expression because he cocked his head and narrowed his eyes, in the slanty way of his new-acquired charm, and said, "And what might be your trouble?"

She said, "Nothing."

He said, "Then could you not get off the floor? Why are you looking like that?" Will pulled his daddy out the door and when Alec had said "I see" to Will, he came back in the house. He told her the faculty'd been plotting their route. They were to take the Lugazi Road if the fighting came closer. It was contingency planning and she was not to be concerned, he said. Whites would not be affected if they kept out of the way—the kabaka has known his hour was coming. There was no room for royalty in independent Africa, he said, everybody knew that. The kabaka was getting no support to speak of.

She said, "While you were gone the ssekibobo came by. He was looking for a place for his grandson and I said Of course."

Alec said, "What grandson? What are you talking about?"

Sylvester, the pork man in his pith helmet, called through the back window. She hoisted Amy up. She slipped on the Lego and Alec pulled Amy away from her and helped her up. She said she would be back but Alec followed her. Amy screeched and Alec's voice was not so calm as she had hoped and his charm had evaporated. He was being insistent: "You stop and tell me what you are talking about. The only grandson I know is the baby kabaka. What are you talking about?"

She said, "Just a minute." She tried to listen to Sylvester who was unwrapping the banana leaves around the wobbly-jelly blobs of pork and saying in Luganda she was lucky, he had saved some pork for her and he couldn't get more because the soldiers made off with his pigs. She could tell he was waiting for Leah, the way he looked around—he could dawdle till Leah came. Alec grabbed her arm and pulled her away. He shoved Amy at Sylvester. Anna fought to find her pocket book and give Sylvester money but Alec steered her in the bedroom, slammed the door, set her on the bed and demanded she explain herself.

She said, "The ssekibobo has to hide his grandson. Whites won't be suspected. He says if Baganda keep the baby they will be found out and killed. He says Europeans won't be bothered."

"So you ARE talking about the baby kabaka," he said. "Are you out of your head?"

She said nothing.

"Can you grasp what you are doing? White families aren't bothered because white families keep out. Has it occurred to you that we'll be shot?"

"That won't happen," she said.

"Have you thought—other whites will be shot?"

"I have not thought other whites will be shot."

"Of course not. You have not thought. You plunge us in headfirst to prop up a medieval farce." He made his eyes go round as plates. White circled his pupils.

She sat taller. She said, "We can not say no to Wilfred."

Alec went loose and looked away. He took his glasses off. His skin was grey around the bushes of his eyebrows. He moved closer. He took her arm, which sat on her lap, in both his hands. He looked in her face. He spoke with slow deliberation. He said, "Anna, I know your feelings. You mean to be heroic."

She closed her eyes, clapped her hand across them.

"An inadvertent hero," he went on. "I am aware of that—you are Southern. But it doesn't matter. What matters is, you are a mother. You are not called to be heroic. I cannot allow your heroism. You do what you say and you put the whole school in danger, all whites in danger. And yourself, me, Will, Amy, Sophie—every one of us. You have to see that. This is tribal war. This is not for Europeans to get involved in. Whites can still do things in Africa precisely because whites aren't involved in tribal wars. You mean to do this for a friend. But this goes far beyond reason and this time you are wrong. I cannot allow it."

She looked out the window. Across the sky, from her

angle, one limb of the mango tree was dark and bent and its big wax leaves were flying in the wind. A black bird screamed and glided in low. It made her shudder. She struggled to stand up, to check on her children. He dropped her arm and pulled back to allow her to. He watched her face. She craned to see out the window. Will was bouncing in the mango tree. Sophie's face was hidden under Sylvester's pith helmet and she was pointing down the hill at strutting s-shaped ibises. Her orange dress was fat with wind. Sylvester was kneeling holding Amy in his arms. He was patting her, cooing to her, trying to stop Amy crying. Black smoke was blowing from the hill across the valley.

Anna sat down before she said, "Allow. Not allow. You assume this is something I want, something I haven't thought about. We don't have a choice."

"No, we don't," he said.

She said, "It isn't mere survival, taking children in. In Africa it's culture. It binds people, most of all when there's danger. Obviously the ssekibobo was afraid to come to whites for that act of humanity. When I said Yes, his voice went trembly. It's obvious that we don't have a choice."

"You see everything as a personal matter," he said. "You confuse the personal with genuine issues. One of us is obligated to look at consequences and if you will not, I will."

"You mean I am to go to the ssekibobo. I am to say, 'Sorry, saving your baby might put us at risk. Forget what I said. We didn't come to Uganda to take risk.' But of course—saying that won't be necessary. As soon as Wilfred sees the car he'll know. He'll see precisely what it means to have white friends."

Alec stood up. "*I* will go," he said.

"Don't do this, Alec."

He was out the door.

Car gears ground along the drive.

She paid Sylvester. She told the children they wouldn't

get a baby brother. She said, "Hush hush" without looking at them because she was adjusting: they could not stay in Uganda. She would have to go back to standing in lines in wretched government offices where when you got to the front of the line you had to start over in another line and where the form you filled out turned out to be last week's form and the ousted minister thought that one up so it didn't work this week.

But what her body was feeling was not that. Her limbs were loosening and her chest was opening, as if a colossus had been lifted off.

She heard their Peugeot at the bottom of the hill. It was too soon. Alec couldn't have reached the ssekibobo's and come back.

She stood. She watched Alec drive up, pull on the car brake and get out. He brushed children away. He took her elbow and led her inside. He said, "I couldn't do it."

The tightness in her chest came back. She nodded. They sat in the living room.

Children clamored at her. They wanted her to play with them, they wanted her to read to them. She told them they would get their baby brother any minute. Will jumped up and down. He squirmed under the sofa for his book. They fought for her lap. Will banged the book. She put him off. She and Alec studied each other. Amy poked her cheek. Will yanked her plait and rattled the book.

She read to keep them quiet. "The children used to go and play in the giant's garden. It was a large lovely garden, with soft green grass. Here and there over the grass stood twelve peach trees. The birds sat on the trees and sang so sweetly that the children used to stop their games in order to listen to them."

She heard a car somewhere down the hill. She knew Alec heard it, but she kept on reading. "One day the giant came back. He had been to visit his friend the Cornish ogre and had stayed with him for seven years. After the seven years were over he had said all that he had to say, for his conversation was limited, and he determined to return to his own castle. When he arrived he saw the children playing in the garden. 'What are you doing there?' he cried in a very gruff voice, and the children ran away. 'My own garden is my own garden,' said the giant."

The car was close.

She had to calm them into this, not only Alec but herself. She stopped reading and looked up.

Alec was in the chair across from them. His arms were folded over his chest. He was looking out the window over their heads. The wind was snapping the veranda vines but Alec wasn't noticing and that moved her: he looked calm. He had grasped they didn't have a choice.

Will said, "We don't have peach trees."

She said, "We have a garden with a mango tree."

She watched Alec push up. He started toward the door. Will ran after him. Amy ran after Will. Sophie slid off her mother's lap and halted in the middle of the room. She stood sucking her finger with her elbow poking up. She stared vacantly, in the direction of the window. Anna looked at the child. She saw the child was in the secret garden still, and for a minute she was caught in Sophie's transfixed eyes. She twisted around to see what Sophie must be seeing, and she and the child held still, and watched the wind in the mango tree.

Then Anna got up from the sofa. She whisked the leaves and sticks and mud from off her skirt. She stooped down to the little girl, heaved her to her hip, and carried her out to meet the baby boy.

Rosa Shand has a novel, The Gravity of Sunlight, *and a story collection with three other writers,* New Southern Harmonies*. She has published more than thirty stories, currently holds a fellowship from the National Endowment for the Arts, and is a five-time winner of the South Carolina Fiction Project.*

Alice Cabaniss

Mercator Projection

Every day after work in the summer, I take my beach chair with the tall back and short legs down to the water and sit there, looking off at the horizon. Much better than a movie, though it's very slow motion, and it turns me back on to living. From my chair I can see 360 degrees of sky if I turn, just as if I were standing on top of the tallest mountain in the world or as if I were on the overpass of a highway through the desert.

Usually I bring a cooler with me, a small one because the white sand is deep in places and carrying anything heavy makes the trip more like work than play. Liquid is essential because the wind blows sand up against me, and I seem to dry out like the sponges that litter the beach.

Most of the time, there's activity on the beach. Fellows beach their catamarans, and grandparents walk their offspring's children for them. There are dog walkers and runners and joggers, and in dead summer, you can hardly see the sand for the day-trippers and the renters with their big families.

Last night I took my chair down about 6:30, after most of the families had stopped playing games and had gone in to take their showers and have their suppers. Digging in my heels near the waterline, I surveyed the horizon as if there might be something new and interesting there. Something other than sails and ships and pelicans. Sure enough, far off, a lump of clouds moved steadily toward me in the shape of a city of towers, Vancouver, Madrid. And last night, as many nights before, my friend came to sit with me.

I hardly remember when he first began to sit there, but we have never spoken to each other. I guess it was about three months ago that he first walked up to a space about twenty feet away from my chair and put his chair on the same parallel.

At first, I thought he would speak. But he just took out his newspaper and read, slapping down the pages when the wind came up until he had finished all four sections and neatly folded them away into a canvas sack.

I tried to imagine what he saw as he settled down twenty feet away. An overweight woman, medium height, medium brown hair, shaded sunglasses, black racing-style swimsuit, barefoot. A tall-backed beach chair with brown and yellow stripes.

He might have chosen this spot because it looked safe; children might not run over him with their bikes or horses with two of us, I guess. He was heavy built, not in the stomach so much as thick though, like a tank, and wearing a maroon bathing suit, getting shiny from long use.

He wore a cap, one of those Greek fisherman things, and I soon found out why. He was about to go bald, and even the late evening sun produced a reddish tinge on my forehead sometimes, a faint burn that stung when I frowned the next day. What hair he had left, around the back of his neck and skipping over his ears to his cheeks, was a feathery grey, not unlike the sandpiper that pecked very close to our feet as the tide brought him bits of food.

When this guy first sat down there, I thought it would be polite to welcome him to the part of the beach I had long staked out as my favorite. But he seemed to have no need of greeting; looking off at the righthand horizon, he seemed quite content. He came back again the following evening, and I decided that he must be a renter who had had second thoughts about all this solitude.

But again he put his chair down on the sand about twenty feet away and proceeded to read, this time a *Newsweek*, which he digested from front to back before dropping it inside his canvas bag. That day I thought surely he would say *something*.

I had never been that close to someone in physical proximity for that length of time without having them hail me in one fashion or another. They would at least comment on the weather, or smile and nod in a friendly way; acknowledge my existence at the minimum.

The third day straight that he brought his chair to the waterslide and placed it close by, I began to resent his taking the liberty of association. Twenty feet away on a subway would be an enormous distance. Twenty feet on a beach where people had room to be two hundred feet apart was, I felt, an intrusion. He couldn't be following me personally. It would be paranoid to think that, even though I worked for the Army Corps of Engineers and occasionally had to handle material marked "classified."

I had been coming down here most weekday afternoons for six years, though, and I guessed it was possible somebody noticed that. Well, it was presumptuous: that's what it was. Probably a Yankee wanting to make friends and didn't know how to go about it. But I was not a prime candidate for picking up on the beach. My bathing suit was a 16, not a six, so I didn't consider myself a logical target for passing lust. Where *had* this interloper come from?

I looked back at the line of front row beach houses, expecting to see a wife or mistress or children appear, drink in hand, to keep him company. I determined to sit and watch where he went when he left. Or I thought I would.

When at 7:45 he had not moved, I became impatient for my TV show and my telephone, and when he still hadn't left at 8:30, I folded up my beach chair for the night.

The next evening, I went to a party for someone in my department at work, and by the time I reached the beach with my chair, the sun had already begun to go down, and he was no longer there. In the sand, though, marks of a beach chair collected water from the incoming tide, and I knew that he had been there.

The fifth evening of this phenomenon, I got to my beach spot by 6 determined this time to ask him what the point was of putting his chair that close to mine when he wasn't going to speak or anything. Did he think he knew me? He couldn't have been a friend of Ben's, although people's appearances do change, just the way landmarks at the beach change from slow erosion. And my husband had been away for seven years.

I say "away" for "divorced" because even though I know what the truth of the situation is, and that Ben is alive and well in Boston with another woman, I don't like the finality of the word divorce.

It makes me feel better to use the word "away," even to myself, since it implies the possibility that he might eventually get tired of Janice and come back home. She is twenty years younger than I am, and pretty spunky, and it will take a long time for him to get tired of her. But it might happen; you never know.

That man, though, on the fifth night, as I said, just wasn't there. The rage I had been building up at his invasion was like one of those sandcastles, and it fell in just like those do. I sat in my chair, waiting and refusing to wait at the same time, feeling cheated that there was no one there to complain to about his behavior. Unless, of course, I had imagined the man. I picked up the brown and yellow chair and moved it way down the beach. Let him come. He wouldn't find me there.

Two women passing by on the beach left a snatch of their conversation. An Airedale came up and sniffed at my crewelwork. I tried not to look down the beach where

I usually put my chair, but I did it anyway.

The next night, after avoiding the hottest part of the afternoon, I made myself a big piña colada and took it with the beach chair down to the shoreline. Where I usually put my chair, a family had spread out a tablecloth and put a picnic on it. I moved up the beach a way and staked out what appeared to be a vacant section.

How restful, away from my daughter Judy's problems. Judy had arrived at my house that morning bringing her apricot poodle, Muffin, for me to keep while she took the twin boys to the mall shopping for new school clothes. Her face was as cloudy as my reflection in the gully was sometimes.

"Jim keeps talking about moving to Augusta," she said, "but we don't know anything for sure yet." Judy's husband was in advertising, and he moved around a fair amount, doing what he called "keeping up with the market."

"I don't want to move to Augusta. All our friends are here, and there aren't any theaters, and there's no beach, and I just don't want to go."

She would go though, if Jim did. Every time she got balky about moving or spending money or whatever, Jim would take her to Hilton Head while I kept the twins, and when she came back she was all smiles and compliance.

Sometimes I wondered if she knew how familiar I was with the patterns of those weekends: the steak dinner by candlelight and the dancing on the terrace under the moon, the barefoot stroll down by the water, the passionate return to the quiet, clean room to undress in a hurry, the sunrise of more lovemaking telling her no quarrel could matter more than the loving. Until, of course, a difference of opinion did matter more than that: until, perhaps, the woman pays for the weekend with money she has earned herself, until the woman's job pays more than his.

The piña colada was all gone. I opened my eyes to find that the man had arrived. He had set his chair about thirty feet away and was reading *The Wall Street Journal* as if he were sitting on his own bloody front porch. As if I were some second cousin visiting, being tolerated. I had always been taught that it was rude to stare. But this was not a usual situation, I thought to myself, and so I will damn well stare as much as I please.

Hostile stare.

Curious stare.

Dissecting stare.

He neither turned his head nor spoke nor gave any sign that I was alive. Now look here, my brain began, who *are* you? But my mouth did not move, nor did his eyes leave the paper in front of him. Vibrations: that would be the answer. I would meditate, the way I learned to in the smoking clinic after twenty-three years of cigarettes.

The vibrations I sent out would invade his space, as they say, and he would have to turn and see me staring at him. I concentrated as hard as I could, repeating the word "man" over and over to myself, scrooching up my eyes and focusing all my attention on the word "speak" until I felt the loose skin of my scalp crawl. Still, he did not acknowledge my presence in any fashion.

I crossed my knees impatiently. Dammit, I would *not* be the first to speak. It had been my custom to come here, for six years, long before he had turned up. His profile was jagged, sharp, with a big nose and powerful jaws. The towel hanging off the arm of his chair was an awful purple color, scattered with red fleur-de-lis. Really tacky. And he had the biggest feet I'd ever seen, all tough and yellow.

When he turned the page of the newspaper, you could see hair on the knuckles of his hands, like a pig's. His chest was hairy, too, though the hair was grey in spots, and his fingernails didn't look too clean. Who was he? I picked up my chair and the empty piña colada glass and got out of there.

Monday was the next time I went down to the beach.

I set up my chair and cooler just short of the water line; and after about twenty minutes of solitude, the man appeared again.

This time he put his chair about forty feet away, settled himself into its plastic webbing, produced some sort of paperback novel and smiled one time. Whether he was smiling at me or at the pelicans diving or at himself, I do not know.

But he began at page one of the book and read it all the way through. When I left at dark, he had closed the book on his chest and was snoring gently. If the tide had been coming in instead of going out, I would have wakened him. I think I would.

Tuesday of that week, I wasn't able to make it to the beach. Wednesday I arrived a little early, and the man did not come that day to sit at all. Thursday, though, he came about 7 o'clock and settled himself about twenty feet from my chair. Still no acknowledgment of my presence or that another human being was anywhere around.

The next day, and the next, and the next—the same procedure, different reading material, occasionally a different towel: a frightful orange or a sad-looking, washed-out blue. Once he brought a radio and played classical symphonic music very softly. Another time he brought a one-man picnic, two gherkins and a chunk of cheese, not offering to share.

Then once, in the sand, above where our chairs usually sit, I found a message in large script: WHERE WERE YOU YESTERDAY? I realized then that the night before, Judy and Jim had taken the boys to Augusta to pick out a new house there, and I had felt so lonely and depressed that I couldn't even take in my usual measure of horizon.

Two or three times after that, I tried to make eye contact with him to see if he would in any way respond. No luck. My rage has gone, though. The curiosity has even left me. It does not matter now, where he had come from or who he is. He is part of my beach and when I am not there, he will be sad.

Alice Cabaniss is a poet, fiction writer, and professor who lives in Camden and in Nice, France. She received degrees in journalism from Winthrop University and English from The Citadel, and a doctoral degree in American Literature from the University of South Carolina. She was coordinator of Sundown Poetry at Piccolo Spoleto, 1978-88 and 1996-97.

Greg Williams

PROCEDURES

You are a refugee in a mall. Dusk is shattered by the
cracks of the lightning and the rumbling thunder. The storm
forced you off the road and into the mall, where the electricity was knocked out. You wait for Andrea, who is in the
restroom. You assume she is ill.

The mall is filling up with dripping people who have
nothing to look at. All the stores have cranked shut their
entrances to guard against looting. You sit next to a penny
fountain jungled with ferns, plastic palmettos and boulders.
The giant cookie booth next to Sears has sold out. A
counter girl from the deli sells hoagies and beer out of
a paper towel box she drags along the floor. You wonder
about this.

You wonder if Andrea will be okay. You have just been
to an abortion clinic with her. You don't want to think about
it. You weren't the father. You wish hard that Andrea could
have kept the child because she needs someone of her own
to hold more than she needs to go to bars or have another
bad relationship. But she has no money, no husband.

The storm isn't stopping. A portion of the Red Lobster
sign from across the parking lot tumbles past the mall
entrance. "Lord, Lord," a heavy woman in a flowered dress
moans as she fans her face with a U-Sell-It tabloid. An
Asian man searches for a crack of light to examine a sales
receipt. A baby cries. A thin female security guard wearing

an oversized belt holds Andrea by the arm and helps her sit down. "Sir, your wife is pretty sick."

"She's not my wife," you say too quickly. "She's just a friend." Andrea pushed back against the seat and stares up at the skylight, which sends in only a grayness. "When can we get out of here?" she asks. "The pills they gave me got me all groggy."

You see strands of gray in her long black hair. You think it is the hair that makes her seem so pale; at least you want to believe this. Her navy blue business suit is wrinkled. She is short, neither thin nor heavy, and her face is small with puffy cheeks that seem younger than her thirty-one years. Her lips coil inward on one side. Her smile is crooked— when she smiles.

"I don't believe I had an abortion," Andrea says. "I don't believe how much it hurt. The doctor wore shorts. A smock and shorts. Can you believe it?"

What you feel is anger. This is not normal for you. Andrea isn't your type—never has been. She gets angry quickly. She's impulsive. She designs windows for a department store and knows nothing about proper landscaping. You're not sure you like her—even as a friend, but you're not in any position to drop imperfect friendships. She's someone to talk to on a dateless Saturday night.

The two of you go to bars, and she picks out other women for you, but you never go up to them even though you are dressed in the latest fashions from Merry-Go-Round or The Gap. You are a failure at single's bars. You are shy. You like your work. At the office with blueprints in front of you, a pencil stuck above your ear and a tape measure in your pocket, you know how to correct problems, abnormalities or inefficiencies. You are a landscape architect and you know nothing about anger.

"Rain should let up soon," you say. You wonder if it is flooding outside.

"I hate Henry," Andrea says. "He's such a jerk." Henry, the father of the child, wouldn't pay for the abortion or escort Andrea to the clinic. You don't know why you volunteered. You thought it would be the right thing to do and perhaps it was, but you wonder if you took her because it was potentially interesting. Perhaps you were a waiting room voyeur. You've no idea if you're responsible for anything.

You want to get Andrea home so the anger will go away and you can slip into your workroom and finish plans for a golf course, a nature trail, a parking lot, anything.

The woman who had said, "Lord, Lord," leans against a window display of shoes and slumps to the floor. A girl with an alligator emblem on her pink shirt screams. A woman in black calls for someone to get an ambulance. You race down a mall aisle and stop the security guard. "A woman's fainted or something," you yell.

The guard clutches her walkie-talkie and rushes toward the woman. You follow. A crowd gathers. The hoagie girl continues to sell sandwiches. She is out of beer. Someone fans the woman with the tabloid. Sweat rises off the paleness of her face. You don't want to see her die.

You decide you've seen too much today. You hurry around the crowd and down a dark corridor of the mall. Stray refugees window shop in the dark. They press their faces against the display windows, attempting to see what is on sale.

"Parking lot's almost a lake," one says. "Waves and all."

Your firm had put in a bid to restructure the parking system in the lot of one of the malls in town. You could make the parking more efficient. Trees could shade the afternoon sun. Shrubbery! You move deeper into the darkened mall and things echo.

The Woman's Center Clinic wasn't unpleasant. In the waiting room, nervousness exhaled with cigarette smoke. The women and girls waiting for the procedure smoked. Their boyfriends, girlfriends and mothers also smoked.

You were on a well-flowered couch that sank too much. An old and frail security guard in a corner sipped coffee.

He was white as Elmer's Glue. You eyed the twenty people in the room as if they were celebrities. You were mindful of their need for privacy, but you were curious. You wanted to see if you could read their thoughts.

Andrea was in an adjacent room having the procedure when the large girl with too much makeup on sat next to you. She filled out a form. When she finished the form, she pulled an ashtray stand next to her.

"You'll have to put that back, Missy," the old security guard said to the large girl.

"Okay," she whispered and lit a cigarette, "After this cigarette."

You watched three boys across the room. They had all tried to sleep while waiting for their girlfriends, but only the youngest succeeded. The other two fidgeted with their cigarettes. They could have been waiting for allergy injections or dental cleaning, but the room was clouded with smoke.

Another girl, a tougher one wearing a Def Leppard T-shirt, was in the chair next to the couch. "How much longer?" she mumbled to her boyfriend, blowing smoke out of her nostrils like steam jets out of an iron.

"I think I'll go out and get a newspaper," her boyfriend said.

"Here," you said. "Read mine."

The boy rubbed the stubble of his junior beard. "Oh, thanks, man. That'll save me a trip."

You handed the kid the paper and realized he had wanted a five-minute walk more than he wanted to read the paper. The door to the examination room opened, then slammed shut. The large girl jumped. A nurse held a clipboard and called off six names. The tough girl coughed smoke, stood and marched with the other girls to the adjacent room as if an inductee at a selective service physical.

The large girl's face tightened. Her eyes were downcast. She hadn't been called. She would have to wait another hour. The large girl was alone. You had nothing to say to her. You felt she was brave to face the procedure alone. She wore a white silky blouse and a gray skirt. She lit another cigarette as her old one smoldered in the tray. You watched her stare deeply into that ashtray, and you knew she didn't see it.

"I need that ashtray back. Now!" the guard said as ashes from his cigarette fell to the floor.

She jumped and the cigarette popped from her hand and landed in the ashtray. "I'm sorry, I'm sorry," she whispered, mostly to herself. She shrank into the couch as much as she could.

You slid your eyes sideways to see if tears were running down her cheeks, but her face was dried petrified. The roto-tiller inside your stomach twisted. You looked away from her. You would remember her face. You realized she was in pain, and you had no grasp of how to measure that pain. You were angry because something was unfair.

Andrea came from behind the wall and flipped her hand at you as if you were a junior business associate. You followed her outside. She was as pale as clouded water. The thunder had begun. The sky flipped inside out. The storm let loose on the highway. You had to stop at the mall.

"Hey, man." A salesman in blue '40s-style trousers, a tie-dyed shirt from the '60s, hair greased back like Elvis in 1956 and a leather tie from Italy trips out from under the Merry-Go-Round gate with a candle and flashes his perfect teeth. "We're having a candlelight sale."

The Merry-Go-Round is where you buy your bar clothes. The sales people are terribly hip and usually dance with themselves while selling clothes. "What's your size?" he asks.

"I don't have a size today."

"Would you like to browse?"

"I can't see anything."

"You ever shopped in a horror movie? You could like

shop…like you're Dracula looking for a cape."

"My credit cards are at home," you lie.

"Layaway?"

"Shut up," you say. "Don't you know we're trapped in here?"

"Wow," he says.

You don't believe he exists. You don't believe you're still in the mall. You move away.

You've always been attracted to malls. They are accessible, efficient and there's no weather. You see yourself rushing deeper into the mall. An emergency light brightens a corner, but only a corner. You might as well be in a mall in Kansas City or Austin or Charleston. They are all the same. But malls in Kansas City have light; they are open. You remember a news item about a storm near Kansas City that sent a flood surging through the main concourse of a mall. You imagine mannequins in their Calvins floating past a B. Dalton's. It was the ultimate use of water in a mall.

You hear wheels behind you, small squeaky ones. You assume it is a baby carriage. You suppose this has significance. Your chest pounds, and you hear rain and rain and more rain. You pass a kitchenware store. There are strainers, bowls, salad forks and zucchini corers.

"Someone said they saw a twister," a voice from a rest area says.

"Sink holes. I seen 'em," another voice answers. "Eatin' trees, sidewalks."

The center of the mall seems to be coming closer to you.

A crowd is moving toward the door and watching a stretcher being rolled out to a waiting ambulance that lights up the mall like a disco. The female security guard sits on a couch, shaking her head and rubbing her eyes. Andrea is next to her. She seems asleep. You wonder if she is dead.

You rush up to her and shake her shoulder. Her eyes blink. She stares straight ahead, beyond you. "I want to go home. Where have you been? I need you to be here."

You try to swallow to unplug your clogged ears. The

ambulance light disappears. Water is seeping into the mall. You wonder if they should sandbag the front doors with Walden books. You wonder if Andrea had a name for the child, if it is too late for her to have another child. You worry about the old woman.

And you wonder if you'll ever have a child or anyone to have a child with. You are twenty-eight years old and you play co-ed softball, you are good at Trivial Pursuit, and you have lost track as to why you would want to get married. You pull at your ear, you tilt your head, but there is nothing to unplug.

You want out. Condensation covers the windows of the front doors. It is dark out. It is dark in.

"That lady's dead," Andrea says.

You are outside, and the wind knocks you over. You crawl behind cars that are parked scatterbrained, as if in a junkyard. The water is above your ankles. You find your car and get an industrial tape measure off the dashboard. The water soaks into your jeans. You run for the entrance to the mall parking lot. The ground is higher and slanted near the entrances.

Your job is to measure the distances between Green B and Orange A. You must determine the proper angle for parking spaces. More parking spaces can be created. You stick the tape measure end into the grass on the edge of the lot and stab it with a stray hubcap. Then you pull. The tape buckles, wails and snaps back into the container. This time you cover the tape end with a rock. The rain slaps your face as you walk across the soggy grass. The roto-tiller in your stomach tightens.

You stop and stand on the tape. You are wet, breathless and teetering on some confused brink. You are afraid it will snap. You are afraid. You are wet and petrified because Andrea is not well, because the large girl's face has swollen too much in your mind, because some lady whose face you don't remember is dead, and because there is no reality in measurement.

And you stand wavering, windblown, a refugee on soggy grass, and you feel like an old lighthouse keeper searching endlessly for something to come out of the fog, but you have no light.

Greg Williams has a Master of Fine Arts degree in creative writing from the University of Oregon. He is currently curator of photographs for the San Diego Historical Society and has held archival positions in Charleston, New Jersey, Oregon, and Williamsburg, Virginia. He lives in Solana Beach, California, with his daughter, Anna.

Susan Beckham Jackson

LAW'S PASSAGE

Law called Janie on the phone that night and started talking like he hadn't been anywhere. Like he didn't know himself he'd been gone two weeks from school. Janie asked where in the world he had been, if he knew the Democrats had come to power, but he skipped her question and said he had missed her. Then he called her Bee Bee, and she knew he needed her.

When they were kids across the street from each other and just starting to be friends, he gave her that name. She had stepped right into a yellow jacket's nest when they were walking in her back lot. She had screamed, "bees," over and over because they were all in her hair and stinging her scalp. Law ripped out her ponytail and chased them out with his fingers. And then he was screaming too. Later, when they were mending from the stings, he said she was his Bee Bee.

"What is it?" she asked him now. Most times he wanted something silly, getting her help with little things he'd rather avoid. Not long ago he'd put her up to calling his mother for extra allowance. He had pulled up to the pay phone at the Quick Stop and stood close, his ear beside hers so he could listen too.

"Darling Janie, how sweet to hear from you," his mother's voice rushed at her. "Is everything okay? Are you taking care of Law for me?" Then Janie explained how Law needed money. It was so easy because his mother gave him anything.

But the way he said her name now, she knew he didn't just need her help with an errand. He needed her. But she didn't want to talk, no matter how she cared. Two weeks was a long time for no one to know where he was, even if she was relieved to hear Law's soft voice in her ear.

Ever since Tricia had broken things off with him, he had been off center, even for Law. He drank more for one thing. And he never went to class. He couldn't stay focused on anything for very long except for thinking about Tricia.

He had gone completely berserk a few weeks ago when he saw the boy Tricia was going out with. He ran right up on the boy in the front lobby of Janie's college dorm when he came to pick up Janie.

Thrusting himself into the room, Law had picked up the nearest thing, the trashcan, and hurled it. The boy saw what was coming and ducked but got bashed in the shoulder anyway. The boy's fist of Gerald Ford stickers scattered, paper flew out and pencil shavings littered the air.

Somehow, Janie had pulled Law from the room. She told him to stop all this craziness. She said they should go do what he came for, to ride with the top down on his little red car on the first warm day. After awhile he calmed down.

"Come on, Bee Bee, please," she could hear him now over the phone. "I really want to see you. My kissing cousin."

She knew he'd be sitting at the kitchen table at the A-frame river house he rented with his roommates. She knew he'd have an ashtray flowing over, and tiny bits of ash, scattered everywhere likes spots in the pattern of the Formica tabletop. And the newspaper, maybe, and beer cans, lots of beer cans.

His voice was cool but eager too. It told her how he looked. He crinkled his brow when he was really fired up or wanted something. And his John Lennon glasses slipped down his nose. He always pushed them with one finger back up his nose, over and over, gaining more and more speed, the more he talked.

He hadn't had the glasses yet when they were little, and he announced out of nowhere he thought they were cousins. "Maybe third or fourth. I'm sure of it," he said. "I asked Mama, and she said it could be because your eyes are the same blue as mine. She said you hair is caramel colored too."

"No, we're not," she had laughed at him and touched his shiny brown bangs that hung down over his forehead. "You're just my friend." But she could still feel sometimes, grown as she was in college, the aching wish that what he said was true.

"So, can I kiss you anyway? Even if you're just my friend, but I still can believe you're my cousin," he said.

And she told him yes, just that one time, and he had bent toward her, his brow crinkling up. He pulled her awkwardly by the shoulders and touched his lips to her cheek, and he kissed her mouth like he was a grown up.

But there was nothing awkward about his kisses or his ways now. Or at least she figured that from watching all the girls who had adored him. That sweetness always stayed with him. He knew it too, and drew people to him.

Except Tricia. Tricia had finally needed something else. Something Law couldn't provide her. An order. A form. But Janie believed that part of him would come. Things worked out with time. Some people just got there later.

"Come on out here tonight," he said. "I've brought back stuff for a party. Hey, a victory party for Mr. Carter and a new start. I've already told the guys." The guys were his four roommates.

"What stuff? Forget it. I guess I know. Is that what you've been doing all this time, just roaming around and doping?"

"More or less," he said, "But nah, that's not all," he added quickly. "I had some things to do."

"What things? You're making that up. What are you doing about your classes?"

"Going to sit in the class, I guess. Listen, what are you doing right now?"

"I'm studying."

"Pack an overnight bag," he said. "You don't want to drive that dark road back into town late. Why don't you bring Lucy, too? You think I'd like her? Would she want to go out with me?" One sentence piled on top of another, and she wondered if maybe he was already into stuff, the grass or the acid. It always amazed her he got these things so easily. Things she'd be scared to death to do.

"Maybe. But Law. I don't know. What are you thinking all this time? How are you going to catch up? Can you even pass the semester?" She'd thought about getting Lucy, her roommate, new this semester, involved with him but it wasn't a good idea for Lucy.

"Probably not." He laughed low and muffled in his frog-throated way. "So, why worry about it now? It'll work out," he said.

A part of her wanted to go out there. She missed him. But if she didn't go, it would say something to him. Wouldn't it? She stared down into her lap. She was sitting on her bed, legs crossed, her feet on her thighs, the way she did when she studied and concentrated. She ran her fingers along the creases that formed in her jeans at the tops of her bent legs. She wandered off thinking of him, what to do.

"Hey, are you there? Where'd you go? You know I've got that extra toothbrush for you," he said.

She came back to him and reached her hand up to grasp the receiver, balancing it while she raked her fingertips through the short hair. She thought of him smiling. And showing that line of straight, squared teeth, off color just enough to prove they were genuine.

"You remember. I said I'd get it after last time you were here," he said.

She hadn't meant to stay that night, but Law worked it out that way. She'd been to a dance with a boy she had just met. And she saw Law there, too, dancing with everybody.

He came to her and said, "My favorite girl." Then, he swirled her in the air. She could feel now that same little tremble she felt from the dance that night, and she fought it away.

She said sharp into the phone, "The things you do for me."

"Hey, now, what about that guy you were with? Didn't I look out for you?" he asked.

Her date, Joe, hadn't known what to make of him at first. Breaking in that way and making a show. But Law won him quickly and invited them out to the river house. Joe got drunk, very drunk. He went to bed. And it got late.

So late, that Janie had to go to bed, too. When she looked for a bed, they were all full with Law's roommates and their girlfriends, so she just ended up on the other side of the bed from Joe. Law had followed into the room behind her, still on his feet. "Now you be careful with Bee Bee," he told Joe even though Joe couldn't have been listening. "She's my cousin, and nothing can happen to her." It was all so silly, him always acting like her great protector, but she never stopped him.

After a little while Joe had come to and decided if she was in the bed with him, well it must be okay to see where it'd lead, and he started rubbing her knee.

She scrambled out of the bed and climbed up to the loft where Law slept and slipped in. In the morning, he woke her. He was brushing his teeth, and he said through his mouth of paste and foam that Joe said to say goodbye.

"You need a toothbrush?" he had mouthed to her then. "You use mine, and I'll buy you one for next time you need it."

He was working on her now, reminding her of these things. Getting her out of her anger. It was the way Law could do. So she played back at him, in spite of herself. "Coming out there might get me in trouble," she said.

"You're just leading me on," he said, playing back. "But you stay there and study like a good girl, and I will call you soon."

Later, near the edge of sleep, she didn't pay attention to the steady knocking for a while. Finally, she started up, thinking it was Lucy with no key, but then she heard Law calling her from the other side of her dormitory door.

"I can't believe you did this," she said, breathless, coming awake, stumbling over clothes to let him in. "Ssshh. This whole dorm is probably asleep."

"No, it's not. You don't want to be a stick in the mud. I won't let you. Really, it's early. It's election night. Come with me," he said. And he was picking up her jeans and holding them out. "Please, Bee Bee. You make me feel good. I need you to be with me."

In the car, he talked for a while about how much fun everyone was having back at the river house. How she'd be so glad she came instead of sleeping.

When he stopped talking, she was quiet. "You aren't still mad are you?" he said.

"No," she said and it was the truth, but still she couldn't completely stop this weariness from crouching on her.

"Well, let's just look at the night, then," he said. He reached over and touched her arm.

"It is pretty," she said. The moon hung full and red streaked in front of them in a clear sky where the stars shone out like hot white sparks. "I just care about you is all," she said finally.

"I know you do. And I care about you. But let's don't worry. Not tonight."

"Law," Janie said suddenly. "Pull over. Don't you see the light? Revolving in the mirror? You'd better stop."

"What the hell," he said, and his first impulse was to speed up.

"Stop, Law. You can't do that. What's the matter with you?"

He pulled to the shoulder, so changed in a moment, his hands wildly jumping on his thighs. "What is going on?" she said again.

"Just be quiet, will you? Don't say anything."

"What would I say?" His agitation frightened her.

Janie looked at Law curling his fingers under to control his hands as the officer talked. But the whole thing turned out to be nearly nothing. Just a taillight was out.

When the officer pulled away, Law stretched his fingers out and smoothed them down his thighs. But he was sweating down the sides of his temples.

"There's something in this car, isn't there?" asked Janie.

"Yeah, I guess there is," he said. "Under your seat."

"My seat?" And she reached under and pulled out a shoebox. Inside were little plastic bags with pills and powder.

"Back, I want to go back now," Janie told him.

"I know. I'm sorry. Really I am. You know I'd never hurt you."

"But you would have. Having this stuff and me in the car. You've gone crazy, Law. This is too much for a party. You're dealing this stuff." Later, she tried to remember what she'd said to him when she got back to her dorm and left him, but she couldn't.

Three days later Lucy drove her to his place at the river and dropped her off. She stood on charred wood and debris where the house had been, where seven people had died. Everybody who'd stayed the night. The thought gave her one of those quick cold chills that ran up her spine and down her arms. She thought this wouldn't have happened if she had been there. She wouldn't have let it.

She hadn't thought she could bear coming here; she didn't want to see. She came because Law's mama, in her town two hours away, asked her to get his car.

The whole place was gone except part of the chimney, still red, without a stain of smoke on it. How could that be? She bent down and picked up a handful of lumps and ashes. In the debris she grabbed—some remaining part of an object, something pointed, stuck her hand. It jabbed into soft flesh, and she clenched her blackened hand. A single, full and perfectly round drop of blood formed in her palm and then another.

She felt strange and unreal, so disconnected from herself in all this smoky dustiness of a crumbled world around her. She stepped around in the open space and walked through where a wall had been from the kitchen to the den. She stepped over metal springs, and her feet dropped into soft soot that swirled in little gray clouds.

She gasped to realize this was Law's fat armchair. A shabby thing covered in huge red poppies that he adored. That he dickered joyfully for in a secondhand store downtown. Her arm dangled out beside her, reaching air where the little table beside the chair had been. Where Law always left his glasses and ring, his grandfather's signet ring. "Please," she heard herself calling.

She gripped the car keys hard, and her hand throbbed. She concentrated on the pain in the hand. She liked feeling the pain and seeing the blood. It was real. It made her cry out.

What was real and unreal and what she'd never dared to think ran together in her head. She cried out in trembling noises, holding her aching hand, until words finally came and she cried, "I loved you, Law, I loved you."

Susan Beckham Jackson is on the English faculty at Spartanburg Technical College. Her fiction writing awards include the South Carolina Fiction Project, Porter Fleming Writing Competition and runner-up in the Hub City Hardegree Fiction Contest.

Fred Thompson III

THE RECKONING

I dress quickly in a lime green polo shirt and find a pair of yellow Sansabelt slacks. I put on my Bulldog baseball cap. I slip on white socks and my penny loafers. Just the thought of not going to the office and not dealing with the files stacked up on my desk and the empty checkbook has made me giddy. My giddiness inexplicably flowers into a sense of happiness. But I'm all alone and don't have anyone to share this warm glowing euphoria. I can fix that, though.

I get to my car, a Mustang convertible, and I labor to pull the top down. It's now 8:00 a.m., and I need to hurry if I'm going to make it on time. I drive out purposefully through the city streets in the rush hour traffic, fretting at the lights and the stop-and-go pace. I get to the school just in time. Just as I pull into the faculty parking lot, I hear a final 8:20 a.m. bell. I park and race to the lower school administration office.

"I'm William Blanton. I need to pick up my son, William, Jr., for a dentist's appointment."

The secretary is an elderly woman with a broach on her collar. She's a lifer, spent every day for thirty years right here, I bet. She's looking at me with distrust. I haven't been to William's school that much, so she doesn't know me.

"Mr. Blanton, we're aware of your separation from your wife. She asked us to contact her in the event that any requests were made regarding William, Jr."

So, Janice, you're thinking ahead, as always. I turn on my most impressive manner. "Yes, you're very correct. William's mother and I have had a very mature and amicable separation. We're both very involved with the child and his best interest. If you need to call her, of course, please do." Please don't, I think to myself.

While I'm talking, the secretary spies a note on her bulletin board. "It says here that William, Jr. is to get out of school today at 12:00 for some appointment. It says his mother will pick him up."

So, they're planning to bring William, Jr. to court. "Oh, yes," I say. "That's for the dentist appointment. He called and asked if we could change from 12:30 to 9:00. William's Mom couldn't make it, but she asked if I could rearrange. So I'm elected." I smile a warm and ingratiating smile. She relents. She goes to the PA system and flips a toggle switch. I hear the echo of her amplified voice calling William, Jr. to the office. We wait in silence.

When the door opens, I see William, Jr's small head round the corner. He has tousled dirty blond hair and is short for his age. He has a scrawny, wiry thin little body on top of dowel legs. I haven't seen much of him these last few weeks and he didn't expect me. His face is wary, suspicious when he sees me. "Billy, I'm here to pick you up." I am effusive, I dominate. William shrinks.

"I thought Mom was going to pick me up at noon."

"We've changed plans. I'm supposed to pick you up now." I smile. I open my hands. See, I'm not hiding anything. William stands still and stares at me like I'm a tree. He says nothing.

The secretary speaks. "William? Is it okay?"

That prods him, and he responds. "Yeah, sure, fine."

"Well, okay, son, do you have your things?" I ask and at the same time start edging him out the door.

"Wait. You have to sign him out," the secretary says. I'm eager to be gone, so I scrawl my name without delay and then we're out the door.

She calls to William as the door closes. "Good luck at the dentist's!"

As we walk, William says, "What did she mean, dentist? I don't have a dentist's appointment. I'm supposed to be going to the lawyer's office with Mom and then to court to talk to the judge."

"Son, I'm a lawyer, too, and I know all about these things. So don't worry. What I really came for is to get you so we can go out and enjoy the morning together. Let's go to the National and play off the regular tees."

I'm walking fast, and I've got William's hand in mine. He's half walking, half skipping to keep up. I'm gripping him pretty tight.

"Dad, I've got a test next period in English. I can't just go out to play golf."

"Of course you can, Son. I'll write you an excuse. I've got your clubs in the trunk. You can make up a little school-work anytime. We've got to seize the Moment."

We reach the car. I toss William's books into the back seat. I grab the passenger door for him. For a moment, my eyes meet his. He is a raccoon frozen in headlights, unable to move out of the way. I jerk my head toward the seat to break the spell, and he gets in.

We speed off, out and over the bridges past the suburban strip malls. There's no conversation because of the wind noise. William, Jr. just stares out to the right. I see only the back of his head.

We make the right turn through the white picket fence gate and into the golf course. The sunny, clear day has drawn a crowd to the course; a young attendant drives up in an electric cart once I've parked. I pull out my clubs and William, Jr.'s cut down set. While the attendant hooks the clubs onto the cart, I stroll toward the clubhouse. William stays in the cart; he hasn't spoken since the school.

Several groups of golfers are lined up, waiting at the first tee. I spy the assistant pro, a social climbing personality, who bubbles over when he sees me.

"Mr. Blanton, how are you?"

"Fine, fine, Ronnie. I'm out with my son. Can you let us go off as a two-some?" I smile a broad, male grin that connects.

Ronnie's face suddenly is serious. "Gosh, Mr. Blanton, we're packed. We're playing all foursomes. If you don't have a starting time, I don't know. He squints, runs his finger down the sign-up ledger. Then he lets his finger stop and taps the page. He looks up, smiling back at me now. "I tell you what, if you don't mind, I've got an older couple from up North, a husband and wife. They're out on the driving range. I can pair you up. Billy and the woman can play off the reds. I can let you go off on the back nine."

"Fine. Great!" I say. I hadn't pictured my fine morning to be so crowded, but I'm still feeling good. I pay with my corporate American Express card, get my complimentary tees and a new black glove, and saunter out to the cart. William sits in the cart, tiny and forlorn. I put on my golf shoes; white Reebok pumps. "Don't look so down in the mouth," I kid him, "you look like you've got the weight of the world on your shoulders."

He tries a smile, but it dies below his eyes. He looks at me as though I'm a stranger. I feel a tiny chill in my mood. "Come on, son, we're playing with another couple. I want you to show some personality, you hear?"

"Yes, sir," is all he says.

We reach the tee and meet the Masons from Ohio, cartoon characters drawn to be friendly, generous, contented, devoted lifetime partners. George is retired and he and Winnie travel all over; married forty-five years; four children and six grandchildren. Winnie has pictures of them all in her purse.

The tenth hole is a par four, slight dogleg left, marsh on the left from tee to green. Large traps guard the right side. From the regular tees, the hole plays 385 yards; from the woman's tees, it plays around 290. George lets me go first. I've taken no warmup, but I tee it up and hit a low fade that stays in the right side of the fairway. I hit my graphite driver a ton, and even though I'm a little off on this first shot, I'm out about 240 or so. George and Winnie congratulate me; then George hits a low drive so straight it is as if it were on a string. He is short off the tee, only about 190 or 200, but with those shots, he'll never be in trouble. An old man's game, I think, no terror, but no triumphs either.

William stands on the women's tee with his cut down Taylor-Made metal wood I bought him last Christmas just after I left home. I'd thought then that this would be how I'd keep up with him, playing a man's game together, but we haven't played but twice since then. He's got a sweet swing. Two summers ago, sandwiched between soccer and baseball, we'd sent him to a day golf camp run by Ronnie. He hits straight down the middle, about 150 yards.

"You the man!" I call.

"Oh excellent shot," George says.

William winces, then smiles shyly.

We play out the hole.

We wait on the eleventh tee, a par three, for the group ahead to clear the green.

"Hit and wait today," I say.

Winnie talks to William. "William, young man, how nice to see you spending time with your father. But how did you get out of school. Is it a vacation?"

"No, ma'am," Williams says. "My Dad came and got me out of school. We're supposed to go to court this afternoon." He volunteers nothing further; I see their eyes glance at each other. I'd better say something.

"My wife and I are separated and we've got a hearing this afternoon. We're just out here trying to relax." I'm feeling forced now, like I'm having to explain things to people I don't know. "Let's play some golf and have fun, okay?" That comes out badly.

We play the eleventh and twelfth with no conversation, only golf etiquette. "You're away, nice putt," etc. But on the thirteenth something strange happens. The thirteenth is a straight, short par five. With my distance off the tee, I can sometimes reach the green in two strokes and have a chance at an eagle, and a good opportunity to birdie. Today, though, I'm distracted and I miss the green into the trap. I can't get up and down, and I get bogey.

"That's par five for me," George happily announces. Suddenly from out of view I hear Winnie, angry. "That's six and you know it. You were in the trap off the tee and took an extra stroke getting out."

George's face darkens with amazing speed and he snaps, "God damn it, I did not. If you're so intent on following me around and counting my stokes behind me, just quit playing yourself!"

Winnie isn't cowed. "George, you're cheating again, just like always, and I'm fed up with it!"

They realize William is gaping at them, and they stomp off the green in sullen silence.

"Dad," William says when we're in our cart out of earshot. "They're really mad at each other."

"Yes, it seems like it."

"Did George really cheat?" he asks.

"I don't know." I say. "But it can't matter. We're not betting on anything. We're really not even keeping score."

William says, "It sure seems to matter to them a lot."

We arrive at the next tee. George is glowering at Winnie, Winnie stopping in mid-sentence when we pull alongside.

George sits silent, the sides of his jaws working in and out. He doesn't get out of the cart. Winnie speaks. "We're a little tired from the trip down. We're going to go on in."

At that she pushes the throttle and off they go. No good luck; no thank you very much; no nothing. As soon as they start off, they're talking in each other's ears. Their faces drawn and hard. I look at William. I see suddenly that he's on the verge of crying.

"Dad," he says, trying to blink back tears, "Why did you really go away from us?"

I look into his eyes and I know he deserves an answer.

He deserves the truth. I feel a lump in my throat like a big rubber ball, like I can't breathe, and I know that I can't tell him the truth. Not now, not never, because I don't have a truth in me. What do I say? That it is a no-fault divorce? No fault. What a great legal phrase, I love it the way it rolls off the lips—no fault. What went wrong? Why is your marriage over? Why are your children going to go through the wringer of knowing that life is dangerous and that nothing is going to be permanent for them? Why, it's nobody's fault, it just happens! I love it; I embrace the whole concept of no fault. You've got to roll with the punches, little boy, because your Mom and Dad have decided, through nobody's fault, to fork in the road.

But I look at those eyes and I know I'm not the man to tell him that, so I say, "William, I just don't know."

William looks at me as though I have stabbed him. Without a word, he gets off the cart and backs away from me, keeping his body square facing me, and his eyes on me.

"William, I…"

But he keeps backing up and then when he's ten yards away, he turns and runs for the woods behind the tee box.

"William!" I call but he doesn't look back.

I get down and start to go after him, but another golf cart drives up. "Any trouble?"

"No, no, fine, my son just needs to use the bathroom. You guys play through."

When I turn back, William is gone.

I'm crazy now. I'm crashing through the woods. "William, William!" "William, please come back!" But no voice returns. I look and look. I jump a drainage ditch and fall to my knees in the muddy bank. I come out of the woods into the new construction skeletons of the country club houses being built back on another fairway. I walk around each one. I search without thinking, until I sit down on a pile of bricks. Finally it occurs to me that William has undoubtedly gone back to the pro shop. He's probably cooled down, has a Coke and is ready to talk. I notice the time. I'm stunned. It's already past one o'clock. The hearing is at 2:00. I run back to the abandoned cart and drive it back to the clubhouse. I try to assume a healthy demeanor. It is hard with the briar scratches on my arm and the muddy knees on my yellow pants.

Ronnie meets me with a serious tone, "Mr. Blanton. What's going on here? Your son came in and used the phone. He went outside and wouldn't talk to me at all. Then he was picked up by a woman in a station wagon. Should I have stopped him?"

William has been picked up by my wife. I look at my watch. It's ten till two. I say, "No, no, Ronnie. Everything's fine." I turn and run out to the car. I jump in and crank up. As I accelerate through the gravel paved lot, spinning tires and throwing up rocks, the attendant runs behind.

"Mr. Blanton, your clubs, your shoes!"

No time. I've got to go. I look down. I'm wearing my golf shoes and I have my golf glove on. I strip the glove off and throw it overboard.

I'm driving very fast as I retrace my route to town. My Mustang roars its approval as I weave in and out of the slow traffic. I drive into the County Court parking garage at ten after two. I think, these judges are always late from lunch, maybe I've made it. But when I get to the door of the court waiting room and give my name to the guard, he says, "Mr. Blanton, you're late, they've already started."

I try to rush through but the metal detector at the guard station sounds an alarm. Everyone waiting looks over at me. I start taking out keys and ball markers and sunglasses, even my wallet, but the alarm sounds again. This time I notice the two guards looking at me with hard, tense eyes. My eyes follow theirs to my feet. I'm still wearing my golf shoes. I smile and shrug. Toe to heel, I drag one off and step on the other heel to pull out the other. I walk through and the alarm mercifully stays silent. The guards are indecisive. What they see is a man in a lime green shirt with scratches on his arms, muddy knees on his yellow polyester golf pants, and white stocking feet, muddy at the ankles. I then re-member my baseball cap. I reach up and drag it off slowly. I smile and keep moving. "I'm late, guys, Blanton versus Blanton, Courtroom C, right?"

They trail along behind, unsure of whether to shoot me or escort me, as I, shoes in hand, run down the hall to the court and my family.

Fred Thompson lives on Sullivan's Island with his wife, Dr. Carolyn Thiedke, and two sons, John and Edward. He was born in Charleston and graduated from Yale University in 1973 and from Duke University School of Law in 1979. He is a practicing lawyer in Mount Pleasant.

Debra A. Daniel

Signs of Deer

This morning before my mother left for work, she found me staring at myself in the bathroom mirror. She stood behind me, took my hunting cap off my head and tried to fluff my hair. It was no use. "Let's try a permanent," she said. I put the cap on again. She looked like she was drinking from a well of blue sadness. Then she said, "Orange isn't your color."

I told her, "People who wear orange are less likely to be murdered." Our faces stared into the mirror.

"I'm not worried about you being murdered," she said. Then she says what she always says, "Billie, I worry about you rambling in the woods by yourself all day. You should be with your friends and act like a girl."

My mother has never had friendship problems. She's on the phone and out to dinner all the time. One Saturday a month she meets her "lunch bunch." Sometimes she drags me along to their favorite tearoom where models in cocktail dresses glide to your table, let you feel the fabric, and gush over the new colors.

She doesn't leave my father out either. He grills burgers or barbecues chickens for her cookouts. She crowds the yard with white-legged men in shorts and women with phony laughs. People love my mother. That's important to her. She's charming, pretty, and has a welcoming face. Naturally, people like her.

My mother, whose hair slow dances around her face, whose eyes seem as delicious as blueberries, whose nose and cheekbones are delicate ice carvings never expected a daughter like me. It's true that love is blind. My mother doesn't realize how I really look.

But people who don't love me have noticed my uncommon face and have started to leave me out. My mother knows Caralyn doesn't call and that I haven't begged for a camping sleepover in the woods, but she hasn't figured out why. What she likes is for the house to be filled with giggling girls and for me to go to parties. She likes for me to be surrounded by friends. It would be hard for her to know the truth. Luckily, when the school bus drops me off, she's not there to see me walk home alone. For her, being alone is punishment. For me, it's a relief. Seventh grade is torture for a girl who isn't pretty.

On the far side of our thirty-nine acres, my father is clearing fields of his swearing rocks. He's convinced they sprout and cover ground faster than cucumber vines after a July rain. "Fine crop of damn rocks this year," he'll say. "Forget fertilizer. Just blink and up they come. Damn rocks."

Until last year, I helped toss those hateful rocks into his wagon, making the field safe for his plow blades. Sometimes after he bush-hogged a new road through the woods, I'd take the lopper and clear out trip-stumps that could stub your boot and land you on your face. My father says when you walk through woods before daylight, your feet have to trust your path. After the pines were harvested, I stepped next to him for hours handing him seedlings while he used the dibble to wedge the soil apart. Then I'd stoop to tamp the dirt around the tiny thread-roots. We were birthing a new forest, he said, not the hardwood kind where a person can forget their problems, but the kind that could become paper for a love letter or a great novel. Until last year, I felt important and sure.

Now I'm thirteen and things have changed. I've been

banned from what my mother calls "farmhand chores." My father stopped trying to talk sense into her. He says it's like hammering your own finger. Life is so mixed up that every afternoon I need what my father calls "a dose of hardwood forest."

So this afternoon while my father minds the business of the farm, I pack a knapsack with apples, binoculars, and two mirrors. Then I leave the house to track deer, to climb the tree stand in deep wintered woods where I can watch for the piebald buck and think sorrowful thoughts about myself.

The woods don't care how I look. They don't care that my hair can't be fluffed. Trees don't notice my face is different or whisper about me. I hear wind and forest murmurs. I can sit with trees and not be left out. In the woods, being alone doesn't bother me at all.

September, a year ago, was when I first saw the piebald buck. A group of does were browsing beneath the tree stand where my father and I had been sitting since before daybreak. The ghost of night still haunted the forest, its misty spirit hovering around trees and fingering the deer as they grazed on mushrooms. Summer was dying, leaving a sweet-damp scent of decaying leaves and sassafras to remember her by. It was so quiet we could hear the deer's soft chewing. Then, as if on cue, the does raised their heads and turned toward the creek. My father and I looked, too, turning our heads slowly so as not to spook the animals. And there he was, the piebald buck, standing where the deer trail opened onto the hollow.

I felt a gasp rising, my mouth dropping, my eyes widening; then, on my arm, the hand of my father, stilling me. I drew back inside myself and made my breathing easy again.

The buck's hide was dappled in browns, tans, and beiges like a map showing the acres where he had spent his life. He entered the clearing like a nobleman. There should've been trumpets. As he passed, drab-coated deer bent back to feeding and he moved with a rustling step through the hollow and out of sight.

Later, when the does had gone and we could speak again, my father told me I'd seen his secret, that he'd been watching the piebald buck for many seasons. "Old Calico," as he called him, was wily, cautious and such a close look was rare. He said it spoke well of our woodland skills that the old buck hadn't detected us and I shouldn't expect to always be so lucky.

He was right. Since then I've only glimpsed Old Calico at the field's edge. I've seen what might've been his white flash of tail vanish through the brush. But I never stop searching. He's always on my hope list. It's the same today.

It's Friday after Thanksgiving and people are joyful and expectant, but on the land, I hear November sighing. Our garden plots stand neglected as stray dogs. Leaves cover the ground, but they're no longer color-splattered by October. Instead they've surrendered to brown, rustling and muttering their last requests. November has discouraged the briars that in summer snap at my heels, reach up and snatch rips in my jeans.

It's cold, not the blinding bright-cold of an open field. It's the kind of muffled-cold that wraps around the woods but doesn't lay itself against your skin. November has peeled the forest to its framework. The cluttered tangle is gone. Getting a foothold is easier, so is seeing the sky.

I head to the hardwood hollow where life seems simple and I think the cleanest. Along the way I search for the signs of deer my father has shown me like heart-shaped spoors proving passage through plowed fields. I spot a fresh rub on a pine sapling. A buck, maybe Old Calico, has been polishing his antlers. On the ground beneath chewed-off branches, leaves have been scraped from the path by a buck's front feet. My father says they do that when they're in rut, ready to mate and feeling frisky. He'll be pleased as to my scouting report and say that Old Calico must be kicking up his heels. I walk on spotting droppings, shiny and wet, evidence it hasn't been long since the deer was here. I could've spooked him myself.

I examine the scat, amazed that a large animal leaves such droppings, only raisin-sized pellets. If my father were here, he'd actually pick up a pellet to check its freshness, laughing when I refuse to touch it, telling me my mother doesn't have to worry that I act like a girl. I smile, imagining my mother's horror if my father surprised her with a handful of deer scat. I think of her shrieking through the woods scaring rabbits, squirrels, and even the Indian ghosts on the spearpoint ridge.

The hollow feels sheltered, insulated from people noise. It's shadowy here and already on the way to dark. The groundcover is slicker. I ease my feet along so I don't slip and imagine my classmates at the skating rink tonight. I could go. It's for all seventh graders, but I feel too uncomfortable in myself these days.

Until this year, I didn't know I looked different from the others. All through grammar school I played kickball and seven-up at recess and ate lunch with friends everyday. I went to birthday parties and invited classmates for Saturdays on the farm. But when we went to seventh grade the same kids I had known my whole life started asking questions and saying things that made my face burn, that made me want to hide.

In gym one day, Caralyn asked me why my face was so flat. Caralyn, my friend since first grade, looked at me like I smelled bad. But that wasn't all. When we studied the colonies in history, Mrs. Hagin assigned us to find about our heritage. When she called on me, I told her Scotch-English-Irish, like my mother had said. She tapped her pen against her cheek and stared at me. Then she said, "Your parents told you that?" like I was making it up. Later Deeny Morgan, who is popular and pretty, said my father must've brought me home from a foreign country like Korea or Vietnam. He was in the army, she said, so it could have happened. Then people nodded like she had the answer to an extra credit question. A boy asked me if I was dropped on my face when I was a baby and Joe Blume laughed that I must have been mowed down by a Mack truck. I'd see groups of kids at chorus practice and in study hall watch me and whisper. For awhile, I ignored them, but it got too hard.

Now I'm alone a lot even when I'm standing in line at the canteen after lunch or sitting in the commons watching science on educational television with a hundred seventh graders. I pretend I'm concentrating on my book, deep into pre-algebra or the conjugation of a verb. I try to look busy.

Lunchtime is the worst. The cafeteria is crammed with kids wanting to sit where the popular crowd discusses what is cool. At the beginning of the year I ate with Caralyn, but now she sits with Deeny and some eighth grade boys. Sometimes she says she's sorry the table filled before I got my tray, but I see her roll her eyes as I walk away. Lots of days I skip lunch, go to the library and pretend a book report is due. I pray for three o'clock so I can go home and lose myself in the woods.

When I was younger, my father taught me forest lessons: how to recognize tracks, why quail roost in a circle, the importance of silence. I trekked after him before dawn into the smoky gray darkness of the woods to scout the albino turkey.

And when I got scared, like the first times I climbed twelve feet to the tree stand, he made me keep trying. My father climbed right behind me. I could see his arms on either side of me and hear him counting steps. "Four more, Billie. Three. Only two." My best times have been in the tree stand with my father, quiet for hours. There is always reward for patience and silence, he says. I believe him.

We'd sit camouflaged and still, spying on forest animals. I'd hold my breath while deer tripped along, uprooting mushrooms or munching on acorns. I've seen bobcats, fox squirrels, and five kinds of woodpeckers. When my mother took away my farmhand chores, I started going to the tree stand alone, encouraging myself up the steps, hearing my father's voice inside my head.

My mother's afraid of heights and can't understand how I'm content so far from the ground. She tells my father he shouldn't have allowed me to climb, shoot a BB gun, and do boy things. My father laughs and says, "A girl as pretty as Billie won't ever be mistaken for a boy. Being high above the earth will give her perspective." My mother says, "It'll give her nosebleeds." She comes home with magazines for teenage girls and marks pages with clothes and hairstyles she says will accent my features. But I want to hide my features. I look at my parents and I can't figure it out. They are beautiful; my mother as feminine as wisteria and my father, tall and lean, rugged and pure like the forest. I don't know what happened to me.

Once I'm in the stand, I take out the mirrors. I turn my orange hat backwards to hold my hair, tilting my head to examine the planes and angles. Flatness juts out and all my features line up in one pale surface.

If I took my face apart like a jigsaw puzzle, each feature alone would be faintly pretty. My eyes are green like holly. My nose is small and straight, and my lips aren't thin and stingy, but they do point downward at the corners, the same as my father's. Sometimes it makes him look sad even when he isn't.

Mother says I have fine cheekbones and my face will grow to fit my oversized teeth. My hair is blacker than the night forest. Maybe that's why I'm asked if I'm Korean, Chinese, or Indian. But other dark-haired kids don't get those questions.

I hold the mirrors to show my profile: narrow forehead slanting back into my hairline, eyebrows in a stern black line, eyes shielding the almost non-existent bridge of my nose. The cheekbones that please my mother rise out of my face to camouflage all but the end of my nose.

It isn't my father's fault he doesn't have money now for braces, but that doesn't stop my front teeth from protruding, pushing my upper lip out almost as far as the tip of my nose. The sad curve of my lips draws attention to my chin, pointy but unconvincing. Altogether there is flatness, flatness surrounded by hair black as used motor oil and straight as pine needles. I know my face by heart. I see what they see.

I brood until I hear my father's quail call. I answer back, one call, then scan the woods for my camouflaged father until I see a flash of orange through the branches.

He climbs up to join me. I tell him about the rub, the scrape, the droppings. He says it could be Old Calico or any ordinary buck, just as easy. I hand him an apple. He sees the mirrors.

"That's your mother's vanity mirror." He waits. Patient. Silent. Soon I cry. He doesn't hug me tight and smothering but puts one arm around my shoulder and shifts over. Then it pours out, the misery of being thirteen.

My father listens, letting me be forlorn, letting me be his little girl. Then he speaks in his forest whisper. "I could tell you things will be fine, but that won't change your friends. I could say you're just like everybody else, but you're not. Truth is, you have a different look, one people notice."

I lean against his shoulder. He pats my arm. "You're a rarity like that albino turkey and Old Calico. They don't look like other turkeys and deer. And while their beauty makes them stand out, it sure makes them easier to shoot down."

I sit up, turn my hat to the front. My father turns his apple in his hands. "We'd wait years for a rare sight like Old Calico, count ourselves lucky, make him a legend. Less discriminating hunters want only to hang him on a wall.

"You'll be all right, Billie. You'll grow content with yourself like you came to be content in the woods."

We settle as the forest goes easy into gray, watch the creek, and wait for the piebald deer.

Debra Daniel has received fellowships in fiction and/or poetry from the South Carolina Arts Commission and the South Carolina Academy of Authors. She has written five winning Fiction Project stories and was awarded the first DuBose and Dorothy Heyward Society Prize from the Poetry Society of South Carolina.

Ceille Baird Welch

City Bus

Ellie McCants sat quietly for a long time, her purse in her lap. Then she plopped the purse to the floor beside the seat and reached up, to run her fingers down the sides of her red knit cap, scrunching it down over her ears and squashing sprigs of nearly colorless hair out on each side. Her nails were bitten to the quick and her fingers were short and plump. Nobody would ever have taken them for piano playing fingers, but they were. She used to play all the time at Sunday school in Swansea before Glorie Shumpert joined. Word was that Glorie Shumpert once had piano lessons. Three years of them, to be exact. But when Ellie used to play, way back, people stood up and took notice. "Real Baptist playin'," they would say, their heads bobbing up and down. "Real fine chords."

Ellie lifted her left little finger, spreading it, as best she could, away from the others, to hit an imaginary note. She followed it with two "real fine" imaginary chords and she heard the fullness of the "plunk plunk" and smiled. "One day I'm gon' learn the boogie woogie," she said out loud. "One day I'm gon' learn 'bout black notes."

For the fat man driving, Columbia came straight on except to stop and go with the traffic lights, or to stop and go with the little bench shelters all strewn and disheveled with people holding Hardee's wrappers. At every stop some of the people would rush to mount the bus steps and drop their noisy quarters in the slot, leaving the wrappers abandoned on the benches while Columbia glowed ahead like a dimestore jewel. The fat man pulled the visor down and raised his head a little hoping to make the glare go away.

It was different for Ellie. She pushed her face against the window and watched Columbia pass in frames and snatches like a slowed-down cartoon. There was no glare. The glare was all in the fat man's face. For Ellie there were long shadows stretching across sidewalks, and there were buildings, old and new snapping by. There were green dumpsters and parked cars and men clutching bags of hidden whiskey and women strolling in bright coats.

Roger Salters sat on the aisle seat beside her although he didn't know her. He noticed her fingers and how when they were held straight out to hit a "chord" they seemed not to have any knuckles at all. They were pink and smooth. Roger liked that about her fingers. "Gon' learn the boogie woogie, are ya?"

"Gon' learn 'bout black notes, too."

"I don't know as I believe black notes are all that necessary," Roger said after pausing a minute to two or however long it takes to travel twenty years back to a parlor in Elloree. "Had a Aunt played like nobody's business and didn't know nothin' 'bout black notes. Couldn't figure the need for 'em. Said she tried t' use 'em once but the song come out so sad she cried like a baby and never touched a black note again."

"That makes a lot o' sense," said Ellie.

"No sir, never again. She's gone now."

"Where'd she go to?" Ellie asked, picking a little ball of red fuzz from the cap she'd taken off whenever Roger first spoke to her. She held the cap now and kind of stuffed it between her knees along with the lap of her skirt.

"Heaven, I hope."

"You mean she's dead?" asked Ellie, rolling the pill of the knit between her palms.

"Passed away," said Roger. He leaned forward and

around her like he was interested in something outside the window. "They laid her out. Right in the parlor. In Elloree." And Roger was there, standing red-eyed in a black suit with sleeves too long. He was looking into his Aunt Mazie's coffin and wondering what the Devil was all that blue stuff in her hair. The piano was behind him but he dared not look at it, for sure if he did he'd start crying all over again.

"I went to Elloree once," Ellie said. And suddenly, she was there too. Not in Roger's Aunt Mazie's parlor, but standing on a long white porch overrun with hanging ferns and rocking chairs. She was sipping iced tea out of a jelly glass and listening to her Mama talk church talk to somebody she couldn't quite make out anymore.

A boy on the seat behind them snickered through his nose and the girl beside him made a soft flirting sound. Ellie looked over her shoulder meeting the girl's narrow secret eyes. "You got anybody?" Roger asked Ellie out of the blue.

Ellie giggled. "You mean like a boyfriend or something? Nooo," she said, stretching the word, raising it up like a little expectant song.

"I guess I mean like family."

"Oh. Well, I got my Mama," she said. "And my Daddy. An' I think there's four aunts on my Mama's side. An' I got my Uncle Bud. An' somewhere 'round umpteen cousins. An' I got my little dog, Rosco, but he stinks kinda bad so I don't pet him much."

"Great Dow!" said Roger, slipping into that parlor in Elloree and hoping he'd washed his face good enough, all by himself for the first time. He swept the tear on his cheek with his too-long sleeve leaving a little clean upward streak. He turned bravely. Facing the piano. "You shoulda seen it," he told Ellie. "Had a long ole lace cloth runnin' on it. Made by her Grand Mama she said. An' pictures? I mean that piano was crowded up with 'em. I believe if you'da walked by it fast and snagged that cloth chances are you'da knocked a dozen or so pictures on the floor. Family, she said. All of 'em. Family."

"I bet you gon' tell me you knocked 'em all off and broke 'em. What a story," said Ellie laughing.

"I'm not gon' tell you no such thing. I'm gon' tell you I didn't never have nobody but my Aunt Mazie. I'm gon' tell you I don't have no inklin' 'bout who those people on that piano coulda been 'cause I never met a one of 'em. 'They real busy,' she told me, 'An' they live real far off.'"

"Really?"

"I tried t' look some of 'em up after she passed. But you can't look nobody up from a picture."

"You know what?" said Ellie, "you shoulda got a-hold o' that TV show. You know that show. I saw one time 'bout these two twins? Separated at birth, they called 'um. Well, one of these two twins got a-hold of that show wantin' to get back together? An' you not gon' believe where those TV people found that other twin." She blurted. "Livin' right next door!"

"Shoot," said Roger.

"If I'm lyin', I'm dyin'," Ellie said.

"My Aunt had this picture of a man in a Army uniform," said Roger, craning around her like he was speaking to something outside the window, something in the snapping cartoon. "A real fine looking man with medals on his coat. She claimed it t' be my Daddy, but it turned out not t' be true."

"You looked him up?" asked Ellie

"Didn't have to," said Roger, leaning over to examine the side of his shoe. "Stepped in some bubble gum."

"How'd you find your Daddy?"

"I didn't. That picture wad'n nobody."

Ellie thought for a minute. "Hunh," she said, "Seem like a picture gotta be *somebody*."

"Wad'n none o' them pictures nobody," said Roger.

"How can that be?"

"When I took them pictures out o' the frame they wadn't even hardly pictures."

"I don't get it," Ellie said.

"These pictures was real thin an' krinkly soundin'.
A picture's kinda hard, right? And stiff?" The boy behind
Roger was tickling the girl beside him, jarring the seat but
Roger didn't feel it. He was leaned way over pulling at the
gum on his shoe. "If I had some Kleenex, I might could
get this off."

Ellie flicked the fuzz ball and she leaned too, reaching
her plump pink fingers into her purse. She pulled out a
tissue and handed it to Roger. "Here."

"'Sally Picture Frame Company'," said Roger, dabbing
at the gum. "Stamped on the back. On the back o' every
one o' them pictures. 'Sally Picture Frame Company. When
displayin' photos in this frame, be sure to replace the
cardboard backing.' None o' them pictures wad'n *nobody*.
None o' them pictures wad'n nothin' but the picture that
come in the frame. An' Aunt Mazie holdin' out they was
family! I guess they was just so fine she didn't have the
heart t' change 'em." He looked at Ellie and laughed, but
the look and the laughing matched up strangely and awkwardly, like his clothes. "Either that or I didn't have no
family t' speak of and she didn't want t' let on."

"What you tellin' me don't mean nothin'," Ellie said.

"Means they wad'n family," said Roger matter-of-factly,
crossing his leg squarely with the other, trying to figure how
to get gum *and* tissue off a shoe.

"Don't mean no such thing," said Ellie. She looked at
him with wide blue eyes. "Just 'cause them people come
in the frame don't have nothin' to do with them not bein'
family. People is people whether they come in a frame or
not. *Everybody* gotta be *somebody* an' I suspect every one
of them people is *somebody's* family. Who says they couldn't
o' been yours?"

"I never thought like that," said Roger. He balled up
the tissue shreds and hid them in his hand. He put his right
foot back, a little behind the other so he wouldn't have to
look at it anymore. "What's your people like?"

"Fat."

"Your Mama too?"

"Fat."

"Fat as the bus driver?"

"Fatter. But in different places. She's a real nice Mama though. She don't mind at all I'm a little…" Ellie dragged out the word. She said it like she was *supposed* to drag it out "…slow."

"You are not," said Roger.

"Am too," she said, "An' I play the piano sometime when I'm not s'posed to…You know, like I was doin' while ago. I know the difference, though, between when a piano's there an' when one's not, but some people don't think I do."

"When you was doin' that I didn't think nothin' of it," Roger said. "An' you know, I decided you was real smart. That seemed real smart what you said 'bout them pictures."

Ellie put her cap back on and scrunched it down. She picked up her purse from the floor and placed it against her knees, holding the handle with both hands. "I know in my heart they was pictures of your family," she said. "I know it just like I know I'm sittin' here."

Roger bunched his already close eyebrows together. "You act like you fixin' t' go."

"My Mama come downtown way early this mornin' to witness at the tent revival on Two Notch Road an' now I'm meetin' my Mama at the Do Duck In. She's gon' buy me a hamburger. I gotta get off soon." Ellie opened her purse and took out a lipstick. "Where you goin'?" she asked.

"Goin' is all. Ridin'."

Ellie turned the lipstick tube carefully and just a little. "You can't roll a lipstick out too far it'll break."

Roger stretched his bubble-gum foot forward to examine it again, then he looked up quickly, meeting Ellie eye to eye. "Don't put that on. I want t' kiss you," he said.

"You do?"

"I want t' kiss you for givin' me somethin' t' think about."

"You do?"

"You give me somethin' t' think about when you said what you did. Here I been carryin' on all my life like I was a orphan. Carryin' on like a fool an' could be..." He cut his deep eyes away from her, deciding. With his thumb he flattened his bottom lip then rubbed the thumb against his teeth. "You know," he said, "You mighta hit the nail on the head. People in them pictures *gotta* be *somebody*. More'n likely somebody's family. Coulda even been mine."

"Your Aunt Mazie wouldn't of lied," said Ellie and her tone and words so were final they would have been hard for anybody to argue with.

Roger faced her. "It was them for sure," he said absolutely. "And it was fate I come on this bus. T' ride. An' that you come on it too. Goin' t' meet your Mama at the Do Duck In."

"You know what I was thinkin' about? I was thinkin' 'bout fate too. Listen to this. My name's Ellie! What do you make of that? Ellie?...Elloree?...Almost the same. That's why I was thinkin' it was fate."

The bus driver automatically reached out to the door lever and made a little motion like he was turning in his seat without turning at all. "Next stop—Do Duck In," he said.

The snorting boy pulled the flirting girl up beside him. He walked her down the aisle of the still moving bus. He escorted her like in a little wedding ceremony except that they were jostling from side to side, bouncing their hips off one another and giggling.

Ellie thought about playing piano for them, giving them something to march to, but she stood instead and dropped the lipstick back into her purse. "No use in puttin' on lipstick," she said, "I'll just go an' eat it all off anyway." She squeezed by Roger, facing him, and Roger stood too, no less than a gentleman at the theater, for her to pass. The bus gave a long sucking sound that suspended Ellie for a moment, making her weightless. It stopped and she let the stop swing her against the seat-back behind her. She let it swing her, like a little pendulum, forward, swaying her toward him, and she calculated quickly, shifting her purse to one side and bumping her lips on his.

Ceille Baird Welch holds a Master of Education from the University of South Carolina and a Doctor of Arts from Lander University. She is a licensed professional counselor. She is also mother, grandmother, poet, songwriter, storyteller and playwright and is married to Jim Welch of the Public Television series NatureScene.

Cecile Hanna Goding

Inheritance

It was one of my Friday night visits. Papa was disgusted with everything that night—the supper, the way I looked, the planet. Finally, over coffee, he tipped back in his chair and came out with it. "Another Ng got hired today." He groped at his chest for his one daily cigarette. "And McNulty took early retirement. Not that I didn't see it coming. Maria, are you listening?"

"*Si*-yes, I do remember. You saw it coming," said Ma, passing me the sugar bowl. Though Ma had lived in California all her life, English would always be her second language.

"What I saw was..." Papa lurched forward, banging the chair on the hard linoleum. Ma jerked her hand back, like she'd been hit or burned. So I didn't get any sugar. "...another one of those garlic-eating little..."

"What did you say his name was, Papa?" I asked, as I poured sweet canned milk into my coffee, thinking, this is how Tu likes it. Maybe Tu knows this guy from English class.

"I don't know—Li something. That's what we call him anyway." I saw Ma flinch as the chair legs creaked. "Hell, if McNulty was having trouble, why didn't he come to me for help? I woulda covered for him."

"Maybe he was ready to retire?" Ma tried, just in case he expected an answer. Pa batted at her words with his cigarette hand. "Naah." The smoke scattered, then spread in a fog over our heads.

Ma started coughing and got up. She squeezed the forks and spoons in her short brown fingers. I normally helped her. But this time, I didn't because it would mean turning my back on Papa. It had nothing to do with love.

Papa sat and smoked for a while, looking at me. I saw fear or indigestion spasm across his face. I thought, now he is going to ask me. And I'll say, yes, it's true, but Papa...But Papa slipped a hand under his belt, shifted in his chair, and put off the question I was waiting for. Instead, he scraped his chair back and stood up. I collected dirty napkins, picked at crumbs.

"I shoulda stayed in Chicago," I heard, as he walked out of the kitchen. So, I thought, that's what it's all about. Retirement. And then what? Sitting around, waiting to get sick, blaming everything that went wrong in his life on the Vietnamese and the Cambodians?

Papa was only fifty. He'd hated the same job for twenty years. I was twenty and pregnant. And anything that happened to us was mostly our own fault—not somebody else's.

"Bye, Papa," I said. "Thanks for supper." I picked up a dishtowel and started clearing the rack.

"You know, *Beta*," Ma spoke in Spanish now. "You and Papa have been getting along a lot better these days."

"*Pues*," I shrugged. "A lot of things just don't matter so much." I took the slippery plate she offered, tried not to see her eyes at my waist.

"That's everything, little chicken." Ma looked tired and rumpled. I saw more grey than I remembered.

"Listen, *Beta*," Ma said. "I said I wouldn't—but you got to tell Papa sometime—pretty soon you won't be able to..."

It was time to leave. "Bye, Ma," I said, bending a little to give her a kiss. I got my figure from my Ma and Papa, and my height from a grandfather I never met. "*Luega*." Later.

Later, I watched Ong Tu drink tea in my kitchen. It was hot, and he sat there with his shirt open, so I could see his pale gold chest—scarred and beautiful, ribbed and clean. But he was already old, a lot older than I'd guessed. And once upon a time, he said, he was a doctor. Before California, he'd never even been in a factory.

The smoke from his cigarette rose up with the incense on the table. I wanted him to quit smoking, but whenever I said anything, he shrugged, the way Papa shrugged off Ma. When they did stop—Tu and Papa—it was not for anything Ma or I said.

Tu and I didn't say much to each other—there were a lot of things he didn't want to talk about or remember. Over here, in California, all he had to remember was which tool to pick up.

There were six of them in the plant. Everybody knew they worked hard and were willing to start at the bottom. Tu and I were right on the same floor: me in inventory and Tu out on the line. But he never came back to my desk. "Come on," I said once. "This is America."

"I know," he said. He heard things I refused to hear. How people were talking. Whole sections of San Jose were changing fast—there were strange new foods and exotic billboards, unpronounced vowels in the wrong places. When the first big layoff came in the plant, people got nervous. "Lost my best buddy over there in Nam," said Jim Thompson. "That's enough. Don't need to keep paying for it back home." That I did hear.

Tu said people would talk about us. That it was too soon after the war. So we met at my place instead, where there was no war. There was just quiet. There was just Tu—not talking, sometimes sleeping in the next room.

Sometimes he cried in his sleep. He had dreams, he said.

I am one of those people who never dream. Or if I do, I don't remember, so it doesn't matter. "I wish I am like you," he said. But he told me one of the dreams. He told me because I asked him.

Tu—and the Lady, he called her—but I know it's his
wife—are walking fast through a maze of streets. There's
a lot of fire and noise, and they can't see where to go. So
finally he stops and he feels her against him (her stomach,
Tu said, curving his hands in the air on top of his body,
showing me the shape). He tells her to wait while he runs
ahead.

Tu runs on and when he gets to a corner, he looks back.
But the smoke blows in between them. He can still see
her, but she is so pale, thinner than he remembers. Then
the smoke covers her, and when the air clears, she is almost
gone. More than nothing, less than smoke, he said.

("Wake up in your dream," I said. "Say you will not
be a part of it." But Tu said, "If you are there, you are part
of it.")

He woke up, he said, when the baby cried next door.

"Never again," I said. "I will never ask again."

The night I got back from my folks, Tu stayed for a
while. But he couldn't rest. He had to go to Immigration,
he said, in the morning, before his shift. Something about
one of his brothers, the one without the legs.

"Stay," I said. "We'll watch TV."

"Okay," he said. "For one hour." He buttoned his shirt.

I went into the bathroom and looked in the mirror. I'm
a bunch of ill-fitting parts, I thought. And as I stood there,
it was like I could see the baby through my skin, see her
floating in a big pool, swirling with stars. As the stars
cartwheeled around her, some stuck to her at random—
became eyes and toes and hair. She is going to be beautiful,
I thought.

When I went back into the kitchen, the TV was on. Tu
watched almost anything, but only with the sound turned
off. We watched a three-foot black child moving his mouth
while four white adults listened.

Tu poured canned milk carefully into my tea, swirling it

into the dark liquid like a painter. He never touched me like a boyfriend—you know, never held my hand.

Everyone was hugging the kid on TV.

"Tell me about your family," Tu said suddenly.

"Okay," I said. "Papa's Irish—from Chicago. Ma's from Mexico City."

"Many people from Mexico City," Tu said. "I need to learn Spanish." His long fingers curled around my cup.

"I'll teach you. After French, it'll come easy." I was already thinking how I could teach him real slow, so that nothing would change for a long time.

"I have a question," Tu said. "About you." I could feel his eyes. "Are you going—to the house of your father?"

"I could," I said, tasting my tea. It was warm and good. "But I like being on my own."

"Yes, I see," Tu said. Like I was on my own, even then. I watched him bring the cigarette to his mouth, holding it between his thumb and finger. His mouth was smiling, but his black eyes stayed sad. I looked through the smoke into Vietnam. I saw the street. I saw the absence of light.

I remember the TV's sound was still off, and we weren't talking. So the phone didn't ring—it exploded. Tu jumped, and I yanked at the receiver before it went off again. And this is all I recall. Papa's voice, but weak. "Betsy?"

"What's wrong, Papa?"

"Mama. I woke up…and she can't breathe. Yes, *chika*, okay. God, it hurts her, Betsy!" I couldn't believe this was my father, inactive, stupid with fear, calling my number.

"Tu, no, it's Ma—some kind of attack or something, Tu. Papa, call an ambulance. I'm going to hang up. Call now."

Tu was behind me, holding my shoulders. "Rise her head," he said. "Put it back. Keep warm."

"Papa, listen." I gave Tu's orders. "I'm coming. Call 911 *now*." Tu hung up the phone. I looked to be sure I was dressed and grabbed my keys.

I wasn't even thinking of Ma. That's the strange part— that all I thought about on that drive south was Papa, then

Tu. As if I knew that later on there would be enough time for worry and care for Ma, more than I ever needed. But I didn't want it to start yet. Not that night. That night, my mind was on other things, on men.

So I filled my brain with Papa and Tu. Papa's life and Tu's dream. I replayed them over and over. Oh I know now what I was trying to do. I was trying to figure out where I fit in.

We got to the hospital. They said Papa was with her. I stood waiting by the ICU door, but Tu went into the empty waiting room across the hall. He sat down, his black eyes locked on me, never moving. He was still watching when Papa edged out, holding onto the door. I saw he was old. "Go in for a while," he whispered. Our stomachs bumped.

Ma slept under a white plastic tent. There were wires and tubes. I sat down as close as I could to her face. Her breathing fogged the air. I watched her for a long time. I thought that as long as I kept watching, she would be all right.

When our daughter sleeps, I watch her that same way. I can't help it—she's so perfect. Every chromosome in the right place, Tu says.

You have to leave now, said the nurse. When I came out into the hall, I leaned against the ICU door in the dim hallway, looking across into the waiting room. Two men sat there, in the position of waiting, their elbows on their knees. A pair of thin legs lined up with two broad thighs. Cigarettes hung loosely from their hands.

I started across, but what I saw next made me stop, like a child about to enter a room of grownups. Papa's lips were moving, moving. But I couldn't tell if he was talking to Tu or not. Or if he did, if Tu heard.

Then I saw Tu nod, once, expressionless. So I could tell he was listening. What else could he do? As he listened, he looked at something, something I could not see. Then I saw Papa look up, too, and stare in the same direction.

Two pairs of eyes—one black and one a watery blue—looking at something I could not see from the hallway.

Every time I remember that night, I see the waiting room. I see two men, one talking and one listening. They do not look at each other. Later, one or the other, or both, will look at me. Please, look at me. But they can't hear me yet. For what seems like a long time, they just keep staring at whatever it is I cannot see from where I am—up there, where the smoke mingles and swirls around the light.

Before moving to Iowa City in 1996, Cecile Goding was the executive director of the Florence Area Literacy Council. Her most recently published essays focus on adult literacy issues. In 1993, she was awarded the Fellowship in Poetry from the South Carolina Academy of Authors.

WRECKER

The truth is complicated. I don't mean knowing it. Knowing it isn't so hard, sometimes. But getting it told can be next to impossible. The more you try to say it, the farther from it you get. Like pushing the same ends of a magnet towards one another, the more words people say to one another the farther they get from what they are trying to say, until you hear stuff coming out of your mouth and you say to yourself, where the hell did that come from? Or the other person says, what do you mean? And the fact is, you don't have the slightest idea what you mean. Then you get into the explaining, and before it's over the two of you are pushing each other across Colorado when you both know the truth lives in Carolina. Sometimes it's just better to keep your mouth shut.

It's not that you don't know the truth. It's just that when you do know something, and you know that it's true and somebody tells you to explain or to give examples, it just ruins it. We all know some things that are true. It's the telling that gets in the way. But when you love somebody, and you know it's true, and still she wants you to explain to her what love is, the telling screws up the thing you're trying to say. Everything goes wrong. Before it's over you hear yourself yelling things you never intended to say, things that aren't even in the least bit true. Things you'd never say. Things you can never take back.

I want to get it right.

Let me try to give you an example. I've gotten calls from the Highway Patrol at all hours of the night when it's so cold a dog would jump a cat for no reason. So cold I'd have to use ether to get the engine started. I'm hung over sometimes. I leave a warm bed and dress in the dark. If she knows I'm gone, she never says so.

I climb in the cab of my wrecker, and even through the cushion I feel how cold the seat is on the backs of my legs. My breath fills up the whole cab. Sometimes I'm still a little drunk. The gear stick sends an ache through the palm of my hand. When I pull them up from under the seat, my gloves look like chopped off hands. It's that cold. I'm feeling like hell. And I know what I've got to look forward to. I ain't about to get warm. And I'm thinking about what I'm leaving behind. I'm thinking of my wife and the things I don't know how to say to her.

Then heading west, out to Lamar or Timmonsville there are breaks in the sky, and I know that later the sun will be coming up. I have a cup of Sav-Way coffee. Everything is quiet, the way it is in the South when everything is covered with snow and the moon is full. The blower is hot on my knees now and I can turn it down, too. For a second, I'm not thinking about anything or anybody.

Then I start up a hill and the sky is the color of the ocean just before a storm, gray or bluish, maybe slate colored. Then, at the very top of the hill, the moon is right there, sandwiched between the white land and the sky that's like a tide. And for a second you can't catch your breath, and you're glad as hell to be there, and you feel like the whole damned thing was planned just for you, or that you've slipped into a moment not meant for a human to see. And you forget about what waits for you eight or ten miles up the road and about what you've left as many miles behind.

There's just you and all this white world around you. It's early in the morning. You're warm, and there's the sky and the moon and the snow everywhere. What I'm trying to say is it's a feeling. That feeling is what I'm trying to say is what true is. It is that feeling, that thing I feel for her, that I can't get across. It all gets lost in the explaining.

I wish I could tell you what it's like at that time in the morning when you come to a flat stretch before the final curve and see the red and blue lights dancing over the snow way up ahead. I feel a little sick, because of what I know way down deep. But at the same time the lights on the snow, red chasing blue, blue chasing red on the ice and snow, and way back the beginnings of the sun and the receding tide of slate sky above, there is a feeling there. Still, I get that churning in my stomach on account of knowing and not knowing for sure what I've got ahead of me.

She says there's something missing.

When I was a boy, before I knew what those lights really meant, I would've sat at the top of the hill and imagined they were lights on a flying saucer or the second coming of Christ. Now I know what it means if the EMS guys are still there when there's snow. It means somebody's dying, dead, or damned near it. Sometimes it means I've got to move some steel before they can finish their work.

I leave the truck running and the blower on high. We, the EMS guys and me, we take turns aiming the lights mounted on the cab and warming our hands. Sometimes we see it, the way people go out of this world. The cold doesn't make it any easier. Sometimes it is so bad that we have to look for bodies thrown from cars. People don't drive as fast in ice and snow, you'd say. But the ice means they don't slow down either.

Sometimes they aren't all there. Parts of them, I mean, are lost.

I don't get paid for helping the guys look. My job is to haul away what's left of the plastic and steel. That's what I get paid for. But I just can't drive away while the others are out there looking. I couldn't do that. I'm not like that.

You would think that it didn't matter, not to the dead person. But those EMS guys, they just won't give up looking.

It's what we have in common.

Even when a thing is dead it has its parts, and you owe it to make a broken thing whole, even if you can't give it life again. You and I, we have obligations. We take oaths and say vows. Or at least that's what I think.

I take my turn looking for the parts. Nobody talks. We all know what we have to do, and we know that we have to look close, and we hope that it is somebody else who finally says the search is over.

You would think the parts would be found near the point of impact. You'd be surprised. So you look and you think. Even with the bright lights it is hard to see.

You are always walking in your own shadow.

Sometimes I just want to close my eyes and get down on my hands and knees. Feel for what it is I hope I don't find. I wish I could just come out and tell you. If I had words, I'd tell you.

You can either take people at their word or not. It is a choice. It is a real hard choice. Believing somebody's word takes trust on both sides. It means that one person knows what she is saying and is willing to say it. It means the other person can hear through to the meaning and can take it. Both sides are hard. It comes down to this. When somebody tells you something, they either mean what they say, or they mean something else, or they mean nothing at all. The problem is when they say it straight out. The straighter it is, the harder it is to take sometimes. You would think that the hardest thing would be when someone says, "I don't love you." Worse is when she says, "I love you, but…" It can make you say and do things you'll regret the rest of your life. It'll make you want to get down on your knees.

If the job isn't done when the sun really starts to get up, the EMS guys will go back to the van to warm. Nobody says anything. They just know that in the time it takes them to get warm they'll have the light of the sun to see by.

It's true that it's coldest just before the sun comes up.

They are doing the right thing. If there is anything to be found, waiting a half-hour won't make any difference now. Still, after I've been looking I can't go back with the others. They always feel a need to talk. I can't blame them. I feel it too. People feel uneasy when they are together like that and there is nothing but silence. They feel like there is something they ought to be saying. I understand that. But I can't do it. So I search alone, looking down at the snow, moving slowly, worried I'll bury under my boot the thing I'm looking for. Worried that somehow I already have.

Sometimes after staring down at the snow for a long time in the night, my eyes will play tricks on me. I'll be looking down, and suddenly I'm seeing into nothing at all. I'm not saying this right. I'm seeing the very place where the snow and the night come together, see. I'm looking down from high up and everything just goes down and down, forever. I feel dizzy. I stand very still, and the cold seeps into my bones. I get that numb feeling everywhere. I know I have to bring myself out of it.

So when I feel this way, I sometimes think about the warm place I've left and wish with all my heart I could go back to it, and that it would somehow be there when I get home.

Phillip Gardner teaches at Francis Marion University in Florence. He lives in nearby Darlington, where he writes short stories and screenplays. "Wrecker" appears in a novel-in-stories, Someone To Crawl Back To, *published by Boson Books.*

Elizabeth Langland

A Summer Solstice

The heat pulsing up from the ground made her stolid
and stupid. She did not know what to do about the cattle
moving across the cornfield. She reflected idly that she
ought to do something, but nothing she wanted to do
suggested itself.

In the slow sun even the buzzing of the gnats seemed
lazy.

She might try to shoo them out. A wasp droned around
her head.

But the cattle would, when roused, just push around
her, and she hated their big heavy bodies and the warm
moist breath expelled through their nostrils.

She shoved her toe into the dust and watched the grains
of dirt settle on her shoe.

She should tell her aunt.

Annie remembered her first time in the barnyard—
the musky odor of silage and hay, the pungent smell of
manure—picking her way through the droppings to the
barn. The warm laugh of her aunt greeted her arrival at the
stalls where the cows stood patiently enduring the slow
sucking of the machines.

"Well, then, did you come to see your Auntie Kristin?"
The soft face leaning down to hers had felt warm. The red
bandana her aunt wore to protect her hair swept across the
girl's face as her aunt turned briskly. "You can help me now.

Be a big girl and get me that bucket."

Grasping it in her hand, she had held her breath to escape the smell of disinfectant wash for the cow's teat. She watched intently as her aunt rhythmically stroked each teat clean, leaving it pink and dripping. The dry gasp of the milker on an empty teat of another cow had sent her aunt hurrying to release it. Her aunt, strong and competent, had moved about the barn, now washing, now putting on a milker, removing one and emptying it into the 10-gallon can, which stood handy. She could do anything.

Annie wondered now why she didn't tell her aunt about the cows in the cornfield.

And in the house her aunt would hurry as she did in the barn—always strong, always competent. "Set the table now, Annie; the men will be in soon from the barn."

The men came, but it was really only herself and her aunt there. The men were easy. Her aunt was hard. And warm and tough. Her energy spilled over the room as she alternately laughed and clucked in disapproval.

"Run down, Annie, and get some eggs for breakfast. Take the cracked and stained ones."

And the girl had carefully chosen the stained ones for their breakfast, still stinging under the mortification of having her aunt turn on her after the minister's last visit for eggs. "Oh, land. Always choose the best eggs for Reverend Lee. I was ashamed to have you bring those spotted ones."

And they waited on table, reserving their portion for the last so the men could get out into the fields. Until her aunt would say, "You sit down now, Annie, and get something to eat." Always she felt a little guilty because her aunt barely stayed to take her own breakfast before she, too, left to help in the fields.

Cleaning up the dishes, the girl always felt lonely and set apart. She hated not being adequate to anything. But her aunt stood far beyond her.

So she thought of her aunt now lying in the house. And it was Sunday and church time, too, and the cows in the cornfield.

Sunday and church time were always special. Her aunt was up even earlier than her usual 5 o'clock, down in the barn at chores before dawn. And the girl waited on her like a shadow, drowsy in the early light until the soft, cold hand on her brow brought her to. "Why, Annie, you don't need to get up yet. You're still half asleep. Go on now. I don't need you."

And always that was the worst. Not to be needed. She always felt that she hadn't done enough and didn't know to be better.

Even later, when her aunt turned her around and inspected her Sunday dress and shining shoes and black hair ribbon with a pleased light in her eyes, it wasn't enough.

So she stood immobile now, staring at the cows and wishing them out of the field, remembering the pain surrounding her aunt like a halo inside the house.

Church itself was an ordeal. Her aunt commanded the center there, and the girl was alternately pushed aside or subjected to scrutiny.

"Well then, have you been a big help to your aunt this summer?"

"Do you think she'll want you back?"

The stinging red in her face did not subside until she sat in the pew gazing up at her aunt in the choir loft. Kicking her feet softly against the base, she would watch her aunt's proud face and hear her voice lifting above the chorus. And then her aunt would turn her way, look at her and smile until the girl flushed with pleasure. Annie would make her aunt proud. But now the cows confronted her like some immovable destiny. They regarded her lazily, flicking ears and tails at the flies humming around them. Forever munching the corn, chewing their cud to some inner rhythm. As they brushed down the rows, their udders swayed slowly.

She hated cows. Her own flesh was spare and fine, her

bones thin, her body tense. She resented their big hanging udders and their empty eyes.

She remembered her aunt's mission circle. The ladies had sat massive and immovable, chewing on cookies and bars. As she stood staring, her aunt had jogged her. "Shoo now, Annie, get the plate and pass it."

Then her aunt had proudly led her out. "This is my girl for the summer. She's a fine helper to her Auntie Kristin." And the ladies had oohed and clucked over her. Then her aunt had abandoned her in their midst, awkward and silent.

As the attention had drifted away from her, Annie let her mind come back to her aunt. How they all looked up to her—she directed, she supervised, she spoke for them. Annie's heart burned at her own insignificance—burned with love and pride.

"Annie," the high call pierced her, "why are you standing there? Land, what's wrong with you? We've got to get those cows out of the field." Annie stood still, her aunt on the periphery of her vision running toward the field, her face marked by pain and determination.

"Annie, *help* me." The girl's torpor broke, and she turned to run into the field. "No," she was checked, "circle wide around them, or you'll just scare them deeper in."

So she ran fast now, tears welling up as she stumbled over the rows. Her aunt, pale and urgent, was forcing her way around the other side. "Shoo ee. Shoo ee." Even as she tried to force them back, they broke through startled and alert now. Annie didn't dare look at her aunt who was gasping. "Run out farther."

She ran through the rows of young corn that whipped her as she passed. The cows seemed to loom like a shadow on her horizon, always ahead, always massing together. She felt stifled by the corn over which she could barely see. She ran in a green maze, only oriented by the bulky bodies.

"Ho, hey Boss, hey Boss. Easy now. Go easy." The cows were shoving backwards awkward and clumsy toward Annie. She looked and saw Mr. Larsen, their neighbor, waving his hat and pushing forward toward the cows. They gave way to him.

It was over. She and her aunt closed off the sides; he pushed them back from the front. The cows stumbled out of the field, placid and easy now, back to the barnyard.

Her aunt stopped outside the gate. She stood bent and pale and silent. Her breath was dry and short. It seemed to Annie she could hear her aunt's agony speak. Annie, too, stood silent, the violent rush of comfort and love she wanted to unleash imprisoned within her.

She barely heard Mr. Larsen. "Well, that's all then. I guess I'll be gettin' back. Hey there, little girlie, you take care of your auntie."

Annie stood there in the stillness of the heat, rigid and taut.

"Annie," the voice broke their silence. "Annie, dear," the words were labored. "Why didn't you say thank you...Mr. Larsen...when you knew I couldn't?" The tears on her aunt's cheeks streaked Annie's soul. She swallowed the anguish that threatened to choke her.

Elizabeth Langland is Professor of English and Dean of Humanities, Arts & Cultural Studies at the University of California, Davis. She is the author of numerous books and articles on Victorian literature and culture, women writers, feminist theory, and narrative theory. "Summer Solstice" is part of a cycle of stories she is writing.

Melodie Starkey

STARS

The police come to our house. Dad shoos us outside to play while they speak with him, although he's just called us in for the evening. We press our ears to the door, but can't hear anything. After investigating the police car without getting too close—the radio inside growls and mumbles and crackles in bursts—we sit on the front lawn and chew on leaves from the wild spearmint that grows in the junipers.

Though it is only April, it feels like a summer evening, warm and alive with the sounds of insects and the distant voices of people out in their yards. Across the street Mrs. Pauling is peering out between her drapes at the police car. She always knows everything that happens in the neighborhood.

"Is Dad a robber?" I ask Carrie.

"Of course not, Silly." She stretches out on her back, crossing her long legs at the ankles and folding her arms behind her head, as though she couldn't care less about there being policemen at our house, or about getting to stay out later on a Sunday night. I try to copy her pose, squinting up at the orange clouds layered across the purple sky like lasagna, but I can't keep from glancing impatiently at the door.

Finally they come out, smiling at us as they pass by. When they drive away, without sirens or flashing lights or handcuffed captives, we dash inside to find out what is going on. Dad just shakes his head, then shuts himself up in his study.

Mother sits us on the couch, which usually means a lecture is coming. She cleans her glasses on the hem of her blouse, then puts them on and frowns at us. Then, in her "Why don't we all share?" voice she says, "Girls, I want you to be extra good around Daddy for a few days. A very sad thing happened today. Do you remember Daddy's friend, Mr. Lance?"

Of course we do. He always brings us ten-cent jaw-breakers and sets us on his shoulders so we can touch the ceiling.

"This morning he shot himself."

"Why?" Carrie asks.

"How?" I ask. Dad took us shooting once. He stood behind me as a brace, catching me as his shotgun seemed to tear my shoulder from my collarbone. For a week after, I flashed the bruise to my friends on the playground.

"He was very, very unhappy," Mother explains. "His family went away to live somewhere else. He couldn't stand being by himself anymore. He wrote your Daddy a letter…" She shakes her head, looking at the closed study door. "It's very sad."

"How?" I ask again. On television people shoot each other all the time, but not themselves. Did you have to look in the mirror to aim?

She frowns at me. "Why are you such a morbid child, Marti?"

"How?"

"He put the barrel of a shotgun in his mouth and pulled the trigger. Are you satisfied?"

"Oh, how gross!" Carrie exclaims. She says that about everything.

On the way to school the next morning I listen as Carrie tells the story to her friends. Two years older than I, they consider it enough to let me walk with them—I am never included in their conversations. I don't mind though: arriving at school with a bunch of fifth graders makes me feel important. They decide that Mr. Lance must have been an alcoholic. They are learning about alcoholism in their Social Studies class. Why else would his family leave him?

I think about how when Carrie and I are fighting, Dad is quiet for a long time, until suddenly he'll take off one of his slippers and fire it at us like a missile. He never misses. Sometimes, when my head is the target, I tell him that I hate him, then crawl under my bed and think about running away as soon as I get my own bicycle. He isn't an alcoholic, but I still want to leave him. I decide fifth graders aren't really so smart.

I try to remember what Mr. Lance looked like. It has only been a few weeks since we saw him last, but I can't picture his face. His hands were the biggest hands I've ever seen, with marble-like knuckles and blue-worm veins popping out on back. He wore a plain gold ring on one hand and a ring with a black stone on the other. The ring with the stone wouldn't come off: the middle knuckle on the finger was even larger than all the others. He told me that he'd broken it playing basketball. He told me if he could ever get it off he'd turn into a handsome prince and marry me. When he laughed it sounded like gravel being poured into a coffee can.

Mother isn't home when I get there. I pace up and down the walkway in front of the house, practicing not stepping on the cracks at fast speed until Carrie arrives with the key. I creep into my parents' bedroom and pull °the shotgun out of the closet where it is stored behind the plastic sack covering Mother's wedding gown. I stand in front of the full-view mirror and carefully put my mouth around the barrel of the gun. It has a sour taste that re-minds me of going to the dentist. I try to imagine being dead. I close my eyes tightly, until stars flash inside my lids.

The dog barks, announcing that Mother is home. I

shove the gun back in the closet, tearing the plastic sack in the process. Then I rub toothpaste on my tongue to get the memory of the taste out of my mouth.

After dinner we race to the living room to seize the *Valley Herald*. Carrie snatches it up and holds it out of my reach, taunting, "It's mine, Shorty!"

"Ladder Legs." I stick my tongue out at her, then sit down in defeat to wait for her to read the comics. She takes her time, going through the paper page by page, pausing to read the movie advertisements, while I demand, "Hurry up, Stupid."

Finally she turns to the comics page and stretches out leisurely on the couch to read them, saying "Oh, how childish," as she finishes each strip. Dad comes in and turns on the television, but he doesn't seem to be paying much attention to it. He gazes out the front window at the shadowy willow tree with the moon lurking in its branches. I want to tell him not to look so sad, but he seems too far away to talk to.

Carrie finishes the comics and decides she has to read her horoscope. "My turn!" I protest.

Then she has to check her friends' horoscopes. "Give it to me, Dog Breath!" I shout.

Then she needs to check the next day's weather. I lunge at her. At the tearing sound we both freeze, then look at Dad, waiting for the slipper. He frowns at us for a moment, then goes into his study and closes the door.

"Do you ever think of what it would be like if Dad died?" Carrie asks me quietly.

I frown, trying to imagine it. "Would we be orphans then?"

"Of course not. We've got Mother."

"Would we be really poor?"

"No. He's got insurance."

I frown again. It seems like everything would be about the same then. Only he wouldn't be here. Finally I say, "I think we ought to keep him."

"Yeah."

Mother picks us up after school Tuesday to take us shopping. She buys us matching navy blue dresses. Carrie looks almost grown up in hers, with her long legs and her sharp, narrow face. I look like a Martian. The saleswoman calls me a cherub and pinches my cheek. When she turns away I stick out my tongue. Carrie laughs and keeps pinching my cheek all afternoon, even though I kick her with my saddle shoes on.

We go to Farrell's Ice Cream Parlor for a sundae. On the way out I buy a ten-cent jawbreaker, but it doesn't taste like the ones Mr. Lance brought me. I throw it out the car window as we are crossing the bridge.

I ask Mother why Mr. Lance's family left him. "You're too young to understand," she says. She always says that.

I wonder if, should Mother leave Dad, I would go with her or stay with him? He never tells us to make our beds or wash our hands or pick it up after the dog eats a box of crayons and throws up in the hall. But he doesn't know how to make anything except coffee and peanut butter and mayonnaise sandwiches, and he doesn't know how to rub your back just right when you've had a bad dream, or how to get the tangles out of your hair without pulling. These are Mother's special jobs. I decide if it happens, I'll wait and see who Carrie goes with, and I'll take the other one.

When we get home, I climb up the willow tree in the front yard to wait for Dad. The tree is having a bad case of horn worms this spring, so I have to be careful where I put my hands—they are slimier than slugs if you smash them. Carrie and her friends pick them off the trees with a stick and lay them in the street, then run over them with their bicycles.

I shout hello at Dad when he gets out of his car. He looks around, so I shake the branch I'm leaning on to show him where I am. He stands under the tree and looks up at me. "Who's that in my willow tree?"

"Nobody here but us worms."

"Well, Worm, if you fall and break your head your mother is going to tan you."

"She wouldn't spank me if I was bleedin' all over the place. Want to see me jump?"

"So I can pick up the pieces?" He steps out from directly under me.

I hang by my hands for a moment, then drop, landing on my heels with a jolt that goes straight through my teeth. I take a deep bow, and he scoops me up. As he carries me into the house I notice a few white hairs in his black hair, especially in front of his ears. He smells of the Old Spice cologne Carrie and I give him for Christmas every year.

He sets me on his desk and sets his briefcase next to me. "I brought you some more paper." He opens his briefcase and hands me a bundle of the pale green striped computer paper. We draw picture stories on the blank side and unfurl them down the hall for his inspection. I study one of the pages of numbers for a moment, then ask, "Dad, what is your job?"

"I'm a physicist. You know that."

"But what does a fizzlestist do?"

"I help run some very big machines called reactors."

"But what does it do?"

"It makes fuel for very special bombs. And it makes electricity."

"You make bombs?"

"No. I help run the reactor. That's all."

"Was Mr. Lance a fizzlestit, too?"

"Physicist—yes." He is suddenly very busy with some papers on his desk.

"How come Mr. Lance shot himself?"

He has his back to me, looking for something on the bookshelf. I wait, but he doesn't turn back around. "Dad…"

"Why don't you go set the table for Mother, okay?"

After Mother checks to see that I am asleep, I open my curtains and lie back down at the foot of the bed so I can watch for shooting stars. I wonder if Mr. Lance has already gone to Heaven, or if he has to wait until after tomorrow's funeral.

Carrie says that all the stars are the souls of people who've gone to Heaven, but my teacher says they are just suns that are so far away that they look small. I certainly can't see the need for that many suns, so Carrie's answer seems better.

I hear the doorknob turning, so I close my eyes and hold my breath.

"Marti, are you sleeping?" Dad whispers.

"Of course."

He comes in, starting to go to the head of the bed, then noticing that I am at the other end. He sits down next to me, rubbing my hair while he looks out the window.

"Dad, what make the stars shoot?"

He takes a long time to answer, but finally says, "The stars are wishes that haven't been used up yet. Every time you see a star shoot, someone's wish has just come true."

"I wish Mr. Lance was alive again."

He shakes his head slowly.

"Dad, won't you tell me why?"

"I don't know why, Marti. I just don't know. Maybe he was disappointed with himself. Maybe he was just tired of being lonely. Maybe he was just too tired." He sounds so sad it makes my stomach hurt to listen. He sighs, looking back out the window, and speaks again. "The phone rang— Saturday night, very late. It took me a long time to get up. It stopped before I got there. I wasn't in time…"

Suddenly I feel very angry at Mr. Lance for making Dad feel so sad, and frustrated that I can't do anything about it. I stand up on my knees and wrap my arms around his neck. "When I'm president I'll make it against the law for anyone to be lonely."

He gives me a crushing hug, then says, "Go to sleep

now, okay?"

I curl up around my pillow and practice a few loud snores. He pats me, whispering, "Good night."

When he is gone, I turn over onto my back. Outside, crickets gossip busily. Far away a police siren starts up then fades away. I gaze out at all those bright wishes just waiting to be used until my eyes refuse to stay open.

Melodie Starkey's work has appeared in several journals including Porcupine Literary Review *and* The South Carolina Review. *She received a 1994 South Carolina Fiction Project award and a 1999 Illinois Arts Council writer's grant for a novel in progress. She currently lives in Chicagoland, dreaming of sunshine.*

Nichole Potts

DEALING WITH UNCLE ZEKE

When Uncle Zeke came home from work the whole
house would fill up with sorrow. The smell of it got into
our clothes, clung to our skin, and we could even taste it
in the water. When he was home, he'd order us around like
slaves, calling us out of our names—Goathead, Stupid, and
Monkey. Sometimes when he came home he would want
to fight, mad about something that happened out in the
streets. He'd accuse Aunt Leah of nasty woman acts and
then all five of us kids would have to wrap ourselves around
Aunt Leah's body, our fingers holding tight, tight to each
other's arms. We'd hold our breath and squeeze our eyes
shut, bracing ourselves, waiting for the blows with Aunt
Leah pleading in the midst of us. My mind would race to
the hidden place of Aunt Leah's lead pipe just in case he
decided to hurt her anyway.

Aunt Leah took me in after my mama died. Smyrna,
S.C., isn't a long way from York, but it feels like a long ways
down. My mama died from tuberculosis, something folks
ain't suppose to die from anymore. Maybe she wouldn't
have if we had more money. We were poor, but not Uncle
Zeke's type of poor, we had enough and there was peace in
our house. Mama used to say, "Any house without a man is
peaceful." I see this now.

Aunt Leah had once been a pretty girl, the color of a
copper penny. I know this because people would say it when

she was out of earshot and because I could still see it, even though her arms are full of puffy scars and she has cuts on her face from beatings. Aunt Leah was really skinny, so her cheeks looked sunk in. She looked what folks called hard-timey. It made me mad that he would beat her, especially after he spent all the money, rent included, and then Aunt Leah would have to gather all of us children with little bowlegged Baby Zeke in front to go visit Ms. Dupree.

"Please, Ms. Dupree, give us until next month. Don't throw me and these poor children out in the streets. Since my sister died and I took in her two babies, the Lord knows we see it hard."

I hated standing there being pitiful, because everybody knew that Ms. Dupree would never put children outdoors. I'd be so ashamed that I couldn't take my eyes off the chipped red nail polish on her toes and the whole time I'd be mad at Aunt Leah and hating Uncle Zeke.

Ms. Dupree would warn Aunt Leah that she gotta make a living too and that these things couldn't go on and blah, blah, blah. Aunt Leah would stand there nodding her head like a child being fussed out and then Ms. Dupree would slam the door in our faces and you could feel the sigh coming out of Aunt Leah's body.

In the backyard, behind the tall wild bush that Aunt Leah was always begging to have trimmed down, my cousins would circle around me and my brother. They'd eye us like angry dogs. My cousins with faces like Aunt Leah and ways like Uncle Zeke, like fallen angels. My brother's eyes would be shiny with tears and I would place my arm around his neck.

"Ya'll more trouble than you worth," the oldest one would hiss. They'd tell us that it was our fault that there was never enough of anything. My brother, being soft hearted and only eight, would cry and I'd bite my lip to keep from saying the truth, the truth we all knew, part of it being that we received benefits that Uncle Zeke would waste, too, if Aunt Leah didn't spend every cent so fast.

I'd bite my tongue because they already knew the truth; a lie just tasted better.

Uncle Zeke worked for the city, which was supposed to be a good job. We knew that payday came every other Thursday because that's when Uncle Zeke wouldn't come home until Sunday mornings. He'd come dragging home and sit in the kitchen with his head in his hands. As soon as we heard him fall into the chair, we'd get out of our beds and run to press our ears to the kitchen door. Aunt Leah would pour him a cup of coffee and move so quietly about the room that we wouldn't be sure what she was doing. Then we would hear her softly say something like, "Zeke, the rent's due Tuesday. I reckon we better rake together some money." She wouldn't dare ask where he had been or what he had been doing. Aunt Leah always had to ask for the money as soon as she could before he could waste what was left of his paycheck. If he had any money left he'd dig it out of his pocket or sock and throw it on the table. We would hold our breaths as we waited for the coins to stop making their hollow dings on the linoleum table, and then listen for the sound of her hand sweeping up the money. The next seconds were always strained as we listened to Aunt Leah count the change under her breath. Then we would hear Aunt Leah's "shaky-but-trying-not-to-get-mad" voice say something like: "That's all that's left? Oh, Lord God."

"Woman, you shut your mouth about my money."

"But we got these children and they got to eat. If only you would give me the money."

"What you tryna say? I don't know what to do with my own money? I work hard. I deserve some enjoyment."

I'd press my face against the cool door and imagine the sound of Aunt Leah's hand slapping his face. But Aunt Leah was not that type of woman, not the type of woman I wanted to be.

We all knew what happened to Uncle Zeke's money, because we couldn't help but to know and, besides, folks talked. He either passed out drunk with friends and they took all his money, some loose woman took it, or he just gambled it all away. Some people, mostly church members, even pulled Uncle Zeke to the side to try to explain to him what he should do, but he'd blame all the gossip on Aunt Leah. Uncle Zeke didn't like folks knowing that he didn't take care of his home. He'd say Aunt Leah talked too much, put his business in the streets. Mama used to say, "If you do your business in the streets, folks can't help but to see your behind."

Sometimes when Uncle Zeke came home mad, he'd stomp through the house growling and grumbling. Knocking over things and pushing folks around. We'd all try to run outside scattering like bugs, like the people do in them Godzilla movies. But sometimes we were too slow.

"Look," he would say as he held me by the back of my neck and then shook me like a rag doll, "Gracie looks like one of those big eyed, hungry children in Africa." He'd laugh out loud, even though there was no one to join in. They all just look ashamed. "I guess you ain't never gonna make enough for a man." In spite of myself, Uncle Zeke would win and I'd feel pitiful, small. One time I scratched his hand until he yanked away.

"Keep your nasty hands off me," I yelled. He looked shocked and then he laughed until he coughed.

I would've liked to have spooned Uncle Zeke a taste of his own medicine. I'd like to have placed that spoon on his lips, pressed it past his tongue, and shoved his own meanness down his throat. But such thoughts are petty a
nd belong to small people. I've heard people say that I'm going to be an itty-bitty woman like my Mama. I once heard a man tell Mama that he liked her because she'd fit into the palm of his hand. Mama said that she didn't feel small because being small has nothing to do with being strong. Mama said that she had God on the inside and that made here a part of everything and as big as all outdoors. I believed Mama. I had to.

There was a Thursday—a day before payday Thursday—when we didn't expect Uncle Zeke to come home. Aunt Leah sent me over to Aunt Tyree's house to borrow some flour with the promise that she'll get it back. Aunt Tyree was really our cousin but we called her Aunt just the same. Aunt Tyree was always giving and doing for us, worrying over us "precious, sweet thangs."

When I got to Aunt Tyree's house, I knocked and knocked but she didn't come to the door. I knew she was there because her car was in the yard and the front door was open. So, I opened the screen door and went in because I figured she was in the back and couldn't hear good. I stood in the hallway just liking the feel of the house. Aunt Tyree's house had wooden floors with fancy throw rugs. It was an old house so the windows were as high as the doors. The walls were white and it made you feel like the sun was shining. Aunt Tyree had little figurines set up in different places, making up all kinds of scenes in the house. Aunt Tyree always had plenty of flowers and baby dolls everywhere. Aunt Leah always said that Aunt Tyree picked right—she married a man that worked day and night so that she wouldn't have to. Sometimes I wished Aunt Tyree would've offered to take me in, so I wouldn't have to wait until I was grown up to live like this. I walked lightly toward the back of the house, not because I was sneaking, but because the rooms seemed so still it didn't seem right to disturb them. I looked in the kitchen and then thought to look in the back room, where Aunt Tyree likes to take midday naps.

As I neared the back bedroom, I could smell the faint odor of cigarettes burning. I could hear low mumbling and then high rolling laughs being thrown up to the ceiling. Aunt Tyree didn't have a door or a curtain to the back room, she had some of those different colored beads hanging down. And not the cheap dime store type, but the kind that was made out of real crystal and tossed light in all kinda places. Now, I was sneaking because I could feel down in my joints that something wasn't right. At first, I stood there listening to the mumbling and laughing, smelling the burnt, rusty odor of cigarettes and liquor, and listening to somebody on the record player moan: "It's just like pouring water on a drowning man." I peeked into the back room and saw Aunt Tyree sitting on the couch wearing a silky looking black nightgown that had her huge jelly-like breasts hanging out.

She had her head thrown back laughing through thick, shiny red lipstick. The man had his face buried in her chest. He leaned up to say something in her ear. This man, Uncle Zeke. I squeezed my hand over my mouth and slid down on my knees. Why, I don't know. I just couldn't control myself. I shouldn't watch I told myself. I shouldn't watch, but I couldn't turn away. I couldn't even blink. After he'd whisper something he'd place a bill down in her chest and Aunt Tyree would laugh some more. I felt dizzy and damp with sweat, but also cold just like the time we snuck around and dranked homebrew. Uncle Zeke was shiny with sweat. He had his shirt unbuttoned all the way down to where his stomach began to bulge. By the time Aunt Tyree leaned back on the sofa and Uncle Zeke was fumbling with his pants, I felt like I had been hit in the stomach. It was all I could do to crawl away. When I got all the way to the front door for some reason I remembered the flour. I walked back into the kitchen and took the whole canister. On the way home, I sang "Pouring water on a drowning man," and imagined Aunt Tyree's face when she realized when I took the flour.

I laid awake that night thinking about a whole lot of things. Another payday was coming with another hangover Sunday, and more tears. Even though, Aunt Leah did day work and all of us kids did little jobs like ironing and yard work. It just wasn't enough. I figured up one time all the nice things we could have if Uncle Zeke put in. We could have throw rugs, nice sitting chairs, and maybe even a nicer place to stay all together.

I'd heard the preacher say that a man that don't take

care of his family is worse than an infidel. The word infidel sounded like someone stupid, when I asked Aunt Leah to be sure, she said it was like being worse than a man who say's there's no God. Either way, both seemed like Uncle Zeke.

I was thinking about how people at church were always telling Aunt Leah that they're praying for her and how they bring things to the house because they "had too many to-matoes or ears of corn in their garden," or "they just don't have need of this or that anymore." I thought about the visit from the white lady that Aunt Leah works for, the one with mournful brown eyes like the ones that painters give Jesus.

The day she visited, the living room was as it always was—neat and clean but bare with nothing that wasn't given or hand-me-downed. A faint smell of Clorox was in the room because it holds down damp odors. She stood close by the door and wrapped her heavy coat with a fur collar around her as she looked all around the room. Look-ing so hard, even I could see the peeling, yellowing wallpa-per, the mix-match curtains, the tears in the linoleum, and the wobbly straight back chairs placed near the heater. Then she planted those eyes on us. I wanted to disappear and bless her out all at the same time. She came to give us her children's hand-me-downs and when I saw the clothes, in spite of my shame, I was so glad because they were almost like new. There were blouses, jumpers, and even shoes. I felt embarrassed because all five us were grinning and snatching at the clothes like we ain't used to having nothing. I went over to the lady with the Jesus eyes and when I could stop looking at her leather boots, I said a little too loudly, "Thank you."

I thought about Aunt Leah's prayers. I didn't mean to eavesdrop on her conversation with God, but I couldn't pull myself away from the rhyme—rhyme of her voice, explaining to God that winter was coming and so much more would be needed. I heard her ask God to save her husband, change his life. And I heard myself say, "Amen."

Uncle Zeke's getting off time was around 5 o'clock.
I took the lead pipe from beneath Aunt Leah's bed and
decided to meet him at the liquor store. I could see the red
dots on the white building from three blocks away. When
I got close, I could also see a group of men being led into
the liquor store by Uncle Zeke. I placed the pipe beside
the steps of the liquor store and prayed. I waited out front
while Uncle Zeke cashed his check. Aunt Leah had tried
this before, but Uncle Zeke chased her home with a stick.
I stood there thinking about Aunt Leah's prayer and our
broke-down house. When Uncle Zeke came out of the
store with a bunch of men and a brown bag, I stepped
directly in front of him and looked him dead in the eye:

"I come for the rent money."

I thought about the lady with the Jesus eyes and the
people at the church. I thought about him hitting Aunt
Leah and almost being put outdoors. I felt big, ready to
explode. Big enough to knock him down with my own two
hands and take the money. All the men stood looking at
me and Uncle Zeke having a stare down.

"Did Leah send you?" he snarled.

"Nope, she thinks I went over Aunt Tyree's." I felt
a wave of disgust that made me frown deep.

Uncle Zeke didn't act surprised or nothing, but I didn't
care if he hit me in front of all those men. I thought about
his face being buried in Aunt Tyree's chest and about never
having enough of anything. I could have taken a thousand
licks and still been standing.

I stuck my hand out and stared him in the eye, "The
rent money and we need things besides," and then I heard
myself say, "It's what a man ought to do."

Uncle Zeke glanced around at the men, who kinda
shrugged and shuffled off to the side. He gave me one of
those little "umph" laughs, like he was gonna give me the
money to humor me. He reached down into his shirt pocket
and peeled off a $100 bill. I took the money out of his
hands and turned without so much of a look back or "thank

you, dog." I went to get my lead pipe and headed home
to tell Aunt Leah how God moved on Uncle Zeke.

*Nichole Potts, a native of Fort Mill, has received a Mecklenburg Emerging
Artist Award, Rock Hill Artist Grant and a South Carolina Academy of
Authors Award. Her writings have appeared in* Cold Mountain Review,
AIM, Windhover, *and other publications. This story is part of a collection
titled* Every Good-Bye Ain't Gone.

Cameron Sperry

TORPOR

Tom sits on the top porch step and pops his beer, the sound crackling through the summer air like a rifle shot. He pauses a few seconds, listening for the sound of Lois' footsteps on the hardwood floors of the hallway, then, in the silence of the afternoon, he takes a long swallow from the can. The beer is icy, crystallizing from being kept in the crisper drawer of the refrigerator in the garage, where Lois won't find it. Tom swirls the can around a couple times to speed up the melting of the ice, and the half-frozen concoction foams out of the opening of the can, spilling over onto his hand.

The air is still, thick with moisture, typical for almost any August afternoon in the Florida Panhandle. Sometimes it's so humid it's hard to breathe, and the sweat pools under your arms and at the back of your neck, trickling in tiny rivers towards the base of your spine. Tom hates the summer, this oppressive heat, and the way his clothes stick to his damp body even when he isn't exerting himself. The nights offer no relief. He and Lois sleep naked on top of the sheets, but he still wakes up sticky, a sheen coating his body like a basting glaze on a prize ham.

Lois hardly ever sleeps through the night, and when he wakes up in the morning sunlight and finds her side of the bed empty his muscles tighten automatically and his heart speeds up just enough to raise that metallic taste in the back of his throat. It's fear, he knows, and it's gone in a few seconds, as soon as he gets his bearings, hears Lois downstairs banging around in the kitchen. It's fear and he can't help feeling it, can't help expecting the worst, even though she hasn't had a drink now for almost four months.

"Honey," Lois calls from somewhere behind him, inside the house. He stashes the beer in the vines that are encroaching on the back steps, pushing the shiny can beneath the large green leaves until it's completely hidden.

"Hey, will you come help me with something?" Lois is standing on the other side of the screen door, smiling, he sees when he twists his head around to look at her over his shoulder. A bead of sweat slips down the side of his neck, and he swats at it with his open palm. "Are you busy?" she asks, looking around, trying to figure out what he's been doing there on the back steps.

"Nah," he says, being careful not to glance in the direction of the hidden beer can. She's got eyes like a hawk, and she's always on the lookout for things he might be doing that he shouldn't be doing. And she would definitely find a problem with him sitting on the front porch drinking a cold beer. Because she can't. The doctors at the treatment center said she was not psychologically able to have only one drink. If she has one, she will have another, and then another, until she gets so drunk she passes out or does something stupid. Like picking up a stranger in a bar and taking him to a local hotel for a few hours.

Tom has to force himself to stop thinking these thoughts. He glances back up at Lois, then he stands up from the steps and dusts the seat of his pants off with his palms. He flips a little smile toward his wife.

"Whatya got for me, sergeant?" he asks.

As usual, she is not amused. He knows she hates it when he acts like this, but sometimes he can't help it. Sometimes the memories of finding her in that motel with the stranger get to be overpowering, and rather than smack her around or walk out on her, which are two things he's wished for a long time he had the guts to do, he adopts this sarcastic attitude and tone of voice. Her response is always the same. She makes that little "phht…" noise between her pink lips and tries to sneer at him, though what her face looks like is less a sneer than a crude contortion that doesn't seem to have any meaning.

"The light in the bathroom just went out and now I can't get it to come back on," she says as she turns around and leads the way back through the screen door and down the long hallway toward the back of the house. "See if you can fix it."

"Probably a bulb," Tom says, watching one curl of her yellow hair bounce against the back of her head as she walks. He wants to reach out and grab the curl and pull it out straight against his finger, the way he used to when he and Lois would pack a picnic and head over to Panama City Beach for the day, and after they'd swum in the Gulf and eaten their fried chicken and potato salad, they'd lie there on a blanket on the sand, soaking in the rays of the sun and he thought he could see those blond strands on her head curling into their familiar corkscrews as he watched, the light of the sun playing colors of strawberry and copper against her cheeks and forehead. God, he used to love to tangle his fingers up in that mop.

He feels an ache in his belly, and he concentrates on matching his footfalls to Lois' on the dark wood of the floor. Then they are in the bathroom, and Lois is pulling a wooden chair toward the center of the floor for him to stand on.

"It just flickered and went out," she explains. "And now it won't come back on." She stands there in front of the sink and looks expectantly at him.

A rivulet of sweat creeps down his back, tracing his spine, and he twists his shoulders a bit to sop it up with his

T-shirt. He wipes the beads of moisture off his brow with the back of one hand, then he steps up to the chair.

"You try the bulb?" he asks as he reaches up to unscrew the suspect globe.

He looks below his outstretched arm at Lois, whose face suddenly shapes itself into a large O, her eyes, nostrils and lips all at once forming circles as her jaw drops to make her entire face transform into a disc. Then he hears the crack, loud but muffled, as if it came from a long way off, and his body separates itself from his mind and he is gone.

The stranger was a boy who'd come to town looking for carpentry work, and had instead found a job as a waiter at the Crab Pot restaurant, where Lois spent some afternoons downing dry martinis without olives and rattling off her troubles to anyone who got close to her barstool. The stranger had gotten close enough to hear her complaints, and had stayed to give her advice over gin and tonics, then had ended up at the Twilight Motel with her in room seventeen, just around the corner from the pool. Tom had learned all the details during a counseling session at the treatment center. Not that he had needed to hear the details, or the incredible calmness of Lois' voice as she recounted her affair for the sake of the psychologist.

The stranger, only a boy, really, had answered Tom's knock on the door of the motel room, expecting who knows what—room service was out of the question at such a dive— his hips wrapped in a towel and his blond hair damp against his tanned neck. Lois stepped out of the bathroom as the boy pulled the door open wide to give Tom entrance to the lamp lit room. Lois, also towel-wrapped, giggled and hiccupped and gave him a little wave with her tiny hand, and when Tom looked at him the boy just stared at his feet and fingered the doorknob.

"You have no right to keep tabs on me!" she screamed at him as he drove toward home that night. "You don't know what it means to love someone!" He refused to respond in any way, focusing his concentration on the road ahead of him. This was only the gin talking. He'd heard it so many times before. He had learned that it was best to let her scream herself hoarse.

Lois stopped screaming and cold-cocked him as he drove through an intersection near the entrance to their neighborhood. Her little fist caught him on the side of his head near his temple, and for a second he felt a sharp stinging pain, then his eyes went black and he'd barely gotten the car stopped on the shoulder of the road before a swoon overtook him.

He hears Lois' voice calling to him from very far away. He knows his eyes are open but he can't see anything except a white blankness. He blinks to make certain, but nothing changes, except that Lois' voice has gotten closer, buzzing in his left ear like a blue fly. Then she is shrieking at him.

"OH MY GOD, I THOUGHT YOU WERE DEAD!"

He blinks again and sees her face looming over him, her pale hair and skin slowly forming out of the slate of white before his eyes.

"WHAT HAPPENED?" she screams at him over the ringing in his ears. "WHAT DID YOU DO?"

He closes his eyes again and lets the coolness of the bathroom tiles soothe him. He lies still for several seconds, thinking of nothing, then he begins an inventory. An ache in his head throbs just above his right eyebrow, his right hand tingles, and he cannot feel his feet. Words are forming in his head: What happened?

"What happened?" Lois asks again, and he opens his eyes and looks up into her blue eyes, noticing the crow's feet and rough skin across her cheeks, the red tinge splotched over the bridge of her nose. He notices the pale shadow of a mustache above her top lip, the scar at the side of her mouth, result of a teenage auto accident. He can see up into her nostrils.

He hasn't looked at Lois this closely in a long time. For an instant, his brain clouds, and he thinks, curiously, "Who is this?" He starts to shake his head to clear it, but the pain above his eyebrow explodes into another throb across the entire forehead, and he lies still. He thinks about closing his eyes, but instead he watches Lois' face muscles work as she tries to lift him off the floor by one arm. He helps her by sitting up as she tugs at him.

"My God," she's chattering, "I didn't know what was going on. There was a flash and then "CRACK!" then you fell off the chair and started jumping around like a fish or something. Jeez, Tom, you might have been killed! All I could think was you might have been killed. Are you all right?"

He nods. He can't see her face now, only hears her voice coming from close behind his head. She's got her hands under his armpits, trying to lift him into a standing position. He pulls his legs under himself and attempts to stand, but he still can't feel his feet. Lois is gripping his left arm like it's the safety bar on a moving roller coaster. He sees the chair he'd stood on to fix the light and he tilts toward it, then lurches into the seat.

"Are you all right?" Lois asks, looking into his face. "Do you want me to get you something?"

He tries to think of what he might need. What might help. He pictures an ice pack across his brow, his feet propped on the foot rest of an overstuffed brown leather recliner, NFL football on TV, a cold beer icing his hand. He shakes his head.

"I'm all right," he says. "Give me a minute."

"Jeez, Tom, you don't even sound right. I'm calling a doctor."

His head whirls: a morphine drip, a cheerful young nurse.

"Nah, Lois, I'm all right," he tells her. "Just give me a minute."

He keeps sitting there on the wooden chair while she disappears down the hallway. He's looking at the bathroom wall, at nothing, a blank space painted white. There are a few specks of dirt on the wall. A wisp of dust. A tiny gouge. He feels himself leaning toward the wall and the white expanse slipping away from him, and he puts his head into his hands and waits for Lois to come back.

"Do you want some ice water?" Her voice brings him out of a daze. He looks up at her and shakes his head. She's holding a glass full of water and ice. The cubes sparkle in a ray of sun, and he is transfixed by their brilliance. He stares into the glass.

Lois is looking at him. "What can I do?" she says, worried.

Nothing. Nothing you can do will ever change the way I feel, he thinks. He's staring at the sparkling cubes and things are getting clearer, clearer than they've been in months, and he's finding words swimming around in his head and he captures them and places them on his tongue and when he opens his mouth they spill out in a stream of clear liquid, all water and no sound. Melted ice cubes. I loved you, I loved you, why did you hurt me so?

He looks up into her eyes. She tries to smile at him, but the movement seems foreign to her, and she cannot master it. He's watching her try and fail. He's watching her give up.

"I gotta go outside," he says, and he stands up easily, steadies himself a moment, then walks away from her.

Monday morning Lois calls him in sick for work, telling his boss he'd gotten a touch of the stomach flu over the weekend, but should be okay in another day or two. The feeling in his legs is back to normal, and except for a lingering headache, he knows he's fine. Lois had urged him to see a doctor and get checked out just to make sure, but he'd told her he was okay. That which doesn't kill us makes us stronger, is how he'd put it. Lois had not smiled, had not even tried to.

He just can't seem to make himself do anything. He sits on the porch from the time he gets up in the morning until he can't keep his eyes open at night, then he climbs the stairs to the bedroom and takes off his clothes, lays them across a chair, and lies stiffly on the bed beside his naked wife until he sleeps and dreams. His dreams are full of a brilliant white light, flashing and flaring. He wakes up covered with a sticky damp sheen, and Lois is nowhere in sight. The metallic taste in the back of his throat is stronger now, and always present.

He sits on the porch step and looks at nothing and tries to remember things he's been trying to forget. Like the month Lois had spent in the alcohol treatment center: what had he done? He'd worked, puttered around the house, eaten TV dinners and watched football games on the weekends. He'd gone to a bar with some fellows from work one night. He'd slept with the windows open to let in a cool breeze. He'd concentrated on trying to get the picture of Lois and the stranger out of his head. He'd spent a lot of time wondering if they would be able to make it through this, convincing himself that they could.

"Tom?" Lois is standing at the corner of the house, beside the flowerbed, holding a rake, looking toward where he's sitting on the back steps. He's got his hands clasped between his knees and he'd been looking at something across the yard—he doesn't know what. He looks at Lois. She's wearing her green rubber garden shoes and a pair of white shorts that make her legs look very brown. He remembers her in a swimsuit at Panama City Beach, sprinting toward the water as he ran after her. The Gulf had been nothing but sparkles in the sunlight, silver sparkles dancing as far as he could see.

"Is this going to work?" she asks.

Tom doesn't know what to say. He doesn't know the

answer. He looks at her, at her pretty blond curls glowing in the sunlight, at the smudge of dirt on her chin, and one above her right eyebrow. He looks at her and he wonders what to say, tries to find those words and get them into his mouth.

"I don't know," he says. He watches to see what she'll do.

She pushes a curl away from her forehead and looks toward the flowerbed. "I don't know why I bother with this," she says. "Nothing's going to grow here."

It strikes him that she had been asking him about her plantings, and nothing more. Suddenly, he feels a surge of anger rising in his belly and he has the urge to walk down the steps to where she's standing and thump her right between the eyes. His head is so full of words that he can't focus on any one, but finally he finds something.

"No," he tells her. "No, nothing's going to grow there if you don't look after it. You're always planting stuff and then forgetting about it, so it dries up in the sun, or rots in the shade. To make something grow you gotta care about it and take care of it. You gotta make sure you do that, if you want it to be there."

When he runs out of words, he just sits there, staring at his wife.

Lois leans on her rake and returns his stare for several seconds. Then she looks down at the flowerbed.

"What's got into you?" she asks. He sees the muscles around her mouth working, then he watches as she drops the rake and turns away from him and runs, across the yard and into the garage.

He lifts himself off the back steps and goes after her. His head is throbbing, and a flash of light glows just behind his eyes, but he makes it across the yard and through the side door to the garage and finds her leaning against the trunk of the car with her head in her hands, crying.

"I don't know what's wrong with you," she sobs into her

hands. She won't look up at him. "You never say anything, you never want to do anything, you just go along, like nothing ever happened. Nothing fazes you. You almost get electrocuted and you won't even see a doctor. You might have been killed, for Christ sake! But all you do is sit on those steps, like nothing ever happened. God, Tom, what is it? What is wrong with you?"

Now she's looking up at him, her pale face streaked red from the tears and the skin around her eyes showing a bluish tinge in the shadows of the garage. He looks at her for a while. After a few seconds, he says, "I don't know. I don't know what's wrong with me."

She watches his eyes when he speaks. Then her face twists into a knotted mess, and he thinks the tears are going to start again.

"You're never going to forgive me, are you?" she asks. He recognizes the voice from the psychologist's office. The calm voice. The accepting voice. Unwavering. Unapologetic. And then he hears the voice in his own head responding, I loved you, I loved you. How can I ever love you that way again?

Tom is staring at his wife, feeling the fierce light slowly move from behind his eyes to the center of them. The pain in his head is beating a pulse against his left temple. His eyes are stinging, and he wants to swipe them with the back of his hand, but he doesn't.

He turns away and walks slowly across the yard, his head pounding with each step, the brilliance forcing his eyes into slits. He moves carefully up the steps, and sits on the top one. He looks at the flowerbed where Lois has turned the soil in preparation for some planting which won't be done. He shades his eyes with his hand to see the side door to the garage. He wonders for a second what Lois is doing in there. He scouts around for something else to focus his sight on, so the stinging in the corners of his eyes isn't so strong.

The sun glints off of something shiny hidden in the vines beside the steps, and he reaches over and picks up the beer can he'd hidden there three days ago. The warm liquid inside sloshes against the aluminum, and a yellow jacket shimmies quickly out of the mouth of the can, pauses a moment on the lip, then lifts his wings and takes flight. Tom lets his eyes follow the yellow jacket's path through the sky until the insect disappears from sight. Then he sets the beer can on the step between his feet, and he looks at it until he cannot keep the pain away any longer, and he begins to cry.

Cameron Sperry holds a Master of Arts degree from the University of North Carolina at Wilmington, where she taught creative writing for several years before returning to the South Carolina Lowcountry. She is employed by the law firm of Ness, Motley, Loadholt, Richardson & Poole, and lives in Ravenel with her husband and two cats.

Robert Poole

Break

It's like this. It's like someone turned a skillet upside down, and we're all trapped underneath. I gave up sleeping weeks back. The air is over-warm, sweetish-stale with perspiration stink. And so dark you can't see your hand before your face. Guys turn over every few minutes in their sleep, and the beds go scree-scraw. These beds sag in the middle, like each one was the deathbed of a big man. Iron and wire jobs maybe left over from Civil War field hospitals. The darkest hour's just before the dawn—that's what they say. In any case, all I can feel at this time of the night are failure and finality and imminent iron sorrows.

It's like this. You have to strike a deal with the tunnel rats to keep them off your back. They don't have anything to lose, while you have everything. They were on the street before they came in; they're just continuing, understand, but institutionalized now—fronting for the punk loan sharks, dealing some weed. If there's a weakness, then the tunnel boys are right there on it, to get in on the kicks or the folding green.

It's like this. You go in for chow. The dented tin trays and stacks of Wonder Bread from the day-old bakery outlet. Start to work out on a forkful of the greasy-gray matter which passes for meat and your stomach is sick the moment the stuff hits your tongue.

God knows I've been trying to pull some good time in

here. Go out into the yard, in the shadow of the ten-foot cyclone fences, where the hibiscuses are. I put them there. Those beds are smooth and tight as a baby's bottom. The blooms are as big as your open palm, diaphanous and delicate as a young girl's hair. A young girl, like the last one I kissed on the outside.

But then the sun is setting, and the trusty is motioning toward the tunnel. All you can see is the sun's red glow in the rounds of ribbon wire—like uncoiled razor blades—winding through the top of the cyclone fence.

I'm afraid my experiments in pulling good time might be coming to an end. I'm just incapable of maintaining.

Prison. Maybe I could pull a Jack Abbott, get Norman Mailer to spirit my butt out of here. He could pry open the jaws of the beast, and I'd scurry on up, out of the belly. But the beast I'm worried about is the beast between the ears. They make us into beasts here. Dr. Moreau's House of Pain. Some are benign, lumbering beasts; the others aren't benign. The latter prey on the former. It's the Serengeti behind wire mesh and bars, behind the trees, here in the north end of Columbia. It's either the beast-manifest, or the beast-potential. That's all. Oh, I've been working on my beast here, make no mistake. It's taking shape.

Maybe I'm the most independent man south of the Mason-Dixon line right now. I don't need anyone. It started when I was a kid, just out of high school. Break free, something hard and clean, no hypocrisy, deals, pabulum. You know the story. No one understood, except for a couple of friends I made. We put our hands on a van and started traveling. The van died in Alabama; we pulled off the plates and found another van and bolted on the plates and were on our way again. We did what we had to do to keep moving. It was a tolerable life. Swim in the rivers, scramble up the mountains, meet some girls at the local skating rink or Dairy Queen in the small town, move on down the road again.

But things went bad. In Florida it was, someone got

hurt, now I'm here and my friends are somewhere. Fifteen years of straight time—no parole. Eight to go now.

But damn. It's just, back then, no one knew what I was going through. I couldn't imagine anyone being more alone, the possibility of being more alone. How was I to know that what I undertook, to deliver myself from that, would become this? There's a guy in here, has three of those little banner tattoos, the ones with the names in them—of sweethearts, honeys. One on each shoulder, one on his right forearm. But each banner has been inked in solid.

That's how I feel these days with these jail kids in here. Just leave me the hell alone. My banners are inked in solid. Just let me maintain, move my beast around on its own time in here. But the tunnel boys look out for that sort of thing; it's a place to drive in the wedge. Oh, I used to have a buddy, but he's out some two years now. My time for buddies in here is over.

I see how they do when they come in. They stay tight within themselves, at first. Time passes, they're loosening up, settling in, then one day they're spilling it. Sentencing day. The lawyer said this, and the D.A. did this, and the judge gathered in the folds of his robe like this. Big shots for a day, the moment before the iron door slams, yeah, they're all genuine grade-A inmates now. Punks. It makes me sick.

Hey, you're saying, Merle Haggard or Johnny Cash will come down and play sometime. Break things up a little. Or, you're saying, sit in on some of those college transfer courses. Work on an AA degree. Improve on the inner man.

No way. Eight years of straight time. You understand that before you make me understand this and that and the other thing.

Try understanding a few of these things. First, try understanding that we've got a laundry in here. The crazies over on Bull Street soil themselves and their sheets pretty regularly. Those sheets come this way before they end up on those Bull Street beds again. I put in five years on the sheets, forty hours a week at eight dollars a week—I was on a first name basis with excrement, understand—before they let me lend a hand maintaining the trucks. Very big deal, prison grease monkey, eight dollars a week, sure. Five years for that promotion.

Try understanding that every time one of those trucks goes out, the guard at the gate takes a 6-by-10 mirror on a pole and makes a few passes under the chassis of the truck. Just to check the subject out.

Try understanding that I have taken a blacked-out, 3-foot by 4-foot piece of 3/8-inch plywood and placed it between myself and the truck chassis and rear axle. According to my mirror, the guard won't be checking out my subject with his mirror, especially on the truck that pulls out around dusk, and count isn't until three hours after evening chow.

There's a prison band that practices every day at dusk. Today, it's "Born to be Wild." The melody is being mauled mercilessly by sounds approximating those of an Asplundh branch grinder being operated in three-quarter time. This is good, for me. Any distraction impinging on the guard's sensory capacities is an added boon.

The truck pulls up to the guard shack. The brake shoes are squealing, and the rear Firestones are being seized solid in the midst of their revolutions. It's like I'm curled up with them under the covers.

I have no cause for worry. Either I'll be roaming my beast around, out there, or else they'll enclose my beast in the lockup, away from the tunnel rats and wire-rack beds and malodorous bed sheets. A beautiful dilemma.

There's that mirror on the stick, sniffing around underneath me like an elephant's trunk. The muffler's chuffing, and the long drive shaft is spinning flawlessly. The driver and the guard grunt at one another. That's it. The gate creaks along on its length of track; once it's clear of the truck's bumper, we're on our way.

Half a foot below, the asphalt and gravel rush by, and

the uneven tones of "Born to be Wild" recede into the distance. The air is fresh and sweet, and the truck's engine right on song.

When we come to I-20, the truck stops at the light. As it slowly accelerates forward, I hunch my body into a ball and roll down the embankment of the overpass. No one notices, as far as I can tell. I hide my prison boots and gray prison-issue pants in the undergrowth there. I count my road money.

Maybe I'll be back sometime to play the tourist in this Columbia. Maybe I'll roam my beast on over and visit the Bull Street crazies, sheets and all. A regular Southern homecoming. But there are a few other cities and highways I've got to see to first...

Robert Poole is a real estate lawyer in Durham, North Carolina. He reads and writes as time allows.

Rebecca Parke

STUCK!

Right before it happened, this lady woman voice say to me from way back in the back of my head where no voice ain't never spoke to me before, she say, "You better get you black hand out of that garbage, gal."

And I did, too. I snatched my hand out of there like I was pulling it out of the toothy mouth of the Devil hisself. Then I couldn't locomote myself no more. Stuck, paralyzed, welded, I was to the spot in front of the kitchen can. "Gone fool," I said to myself.

There I had been ramming my arm down into the garbage like it was a jackhammer stuck to my shoulder without one itsy, bitsy iota of a idea what I was doing. Trying to shred the garbage into a littler pile? I don't know. Don't know what's got into me of late, unless it's my mama's bad blood. I don't know what I'm doing half the time. I go to pick the peas and I pull up the vine. I wake up in the night my heart slamming against my rib cage like some cheetah trapped in a box.

I be twenty-three years old on this the seventh day of June 1954, and I have been married eight years to a man who still has not found the words to tell me what it feels like to be up inside me, though he has been there plenty enough and made with me four babies. And sometimes I think he do it, somehow, without touching me at all. The only waves of love that have crossed my belly in this marriage have come to me as gifts from my suckling babies. And they all weaned now. And all this has been known for a long, long time. So what is there new now to shake me up so? Nothing. Nothing at all.

And I don't care what my best friend, Sarah Jane, say when she popping off at the mouth. It ain't got nothing to do with Welcome Lasier. I am over him. Besides he be dead. He fell backwards into shallow water from the top of a little bridge he was helping build out in California. So what if he had hands big enough they cupped your soul when he held you? I was fourteen years old then. He was nineteen and hell-bent for adventure, something which my body and soul did not have enough of to hold him. That's a fact plain as a pikestaff because he left.

"Don't want nobody that don't want me," I spit it out plain to Sarah Jane, us sitting up under the grape arbor, me yanking her nappy hair into braids so tight I had her scalp pulled away from her head. I had her squealing. "You too tough. Too tough!" She would've thought I was tough if I'd a yanked on what I thought ought to be yanked on. At fourteen she didn't have no bosoms at all. I thought she could've used a couple of good pulls. What time will do. Now she got a plentitude—more, much more than me.

That's how I let Welcome go, played games with my mind, thought about how Sarah Jane wasn't never going to get no man if she didn't come up with some equipment, thought about anything so as not to think about him. Got married. Come Friday week he be dead one year. I let him go. I be tough.

But when I have nights like I had last night and zombie days like today, I gets to wondering. You see I gone to dreaming about standing in the highway.

When my mama was thirty-five years old she took to standing in the middle of the highway in front of our house of a morning with her gowntail up over her head, its hem all wrapped around her arms, so that she stood in a sack of her own making from the waist up. Her skinny legs from the front looked like two knitting needles stuck in a little white pea—her little cotton panties—and inside the little pooched-out mound beneath those panties was me. She never did fully stop that till my daddy was dead. By then nobody cared if she was cured or not, nobody wanted her, and I was little. They sent her down the highway, fully clothed this time, to the asylum.

That's how my dead daddy's mama, Grandmammy Montine, come to have me when I was so young. She used to make me stand between her fat feet and her square toes and look into her squinched-up face while she whipped me with her tongue telling me that story. When the spite would rise in her she'd say: "You a sassy gal; you going to be left standing naked in the street someday. You better get a change of at'tude." I have sworn all my life never to give her the pleasure of seeing me so.

And damn! One month and thirteen days ago, her square toes turned cold, and from that very first night I found myself standing in the highway in my dreams without so much even as a little cotton panty between me and the on-looking world, and smothering my head in a little black plastic bag.

What can you do with this joke called life but keep on moving? I made myself look into that kitchen can. And what you think I saw? I saw this old tin can top absolutely jellied over with slime rust. I thinks to myself, "Um-huh! I done found the culprit now, thanks to that lady woman voice speaking up in my head." Going crazy ain't all bad. I picks up the nasty little lid with my thumb and forefinger and I was working it down in the middle of the garbage so it wouldn't rip up Seesaw Slaan when he swing off the tailgate piston of the garbage truck early in the morning like he King of the High Wire now and swoop down and grab a hold of the trash bag anywhere, minding nothing but how good he's pimping today, with one shoulder up and one shoulder down, his free arm stiff by his side.

He ain't but sixteen, fresh from trouble in the high school, his own mama's breakfast bacon still probably

hanging on his teeth. He flashes his eyes in their corners in
all neighborhoods, like those few of us women left at home
during working hours got nothing better to do than walk
back and forth before the windows of our houses, shaking
it up for him. You can see the way he's peeping that in his
mind he sees us with our hips going from side-to-side while
our shoulders got that backward-forward motion that
moves our breasts before us. And you know he is cocksure
that one day one or more of us is going to show it to him
for real.

And so he practices swooping down over the big, black
over-stuffed garbage bags provided by the sanitation department and scooping them up two at a time against his chest
like them bags is a couple of us women finally splayed out
in the yard before him instead of us being behind our
kitchen windows minding our chaps. Oh, he grabs up two
bags together like he's man enough to satisfy 'em both at
the same time. Some pretty young thing's going to rip his
heart open soon enough, and I didn't want it to be my
garbage that done it first.

And then's when it happened.

Some of them young'uns must have put that florist
spike from Grandmammy Morine's wreath in that garbage,
and I started making plans right then to shine some young
gentleman's bottom. I mean that thing. Lord, have mercy.
The little arrow on the end of that spike, it jammed into me.
Jammed into me just right there where your hands start to
dome out of your arm.

I jerked my arm out of that garbage can, and that spike
it come up, too still hanging in there. I grab a hold of it and
yank it out a there just like you seen them cowboys yank
them arrows across out of their chests on the TV. You'd
think I'd a bled like a stuck pig. But I didn't. Three little
dribbles of blood. That's all that come.

I was counting my lucky stars and going for a Band-Aid
when the world went black as I am. And when I come to,
my arm was throbbing like Sammy's big bass drum, and it

was so swoll up I hardly did recognize it as my own arm. There I was stretched out on the kitchen floor all by myself.

The clock over the kitchen window said it was time for Seesaw Slaan. And I called at the top of my lungs, "Seesaw Slaan! Seesaw!" And no Seesaw come.

I didn't think I could do it, but I grabbed a hold of the Kelvinator door handle with my good arm and I heaved myself up as best I could. And I got myself over to the window. And I called out the window, "Help me! Help me!"

And here come Sara Jane home from the laundrymat early because Beedy By got the colic, and she rescued me. Sara Jane she see my arm and sets Beedy By on the counter and him just a squalling. She says to me while she propping me up, "Girl, child. What have you done?"

I inform her, "I ain't done nothing. But Grandmanny Morine done took spite out on me and her in the grave."

"What that old biddy do?" say Sarah Jane.

"Done made me stick one of them florist spikes off her graveside wreath in my arm. And it's poison!"

"Gal, I didn't know you was considering committing the suicide! Didn't know you was ready to go that far for Welcome Lasier."

Some fools they ain't no talking to; instead I just fell in a heap on the floor. Then I lifted my head up mean, like any baldheaded buzzard, and looked her in her little chickenshit eye, and I said, "You make my blood pressure rise any higher, and this arm it going to blow and shoot blood and veins and bone all over your face because I going to point it in your direction! Get me to the doctor now!"

And then I went to crying. And all the chaps, hers, mine and the neighborhood's, that had squeezed in through the open back door, took up the chorus, and they went to bawling, too. And Sarah Jane gets all in a tizzy and forgets I'm a invalid, yells, "Come on then!" But Sarah Jane is a good woman and ever mindful of babies. She grabs up all the crawlers, mine, hers and the neighborhood's, and shoos the walkers ahead of her. And some power I couldn't see helped me get off the floor and onto my feet.

That's the second time Lady Woman talk to me. She say, "Never fear." Then somehow Sarah Jane and all the chaps was loaded into her old beat-up, once-upon-a-time telephone van, and we bust in on old Doc Bailey. And he standing in the receptionist's glass cage, looking down at the appointment book or maybe, something May Belle had in her lap for all I know. When he looked up, he say, "Bleeding?"

I say, "No, sir. Not on the outside."

He draw his finger down at me like he about to pop a bullet into my brain and say, "Clinic."

And we turn around and meet the last straggles of the line of young'uns still coming this a way and now we going yonder.

"And hold that arm up high!" He booms from his old big purple lips.

And I shoots it up high as the parade leader's baton in the Christmas parade and all the kids fall in line like magic. And Sarah Jane has to drive me fifteen miles to Rock Hill to this big clinic. And when I walked into that clinic door with this arm held high, I got first-rate service. This nurse, she puts me in this room all to myself. And this doctor he comes whipping round the corner and runs right into the room with me and grabs onto that arm. I let out a yelp.

He goes running right out of the room. In just a minute here he come again with four more doctors. And they all got tape measures and they measure my bad arm and they measure my good arm and they look at they measurements and they shake they heads.

And one of them says, "She bleeding on the inside bad."

And one of them say, "We going to have to send her to Memorial."

And another of them say, with something like glee, "No, let's do experimental surgery here."

And I say through my tears, "What you mean 'experimental surgery'?"

And he say, "If that swelling don't stop, we going to have to cut your arm open and take a look on the inside, maybe tie off an artery."

And I say, "How far you going to cut on my arm?"

And he run his finger most the length of my whole arm. And that made me mad.

And I say, "If you going to make that big a swipe, why don't you just cut on up to the heart and tie it off there and be done."

And he left the room. And I left this world. And when I come to they had me strung up here in this clinic bed in a private room and all my clothes was laying over yonder on a chair and they had me in this nightshirt that's open up the back.

But that ain't the worst of it. They had my bad arm in a cast, and it was hung up from the ceiling, and they had my other arm strapped to the bed with sugar water dripping into it. But they hadn't done no "experimental surgery" because that arm was alive and throbbing. They'd just hung it up there for all the blood to pool in my armpit.

Somehow or other, Sarah Jane had got hold of Daniel at the hosiery mill, and there he stood by my bedside, looking like he's freshly joined the homeless. Just time I opened my eyes, he spews out, "Ornatha, you can't commit suicide. What I going to do with all the chaps by myself?"

Then's when Lady Woman's voice speak to me a third time, "Now you see how he can do it to you and not touch you? He having sex with you, yeh. But he making love to he self."

"There's your mama, Daniel…"

"If there's anybody stepping out on me for good, I'd just as soon it was her," say Daniel.

He don't like his mama. He just goes to her for whatever he can't get from me. She boss him worse than I do.

His name's really George. He gets "Daniel" from potted meat. He'd live off of potted meat if I let him. It's as close to pap as a grown man can eat and retain his honor. Just the same, it going to do him in. There's just so much ground-up cow hair and chicken toes in a swill of grease that a man can run through him before his body revolts.

His stomach rumbles and roars and takes on so folks can hear him coming. And they signify on his paunch. "Stand back, Little Cats, Daniel in the big cat den chewing he fat." So, Daniel he is. But he ain't no hero to me, though I always keep hoping.

"Daniel," I say true, "I feel about as naked helpless as the day I was born."

And by damn, Daniel goes to sniffling. Just when I thought it was going to be my turn, finally. All of a sudden a vast desert opens up before me, and it is my life with Daniel. I flatten the palm of my hung-up hand toward heaven and beg for mercy in my mind. If I was a hosiery mill machine, Daniel would be neck deep in my insides fixing me up. They can't do without him at the mill. Call him all hours and he go running.

I got Mama got out of the asylum last year and think she making sense when she say, "Lucky, lucky, he make you a good living."

"Daniel," I look up from the clinic bed into his eyes, and I say, "Why don't you lay down beside me just a little bit and hold me?" But he shake his head, "No." And his eyes look like the backs of two shiny black beetles; I don't see any man in there at all.

The only manly tenderness I ever have knowed in my life was from a big-handed boy with half-moon eyes on his fingernails so bright I thought they would show me the way home. But I was not as exciting as Death. And when I looked into the casket at his hands for them little moons, they was no more.

How I going to live much longer without tenderness? I close my eyes and let myself drift away from Daniel, propped up on his powerful fists on the side of the bed, waiting for me to give him all the answers and despising me deep down when I do.

Deep in the night above the clanking of the outdoor air conditioner here in my backside room, she come to me for a fourth time; Lady Woman was singing to me this time, in honey black alto, surrounding me, holding me in her voice. She didn't show me no visions.

No, I didn't even see the dancing pigs that come to you when the nurse give you that shot to keep the new baby's coming from tearing you asunder. Didn't see no burning bush, no heavenly light, no long white-haired white man, having his way.

Saw only the little crack of light under the door, the little call bell's red spot shining, and Lady Woman unhooking my arm from the ceiling, undoing that sugar line from my arm, singing, "Follow me. Got to get you free." I thought we was headed for the highway, until we made our first step into mid-air.

Rebecca Parke, a three-time winner of the South Carolina Fiction Project, studied writing at the University of South Carolina.

Jasper Neel

A Life of Crime

Ralph walked slowly through the toy section. This was his first attempt in Dave's Discount, and he wanted to be sure before he made his move. Two old ladies were looking at combs three aisles away, and there were two checkout girls, but none of them was paying attention to him. He settled on one of the baseballs. It would be just the right size.

When he reached the back of the store, he turned, went over two aisles, and then walked through the housewares and small appliances. This took him right through the middle of the store. Except for the old ladies and the checkout girls, he was alone.

About halfway to the front, he reached down and scratched his navel, unbuttoning the shirt button just above his belt. At the front of the store he walked slowly until one of the checkout girls glanced at him. When she did, he stopped, took his money from his pocket, and counted it carefully. Then he put his money back into his pocket, turned up the toys aisle, stopped at the baseballs, and pretended to consider several different toys.

He picked up one of the baseballs, squeezed it, tossed it about a foot in the air and caught it, and then leaned over the counter to pick up a sweatband. As he leaned over the counter, he slipped the ball through the unbuttoned spot in his shirt, rolled the fat on his stomach with his stomach muscles, and put the ball in the space between the two rolls of fat.

The movement was very nonchalant, taking less than a second. He had perfected the move with hundreds of other attempts. He didn't remember where he'd learned how to roll the fat on his stomach to hold things in the space. He'd known how to do it for years. Because he did not look fat, it was the perfect shoplifting technique.

After examining the sweatband, he slipped it back over the rod where it had been hanging and began walking toward the front of the store, stopping briefly at one point to examine model car kits. At the end of the aisle, he turned toward the checkout counter, and the rush started. He could feel it begin in his abdomen and then spread downward to his knees and upward to his chest. It was a warm, throbbing sensation like nothing else in the world.

The checkout girl did not notice. He seemed calm, almost indifferent. That was the point—balancing the inside turmoil against the casual outside.

He walked through the checkout counter, between the two checkout girls, and out the door. The rush was at its highest as he turned left on the sidewalk and started toward his bicycle, which was chained to the No Parking sign in front of the next store. He was about five yards from the bicycle when a hand from behind grabbed the center of his stomach.

He did not struggle or try to run because the grip belonged to someone a lot larger and stronger than he. The grip turned him around. He faced a slender man in a shirt and tie, wearing metal-rimmed glasses. The man said matter-of-factly, "Okay, son, let's go."

The man took the ball out of Ralph's shirt, grabbed him firmly by the back of his belt, and walked him back inside the store. They went across the front of the store past the two checkout girls, who had stopped talking and were watching intently. Then they went down the first aisle and through a door into the back of the store.

The back of the store was really a warehouse. Ralph had never been inside the back part of a discount store before, and he was surprised by its size and contents. It was almost as large and well stocked as the store itself. In one corner of the warehouse was a small office about 10 feet square. The man still held tightly to Ralph's belt and used it to guide Ralph into the office.

The office was neat, almost stark. It had a gray metal desk, a red desk chair, two orange plastic chairs, a black metal filing cabinet, and a gray metal bookcase. The man shut the door to the office, let go of Ralph's belt, and told him to sit down. Then the man sat down in the red chair behind the desk.

"What's your name, son?" he asked.

"Ralph Williams."

"Who's with you?"

"Nobody."

"Is that your bike by the No Parking sign?"

"Yes, sir."

"How many times have you done this before?"

Ralph's strategy came at once. The pause between the last question and the answer that followed was less than three seconds.

He couldn't say this was the first time. The man would never believe that. And he had to seem afraid—like a really good kid from a good family who'd stolen a few things for no good reason, but who was now learning his lesson.

Ralph tilted his head slightly, pretended to be thinking, and said, "Four."

"Where?"

"The first time was a pair of clip-on sunglasses from Revco. Then I got a baseball cap from Penny's and a watchband and a cigarette lighter from K-Mart."

The man got up from behind the desk, walked around in front of it, and sat on the desk. He looked down at Ralph.

"Son, did you read the sign on the front door?"

"No, sir."

"It says shoplifters will be prosecuted to the full extent of the law. I've got to call the police and have them come down here and arrest a boy. How old are you anyway?"

"Twelve."

"A twelve-year-old boy. And you're real good at this. If I hadn't actually seen you put that ball in your shirt, I'd never have caught you."

Ralph still had no idea how the man had seen him. He had looked the store over carefully three times and had never seen the man.

"Have you ever been arrested before?"

"No, sir."

"Do you think you should be arrested now?"

Ralph knew this was the crucial point. The man was about to decide whether he was a juvenile delinquent who belonged in jail or a basically good kid who needed a slap on the wrist. The rush returned stronger than it had ever been before.

"I don't know. I guess so. I did it," he said politely, apologetically.

"What's your father's name?"

"Ralph Williams, too. I'm a junior."

"If I call him, will he come get you?"

"He would, but he's not at home."

"Where is he?"

"He and Mother went to my uncle's. They won't be home until about four o'clock."

The man slid off the desk and began to walk around the office. He talked without looking at Ralph. "Son, when you steal things out of my store, you're stealing from me and my family. I've got to protect my family. I can't afford to have people like you stealing things. It's just like you took that ball from my little boy or a new dress from my wife.

"I don't have stealing in my store. Now, I don't want you to go to jail. But if you're going to steal, that's where you belong, and it's where you'll end up pretty soon. What

I'm going to do is this. I'm going to take your picture and get your name and address. Give me some sort of identification."

Ralph took out his wallet and gave the man his public library card, which had his picture, name, and address.

The man sat back down on the corner of the desk and looked earnestly at Ralph. "When your parents get home, have your dad call me. I'll decide what to do after I talk with him. If he doesn't call me by six o'clock, I'll call the police, give them your name and address and your picture. Do you understand?"

"Yes, sir. And thank you."

"My name's Dave Flynn. The store closes at six. If I haven't heard from your father by then, I'll call the police."

The man took a Polaroid camera from the desk drawer and took Ralph's picture. While the picture was developing, the man wrote his name and telephone number on a blank sales receipt and gave it to Ralph.

After the picture developed, the man told Ralph to get up. Then he took him by the belt again and walked him back down aisle one, in front of the checkout counters, and out the door.

On the sidewalk the man pulled up hard on Ralph's belt and looked down at him. "I don't ever want to see you in here again, understand?"

"Yes, sir," Ralph said as the rush came back but it was weaker this time than last.

"You had the money in your pocket to pay for the ball, didn't you?" the man asked as he turned loose of Ralph's belt.

"Yes, sir," Ralph replied with apparent shame on his face.

"Why steal it then?"

"I don't know," Ralph lied as he walked to his bike.

"Leave the bike there and give me the key. I'll give the bike to your father when he comes down here."

Ralph took the key from his pocket, handed it to the

man, and turned to walk home. He didn't look back to see if the man was still watching him. The rush was tremendous. The most powerful one he'd ever had.

It took about twenty minutes for Ralph to walk home. In his imagination, he began to play out the scene that would follow. There was no way to alter the facts. He'd have to tell his parents, and his father would have to go see the man at Dave's.

His only option was to play the same role with his parents he had played with the man. He was basically a good kid who had stolen a few things as kids sometimes do. He was sorry, and would not do it anymore.

When asked why he stole the ball, he would pretend to be as baffled as anyone else. It would be as if someone else had inhabited his skin briefly, someone who was now and forever expelled. He could not imagine why he would do this. And he was sorry.

The scene with his parents was worse than he had expected. His mother cried hysterically and talked with his father about him as if he were not there. She said again and again that they had tried to be good parents, to set a good example. She could not imagine how a child of theirs could be caught shoplifting like a common thief.

His father wore the long, somber face of suffering and betrayal. He said little and spent most of his time trying to calm Ralph's mother. He kept asking Ralph why he would steal something he had enough money to pay for. He said it didn't make any sense.

Ralph pretended to be as confused by the act as his father, but it took all of his self-control not to say the vulgar curse words that made up most of his interior dialogue. He just wanted to walk out of the house and never return. His contempt for his parents and his disgust at their behavior were almost more than he could manage. But, of course, there was nowhere to go.

His mother was standing at the picture window in the living room crying, and his father walked over to her and put his hand on her shoulder. She turned, and they embraced.

She sobbed and said, "Well, I'd always thought that there were three of us, but from now on I guess there'll just be two."

Although he found the scene revolting, almost nauseating, Ralph knew what was expected. He walked over to his embracing parents, began to cry, put his arms around both of them and said, "Don't count me out. I don't know why I did it, but I won't ever do anything like that again.

"I love you, and I'm sorry. I'll do whatever you want me to. Ground me for as long as you want to. Just please let me back in. I love you."

It worked, just as he knew it would. His mother turned and embraced him as his father reached out to pull him close. His father said that maybe the family had not been spending enough time together and that they would do better. His father promised to arrange at least two outings a week so that the three of them could share things and spend time together.

Ralph said he'd like that, and his heart sank. There was no rush at all now, just a flat sickening numbness as he thought about the coming months of happy family life.

Shoplifting was impossible now, and he had no idea what he could replace it with.

Jasper Neel now serves as Professor of English, Dean of the College, and Vice Provost at Southern Methodist University in Dallas. During his career, he has held appointments at Baylor University, Francis Marion University, New York University, and Vanderbilt University. In addition to writing short stories, he writes about literature and about the history of rhetoric.

BUSINESS

I remember the first time I ever seen a air conditioner. It was in the window of Taber Funeral Home, on the morning of August 2, 1952. That was the day my Momma died.

My brother Charley and me drove up to talk to Mr. Taber. It was a stinking hot morning. I stood in the little parlor in front of that air conditioner, feeling the cool air blowing on my face and arms and thinking what a wonderful thing it was and how I wished I hadn't had to come to Taber's to find it.

Then Mr. Taber come out from his office in the back, looking all grim and sorrowful. And Charley walked up to him, shook his hand real dignified and said, "Mr. Taber, I'm afraid I got some business for you. It's my Momma."

And him and Mr. Taber went in the office and I stayed out in the front room by that air conditioner, thinking about Momma, thinking wherever she was now, it was cooler than being in Lancaster County in August.

Momma died in the hospital in Camden that morning about 5:15. It was cancer. They said there wasn't nothing they could do. Daddy drove back to Kershaw from the hospital a little while later. He musta got pretty drunk somewhere along the way, cause when the shift changed down at the plant at eight, Daddy was across the street from the weave room, throwing rocks through the windows of the Nazareth Holiness Church, smashing them windows and cursing God and cursing Rev. Phillips and cursing everything that was holy, on account of Momma was dead and nobody did nothing to save her.

The shift change come to a complete stop, what with people pouring out of the mill. They stared at Daddy throwing rocks at the church and cursing the heavens, just stared like it was a three-car wreck. Then some of them cursed back at him and some of them laughed and Daddy turned and threw rocks at them. And then Butch Dunn come down the street in his big police cruiser with that siren blaring. And he jumped out and ordered Daddy to get in the back of the car and Daddy cursed him and threw a rock at him and Butch just whipped out his black jack and beat Daddy bloody right there on the street, right there in front of his neighbors and friends. And some of them was laughing and some of them was crying.

Uncle Calvin come over to the house a little later. He told me and Charley to go to Taber's. He'd go down to the jail and bail Daddy out.

I stood by the air conditioner for nearly a hour, til Charley come out of the office, his head down low. "C'mon, Bubba," was all he said, walking out the front door. The late morning sun made my eyes squint so tight I could hardly see. Charley got behind the wheel of the Studebaker and I climbed in the seat beside him. He raced the engine and peeled a tire on the pavement like he always done when he hit the highway. But he didn't grin. He didn't look over at me. He didn't say nothing. His eyes were red. He'd been crying and he didn't want me to see.

We drove back into town, past the mill, past our house. We didn't talk. Charley pulled in behind the Kershaw Feed & Farm Supply and stopped the car. "You wait here," he told me.

He walked up a ramp and into the big loading door. Then he disappeared in the shadows. He was gonna talk to his boss, Mr. Gillespie. And I figured, it being Friday, he was gonna pick up his check. Mr. Gillespie treated Charley pretty good. Charley said he wanted to learn the hardware and farm supply trade and Mr. Gillespie sorta took Charley under his wing. That was one of the things that Charley and Daddy fought about. Daddy said farming was drying up in Lancaster County; there wasn't no future in it. But folks would always need shirts and sheets. Daddy could get Charley a job down at the mill, get him a job fixing looms, where he could make a real living and support a family. And Charley would say something like; "I'd rather be a nigger and pick cotton than work in a mill with a bunch of lint heads like you." And that's when they would start to fight and Momma would come in screaming and pleading for them to stop and sometimes she would have to call Uncle Cal and sometimes Uncle Cal would have to call the police. Charley could always count on Momma when Daddy was beating on him and Momma could count on Charley when Daddy was beating on her. They always had each other.

Charley and Mr. Gillespie come walking out of the shadows, out the big loading door. Mr. Gillespie's arm was 'round Charley's shoulder. They walked down the ramp together real slow, Mr. Gillespie talking, Charley nodding his head. When they got to the ground, Charley turned and they shook hands. Then he got in the Studebaker. He didn't say a word. He just drove around the block to the bank, stopped and went in. When he come out five minutes later, he drove us down the street to Williams' Dry Cleaners. He went inside and come out with three white, starched cotton shirts on hangers. Then, he stripped off that T-shirt and put on one of them crisp, clean shirts. He swept his arm under the front seat and pulled out some maps, Daddy's Smith & Wesson revolver, a red-and-blue checked tie and a cartridge box. He wrapped the tie around his collar and knotted it straight. Then he pushed that other stuff back under the seat, got in the car and headed south, out of town.

"Ain't we going home, Charley?" I asked.

"Ain't nothing at home that cain't wait," he said softly. Then he looked at me for the first time. "Ain't really nothing at home now, Bubba. Nothing to go back to. Don't you know that?" I looked away and felt the hot air blast in my face from the open window.

Charley parked the Studebaker in front of the neat frame house on Clyburn Road. He went up to the small front porch and knocked. When the door opened, Verlie Mae Clyburn stood there in all her freckles and red hair. Charley spoke to her—I couldn't hear what he said—but Verlie Mae threw her arms around him and pulled him inside.

Charley and Verlie Mae had been courting since they was fifteen. Everybody knew they was going to get married some day, but nobody could quite figure out when. It was Verlie Mae that got Charley his job working for her uncle, Mr. Gillespie. And it was Verlie Mae that kept whispering around that her and Charley was gonna tie the knot soon.

The front door opened. Charley and Verlie Mae stepped out in each other's arms, with Verlie Mae's mother standing behind them. The two women was crying. Verlie Mae spied me sitting there in the Studebaker, and run to me, her red hair streaming like fire behind her. "Oh, Bubba, Bubba, Bubba…" She reached through the window and clutched my arm with both hands. "If there's anything we can do… *anything!*"

Friends and relatives started arriving at the house late that afternoon. Along our street there in the village, the word got out that Momma had passed and plates of fried chicken and bowls of green beans and potato salad was filling up the kitchen by three o'clock. It was a good thing, cause by nightfall we had Momma's kin from as far away as Pageland and Columbia coming by to pay their respects. Mr. Harris from the mill come in and talked to Daddy and told him to take a few days off. Rev. Phillips showed up a little later and he said a word or prayer over all of us and then he sorta took up a collection to help Daddy pay for them windows he broke out of the church. Someone brought a kerosene lantern and hung it in the oak tree by the corner of the porch and it lit up the whole yard. While folks was eating fried pork chops and chicken, Daddy's old hound, Sarge, hung around under the porch, waiting for somebody to throw him a bone.

In the house, it was hot as the hinges. Aunt Julie and Aunt Juanita was washing dishes and handling the food. Daddy was sitting in his chair by the radio. The left side of his face was all swole up and blue from when Butch Dunn chopped him with that blackjack. Daddy had been nipping at the vodka all day to kill the pain.

Charley and Verlie Mae was sitting on the sofa. Verlie Mae was wearing a starched, white blouse with a ruffly collar and her hair was all pinned up on the top of her head. I never seen her so quiet and stern looking. Momma's brother, Uncle Ed, was there, and his wife, Aunt Rita. Her hair was done up real nice and she wore earrings. Uncle Ed had him a new linen suit and a gold tiepin with the Chevrolet symbol on it. Uncle Ed run the Chevrolet place over in Pageland and he drove a new Chevy every year.

Daddy's brother Lester come in kinda late with a big mess of crappies he'd just caught. He dressed them out on the back stoop and fried them up on the 'lectric range. Then Uncle Calvin come by with several jars of moonshine whiskey from that still he claimed he didn't know nothing about. The men started passing around them jars of 'shine in the front room and on the porch, mixing it with Pepsi-Cola and whatever they could find to cut the taste. And I guess that's when the trouble started.

Daddy and Uncle Ed was talking about where Mamma ought to be buried and Daddy said she was gonna be laid in the cemetery behind the church. And Uncle Ed said he was taking her back to Pageland so she could rest in the family plot. He said she always wanted to move back to Pageland and, by God, she was gonna have her final rest there.

Uncle Ed was standing over Daddy, standing in the middle of the room, cause there wasn't no place to sit. And he started in, like I'd heard him do before, started talking about how Momma wanted to go back to Pageland, how he coulda got Daddy a job in his Chevrolet place, fixing cars. Talking about how he coulda got Momma a job in the cannery, putting up pickles and beans and she wouldn't of had to work in the mill no more.

"You don't have no respect, Ed," Daddy said. "You don't have no respect for what a man's gotta do to keep a family."

"You didn't show much respect your own self, Floyd," Uncle Ed said. "You didn't have to beat on my little sister like you done."

"What happened between me and Mamie was *our* business," Daddy slurred, coming out of his chair. "I loved her and she loved me and that's all you gotta know. If she wanted to go back to Pageland, she coulda packed her things and put them in that Studebaker and left any day she wanted. I told her so, but she didn't leave, 'cause this is her home and this is where she belongs. She had a husband and two boys here that loved her and we ain't gonna let you take her from us now."

"You beat on her, Floyd. Admit it . . ."

"This is my house—*my* house!" Daddy bellowed. "I'll run my house the way I see fit. Mamie understood that. Mamie understood what I sacrificed for her and them boys. I bought this house from the company. I bought that Studebaker out front. I bought her nice clothes and a Frigidaire and 'lectric range. I bought them things by working sixty hours a week in that goddamn mill, by taking every extra shift I could get."

Then Charley jumped up from the sofa and pushed up against Daddy and said, "Don't make excuses, old man. You beat on Momma and you beat on us and you're nothing but a goddamn little bully."

Daddy's face shot red with blood and he took a right hook and caught Charley square in the left eye. Charley fell out the front door, rolled across the porch and tumbled

down the front steps. Verlie Mae cried. Old Sarge barked
three times. But everybody else got as quiet as a movie
house.

Then Daddy stormed out on the porch. The screen door
slammed behind him and he stood there glaring down at
Charley, who was sitting in the dirt beside the Studebaker.

"Don't hit him again," I yelled, coming up behind
Daddy.

"You stay out this, you little pissant," he screamed at
me. "That boy—" he pointed at Charley down in the dirt
"—that boy thinks he's so damned smart, working downtown, working for Roddy Gillespie. Well, let me tell you
something. Roddy Gillespie ain't nothing but a fancy pants
crook who stole everything he's got. At least I worked for
what I own."

"Let me tell you something else," he said. "You don't
know what it's like to be a man and try to keep a home and
a family together, with everybody pulling it away from you,
trying to take everything you got in the world. You got to
fight for everything every day and just when you think you
got it secure, God hisself reaches down and takes your wife,
kills your wife in front of your eyes, wastes her away..."
Daddy was standing on the front porch screaming into the
night. You could hear him up and down the street.

"Don't kid yourself, old man," Charley said, standing
up and brushing hisself off. "Momma woulda left you
anyway. She was just waiting for the chance. She couldn't
stand it here no more, and neither can we. Bubba and me
is getting out of here. You hear me, Bubba?"

"I hear you, Charley."

"Verlie Mae!" he shouted into the house. Verlie Mae
appeared at the door. "C'mon, baby. We getting out of
this place right now." She ran down the steps to him and
he pushed her toward the Studebaker. "Get in!" he said.
"You get in too, Bubba."

I started to open the rear door, when Daddy hollered,
"Wait just a damn minute. You boys belong right here and

so does that car. You ain't going nowhere til I say so."

Daddy was coming down off the porch, unstrapping his belt. "Get in the car!" Charley shouted, opening his door. But Daddy was all over Charley, whaling on him with that belt. "You boys are my family. You're all I got left in this world. I cain't help what happed to your Momma, but I can sure as hell stop you."

Verlie Mae screamed. I jumped on Daddy's back and pulled him off Charley, but he turned and started whipping me. "Leave him alone!" Verlie Mae cried. "He's just a boy."

"You leave my boys alone, you no-good bitch," Daddy said, turning on her. "You stay away from my sons." He started towards Verlie Mae.

Right then I saw Charley reaching under the front seat of the Studebaker, reaching for something, reaching... "Oh, God, no!" I screamed at Charley. And then there was a shot...

I stood in front of that air conditioner the next morning, feeling the cool air blow against my face and arms, feeling the goose bumps rise. Mr. Taber come out of the back office. He walked up and put his arm over my shoulder.

"Good morning, Mr. Taber," I said. "I'm afraid I got some business for you."

William Moredock is a freelance writer living and working in Myrtle Beach.

David Tillinghast

THE SWIMMER

As soon as Harry Cooper sailed his boat within shouting distance, Mr. Pierce cut off the boathouse siren and strode onto the dock.

"There's no trouble, no storm warning," he called to Harry through a red megaphone. He set the megaphone beside his left leg on the dock and waited, hands on his hips, until Harry came closer.

In front of the boathouse, Harry brought his sailboat around in a tight circle, ducked the boom, and settled the boat against the fire hose nailed to the dock.

"I didn't hear what you wanted," Harry called.

Mr. Pierce held the boat against the dock with his foot on the gunwale. "I didn't want to scare you," he said, "but that was the only way to get your attention. I need to close up the boathouse, and you're the only one left on the lake."

Harry was not sure what—

"I know it's early," Mr. Pierce said, "but it's important. I'll need your help—if you want to go."

Harry looked up at the man standing on the dock. "It's one of those?" he asked. He stirred inside even as he spoke.

"You mentioned you wanted to help sometime. How about now?"

Harry glanced down at Mr. Pierce's foot on the

gunwale. Then he looked all the way across the lake. "I guess so," he said.

"Let's go then. Leave your boat here. It'll be secure," and he disappeared inside the boathouse. Mr. Pierce met him coming out. "Carry this to my car, and I'll meet you there pronto." He handed Harry a square five-gallon paint can with a garden hose wrapped around it and a tire pump. Harry put them in a box strapped to the top of the car. He had seen them there before.

Then he leaned on the fender of the finned old green Cadillac that everybody identified with Mr. Pierce and that always was parked on the grass at the strict edge of the lake beside the boathouse. Harry was not sure what he was getting into. He thought of Mr. Pierce in terms of the man he had been acquainted with for two years, a tall strong man seventy years old, a swimming instructor for forty years at the Orlando Club. He was recognized for his talent in teaching swimming, in particular teaching exceptionally young children to swim, two- and three-year-old children, and for his success at locating the bodies of retired people who had drowned themselves.

Harry felt the metal of the car hot against his skin. A swirling notion came to him that this was something he had to do, for no other reason than to do it.

Mr. Pierce came to the car wearing a brown bathing suit and carrying a wide leather belt with sawed-out chunks of lead tied to it. He laid the belt on the floorboard between his feet, and they drove along the side of the lake through the cypress trees. There was no road. He spoke to Harry as if speaking to himself. "We're looking for an old man, older than me, who lived in South Towers." He took a deep breath. "And I believe I know where he went in."

He drove through the trees dexterously. Harry did not answer him. The trees became thicker, the air moist and heavy, the ground spongy under the tires.

"The city's got the rescue truck coming out," Mr. Pierce

continued, "but I know we can find him before they get here." He still spoke without looking at Harry. "Besides, they don't know where to look." He shifted down a gear, coming to the end of the trees, and then there was a wooden pier Harry had never seen before. The Cadillac stopped itself in a rill of ruts at the foot of the pier. Mr. Pierce turned to Harry, not saying anything. Harry noticed for the first time his clear gray eyes. He imagined he could see all the way to the backs of the man's eyes.

"Let's go," Harry said, cutting the silence.

"All you've got to do is stay on the pier. Don't even have to get your feet wet."

"Let's go," Harry repeated, opening the door.

They got out of the car. Harry stared past the pier into the lake, where the water was smooth.

Mr. Pierce hauled the paint can and hose out of the box and threw the lead belt onto the planks, shaking the pier and making circles around the posts. He walked up and stood beside Harry, hands on hips. "Not like fishing, is it Harry? Sure don't have to worry about scaring them off." He knelt on the pier and screwed the end of the hose into a socket soldered into the side of the five-gallon paint can. He stuck the other end of the hose into a fitting on the tire pump. There was a piece of glass glued over an eye opening cut in the can, and he cleaned it with the heel of his hand.

"This is where they go in—right beside this pier," he said, his back to Harry. "They don't want any mistakes." He took a deep breath. "These old people know how to kill themselves the right way."

Mr. Pierce stood up, strapping the lead belt to his waist. "You know where you are, don't you?" He turned around remembering Harry. "Their condominium's right past those cypresses we drove through. You never think of it from this angle." He regarded Harry, who was still at the spot where he had gotten out of the car. "These people who kill themselves are old, or they wouldn't be in Florida in the first place. They want to make their suicides sure and simple, nothing fancy like gas hoses or hanging by ropes."

Mr. Pierce was standing very straight, shoulders back as he spoke, face to face with Harry. He had not changed position at all. "I can't figure how they know about this pier," he went on, "but I've recovered seven bodies from this exact spot. Only thing I figure is the bank slopes off gradually here, making it easy to walk out into the lake." He was looking past Harry. "Course they don't own boats or anything. But, why the hell would they choose this place? You think they tell each other about it before they kill themselves, and swear to secrecy?" He shook his head and frowned. "It's a mystery. Like elephants or something!"

Harry listened to the man as he stopped talking, regarding him inconspicuously. It seemed that he was thinking over what he'd said. He broke out of it and pointed beside the pier. "Look at that. See how that grass is pushed down. Just like the other ones." He stepped to the edge of the pier and pointed into the water. "They walk out in the lake beside this pier and let out their breath. Then they sit on the bottom and drown."

He turned back to Harry, rubbed his hands together, and picked up the paint can. "I'll go down and see what I can see." He pointed to the tire pump. "Just pump it easy; that'll give me plenty of air. Don't kink the hose."

He spit on the window in the paint can and polished the glass with his fingertips. With his other hand he threw several coils of hose into the lake in front of him. Then he sat on the edge of the pier, fitting the paint can over his head, and slid into the dark water.

A few bubbles floated up, and then the surface cleared off and was calm again. Harry began pumping, watching the hose dilate with the strokes. He thought of how he knew Mr. Pierce, as one who did not render a solid picture, a man who, though Harry was not certain, had few friends beyond family, who was of acquaintance only to most people, an individual who was probably on the edge of attaining that category of local curiosity, and unfortunately knew it.

He was not a dangerous man, but Harry could not be easy around him nor stay very long in his presence. He was somewhere in his life between several conditions, Harry expected, and guessed that when he discovered his transition's end, it could be tragic. He was the sort of person to have to do with circumspectly, a man assigned to instinct and reflex.

The water clouded, and Mr. Pierce surfaced. He removed the paint can from his head and set it upside down on the water. It floated beside him while he gripped the pier to rest.

"Can't find the old man," he said. "Some crap down there's got the water all dingy. Can't see much."

He rested on the pier, blowing a snort of water from his mouth and nose. It was a good time for Harry to say something. "Why don't you quit now and let the rescue squad find him?"

"I'll find him. Mark my word." He glanced at his white knuckles gripping the pier. "This one'll be in a sitting position, stiff as a board. Probably be all dressed up, too. I found one of them down near the hotel that had on a tuxedo, a white one." He grinned at Harry. "Would you believe that?"

Harry shook his head. "No sir! No sir!"

"I'll tell you another thing," Mr. Pierce went on, "to show you that old people are creatures of habit. You know how they all wear glasses, don't you?" He was talking with his hands. "You watch and see if this fellow's glasses aren't in his left breast pocket. The poor souls take them off just before walking into the lake. I don't see what they're saving them for." He blew out a breath of air. "Nobody wants to wear a dead man's glasses."

He looked over his shoulder across the lake. "Another

thing, you can tell what time of day he killed himself by his glasses." He pulled another coil of hose off the pier. "Whether they're sunglasses or regular ones."

Mr. Pierce twisted his body and sized up the spot he wanted to search next. "Give me some more length of hose. This fellow's probably farther out than I figured." He put on the can and slipped under the water into the lake.

As soon as the water smoothed, he resurfaced and said something inside the can Harry couldn't hear. Removing the can from his head, he gave Harry the victory sign and told him to get some rope from the car. He said he had found the body.

Harry came running back with a coil of rope.

"I'll swim down and tie the rope to him. When I jerk, start pulling."

Harry waited for the signal and began to pull, the body rising through the water sluggishly, ponderously, like the time he pulled a lawn chair from the deep end of a swimming pool, a similar resistance. Mr. Pierce swam beside it, and boosted it onto the pier.

Harry swallowed.

It laid on its side, in a stiff sitting posture, knees at right angles, arms bent with the hands close together, fingers hooked as if they'd been locked around the bent knees. The drowned man was in his seventies, short, thin, expensively dressed in a blue suit and vest.

"Well there we are, just like I told you," Mr. Pierce said. He removed a pair of tortoise shell sunglasses from the man's nose and slipped them into a suede case clipped to the coat pocket. "Skin cancer," he continued, "that's why he did it." With his fingertips he parted the hair on the man's head, revealing white splotches that ran down the left side of the neck. The left hand was the same way. There were flecks and red specks on the exposed body parts from fish bites.

The two men stood there, the body between them

locked on its side, listening to the water run out of the clothes and drip through the boards of the pier into the lake.

"That's right," Mr. Pierce said to Harry. He unbuckled his lead belt and placed it ceremoniously on the boards. "All we gotta do now is call the rescue boys to come and haul it off."

"Yessir," Harry said. He was looking across the lake at a boat going into a cove. "You think he did it because he knew he had cancer?"

"Why else?" He glanced up to see what Harry was looking at.

"I don't know," said Harry.

They watched the boat sail along the line of cypress trees. There was still hardly any wind on the lake.

Mr. Pierce turned back to Harry. "I've put you through a grisly mess," he said. "Listen, if we get anything out of this, I'll go fifty-fifty with you."

The boat across the lake went past the cypress trees into the cove.

Harry watched the boat.

The body lay on the pier. All the water had drained out of the clothes. The afternoon hung heavy and silent around them. Harry eyed the body. He tried not to. Something fell from the coat, a coin or button, and plunked into the water.

Harry jumped.

Mr. Pierce was studying the corpse. "Tell me, Harry, do people think I'm crazy?"

"They think you're a great swimming instructor. And sure, some people wonder why you pull these dead people out." Mr. Pierce picked up the lead belt and draped it over his shoulder like a bandolier. "I know it's odd," he said, "but I never thought of it that way. You know, Harry, you gotta have a reason for everything you do. You can't just do something because…"

"That's what we're talking about." Harry looked into

the man's gray eyes. "But why do you like to fish up these bodies?"

"Rescue," Mr. Pierce said. He backed up and took another angle on Harry. "Did it ever occur to you that I don't particularly *like* this job? But that maybe I can perform it more efficiently than anybody else? Somebody's got to keep this going."

"What about the firemen?"

"They're just kids. They don't know where to look."

"How many bodies have you found?"

"In all?"

Harry nodded.

"This makes thirteen."

Mr. Pierce bent over, beginning to lift the drowned man. "Help me with him. Let's get him right." He was trying to make the body sit up straight, but it kept falling onto its side.

"Take his arm, Harry. Let's get him sitting up."

Harry tiptoed up to the body and grasped the left wrist, and a section of yellow skin slid off into his hand. He jumped back, and the body slammed onto its side again.

"What are we doing?" Harry yelled. "Do you know what we're doing?"

Mr. Pierce stared at him. "You better sit down," he said calmly.

Harry looked at the man. "I think I better go. I better leave now."

Mr. Pierce kept staring at Harry, one hand on the dead man's shoulder.

Harry backed up the pier. "Listen, you're doing an awful thing! You better stop and think what you're doing."

He stepped off the pier and walked across the wet ground into the edge of the cypress swamp. He stood behind a tree and watched Mr. Pierce, stoop-shouldered, bent over the body working to balance it in a proper sitting position.

Harry turned, tripped on a cypress knee, caught himself, and waded through the tall weeds into the heart of the swamp until he found a path and followed it all the way to the boathouse. Beyond the boathouse he could see his sailboat, light, moving in the breeze that had just begun to rise.

Born and bred in Memphis, David Tillinghast grew up fishing the Mississippi River oxbow lakes and hunting the hardwood bottomlands of west Tennessee and northern Arkansas. He lives in South Carolina with his brother and cousin, where they operate a sorghum mill and a hunting plantation.

Thomas David Lisk

CUCUMBER RONDO

When Bob does me this way I want to put cucumbers on my eyes and lay down my head hurts so much. Sliced cucumbers not whole ones, one on each eye, one slice, cool and green. They're almost white. Real thin. I never worry about the seeds getting under my contact lens because they're stuck in the cucumbers by like a membrane, which sounds nasty but it's as clear as water and has about that much taste. I don't believe I've ever seen a *loose* cucumber seed unless it was from one of those bright-colored little envelopes you see at seed stores like Horse and Garden. Of course a packet of cucumber seeds isn't bright-colored, it's mostly green.

That watery green makes me think of the pond, where Bob is fishing right now, being the main reason why I have this headache. I forget where I first read about the cucumbers, but everybody tells me it's a well-known beauty secret. Which isn't a secret anymore. It may have been in *Parade* magazine in the *State* paper. Takes out the puffiness, but don't ask me how. Not that he cares. I could puff my eyes up like a frog. He's obviously still in love with her, the way you can be in love with somebody you don't have to live with, otherwise he wouldn't have been acting the way he did when I found that book of his right on the shelf.

I would get up and get it if I didn't have my feet up on

that camel saddle or whatever he brought in the marriage, got wood legs and a leather cushion. I'm looking at that painting *I* bought and he hates, two kids arm and arm looking at a big yellow sun.

He thought, I'm sure he did, that I'd never look at any book of his. I know he's smart, but he's not *that* smart. He probably can't believe I could read anything but those trashy books he gets for me at the check-out at Food Lion. No reason a twenty-eight-year-old woman should be dead, whether he likes it or not. Old for a baby but not old for some other ideas. He can be thankful I get it out of books and not from check-out bag boys like some people. When his own sister, I might as well say it, had her an affair with Joe Cautionberry, I heard his name a million times and I pictured this young stud, pardon me, like the bare-chested roofers with nice big shoulders that were working on the Freeman's house, but I was surprised when Bob introduced him to me at the Rotary Ann dinner and I said to myself this must be his father. But no, he was the one and Bob didn't know anything. It was Joe Junior I saw at the Food Lion. Not one word about it came out of my lips even if he thinks I can't keep a secret to save my life. It wasn't my life he was worried about. Joe Senior had a wave of gray hair that flowed into his bald spot and had his pants under his belly and kept looking like wanted to wink at me and show me the wrinkles around his eye. Both eyes actually. Which he never put a single cucumber or any other vegetables on I can about guarantee. Typical, he gives other people headaches and never has one of his own.

Bob's getting a little that way himself. I mean he still wears 36 waist on his pants but his belt travels a little south of his middle, which is because I feed him too good his mother says. I don't know what stories he's telling her because I hardly feed him at all since I've been working. Maybe he wants her to think I'm a better wife than I am, and if that doesn't hurt my feelings I don't need cucumbers.

And if I'm getting big it's not because I eat too much, and she knows that. It breaks my heart to come home and find the wrappers of a mushroom swiss from Hardee's. But he's the one that says we need the money.

He's standing out there right now with his line in the water and no more hope of catching anything than a cow has of inventing algebra. He gets out there sniffing the breeze and not saying anything and either it's still water runs deep or shallow water gets muddy because it doesn't run at all. There's some cuter way of saying that but I can't remember it exactly. Anyway half the time I don't know what he's thinking.

"Bob, what's on your mind?"

"Nothing."

"Bob, what do you want to do?"

"I'd just as soon sit here and enjoy myself."

But half the time he won't even say that, so how am I supposed to know? It's not that I don't love him. Who buys him his 36 by 32 pants, even if I have to stop on my way home from work when I'm dead dog tired and find those khaki pants with bird heads on their backsides? He's out there wagging that pole over the water with the butt up against his belly and giving me no thought in the world.

"Don't get yourself so worked up," says, which is about the most he does say. "I swear you were vaccinated with a Victor-ola needle," he'd say, because he thinks I can't tell a story short and to the point. He had to explain it to me. How was I supposed to know it was an old fashion stereo? One day I was telling him about how Debbie Iris Louvin had a sonogram of the baby right in her, in her womb. You could see the little arm in one picture and the head in another—look like a white blur shaped like a butterfly. They were all black and white. Gray really. Says, "That story's so long, I don't know how you can remember it."

"I'm not a detail person," says, "I'm a big idea man." But he'll fuss over that tin box of wiggly worms and chrome plated doomaflodgies he tries to trick the poor fish with, and if that isn't detail...And of course when I met him I had no idea he would be the way he can be sometimes. I thought he had the prettiest green eyes and that voice that reminded me of the one in the old Walt Disney movies about wild animals. It was low and it was southern, but sounded like he was from maybe Arkansas, Rex something was his name. Bob told me. He would know that. He sounded real intelligent, not like some of the rednecks I was used to. I should have known when I met him in the library where I was taking back a stack of *Glamours* I had checked out and he was standing there looking serious at one of those crackly covered new books, I should have noticed what he was reading. I should have known he thought he was deep. I was the one that went up to him because I remembered him from the Lowery family reunion.

Now he says, "You're an extrovert," which means I like talking to people, says, "And I'm an introvert," which means he likes fishing. It's not like I never went to college and don't know every bit as much as he does, or I'm not as smart. Some women will love anything, I swear. That's why men are so lucky. We love them even when they get too fat or too skinny. It's a rare one that's just right. But it's like Debbie Iris says whenever she has a piece of pie, "I don't know whether to eat this or slap it right on my thighs." When that happens it's all the men do is dream about their past loves. And that's another thing, all this worrying gives me a appetite and I have to sit here and will myself not to get up and make a batch of cookies which he won't eat but one or two of. Cucumbers don't have calorie one but I can't eat them, and I have *never* had a pica for pickles.

If I like to have cucumbers around so I can take two slices now and then, that leaves a good bit of the cucumber, and the end shrivels up and he won't eat it or even cut off the end and eat the rest. But he'll fish those big old dill pickles out of the jar and chomp down two at a sitting as if vinegar was no more than water to him.

"I'm a good provider, right?" says. "Let me just ask you that."

"What am I doing?" I said. "I'm not sitting here like a bump on a pickle."

He did buy us this acre and a half just before we got married. With a pond right on it, which I thought was beautiful, but then I wasn't thinking about fish. I guess I thought he'd smoke a pipe and read or something. And I was used to living in town. "We're not but four miles from the mall," says, but at first I felt like we were on the moon and I was just scared he'd decide to leave me. Then I remembered I had the Datsun that I brought into the marriage and I felt a little better. I knew if I ever did get pregnant I didn't want to be a hundred miles from Leahy Clemens Hospital.

Even with his college degree he's still on the road a right good bit for the power company, which has been his boss since before started college at the age of twenty-three. Of course, now he's a manager and bosses other people and joined the Rotary. And I don't know if he likes the fact I'm working more than he dislikes where I'm working. Which is at the party shop, or red dot store as he calls it, and I think a red dot means nothing much. But I'll tell you that store is anything but a party. Whew. For all I know Joe Cautionberry had been coming in there all the time and buying him a half pint on Friday night, but I wouldn't have recognized him because I had no idea who he was. Joe Senior, I mean. Betty's friend. Bob's sister Betty that I was mentioning while ago. If he knows I'm there now I wouldn't be a bit surprised if he just purposely stayed away.

So when I come home from four hours in that cigarette-smelly place toting a bag of his pants and he's not home, not *there*, I get lonesome for him and if I don't feel like watching TV what would I do but go to the bookshelves to improve myself and maybe find out a little about this man

I'm married to at the same time. Why I pulled out that particular book I'll never know, but it was fate. It was a thin one I thought I could read maybe, starting slow, and I peeled back the cover. It was a hardcover book with a paper cover over the cloth over the cardboard. The shiny cover, which was a pretty shade of pale green that a woman *would* like, with twiney vines around the edges, made think of how even if a slice of cucumber or a whole cucumber dries up and gets dead the way they do you can stiffen it if you put it in ice cold water (not hot! I put a cucumber in hot water one time and it went limp as a fish) for an hour or more, and then when you slice it it's nice and crisp and fresh, unless it was already sliced. It's too cold to put on your eyes, though. I once put two of those icy slices on my face and they set my sinuses to throbbing so I had a worse headache than I did when I laid down. I always wrap them in a washrag for a minute or two to warm them up before I put them on my eyes.

Water will do wonders. I had that little dogwood out in the yard that I planted two falls ago, and you couldn't tell if it was dead or alive until Bob took out his pin knife and scraped the bark, says, "It's still green in there. Maybe you ought to water it once while." I call it a pin knife but it's a big old thing and that's probably what keeps his pants hung low, the weight of that old knife that his daddy gave him. I ran the hose out there (the green one, not the black one he keeps in his garden that I mistook for a snake that time) and put it just dripping a little bit for all day. He ragged me but good for letting that water run, and I said, "You got a whole pond full," and anyway it didn't take more than a quart dripping that little bit all day.

"We'll see when the water bill comes," says, but when the bill came he conveniently forgot. When I brought it up he changed the subject to how I take so many baths and use all that water so he can't tell how much is trickling out the hose. If I didn't have that cigarette smoke around me all day I wouldn't want to wash it out of my hair and put my clothes in the hamper first thing when I get home. Which I do for him so I'll smell halfway pleasant when he comes in, even if all he does is run outside if it's still light to check how his cucumbers are doing.

So this night I'm talking about I came home and cleaned myself up. Took a nice long bath and enjoyed it. He wasn't there to tell me different. Then went looking for something to read. And just by chance I got my hands on this book which was called *Rubiyat*, which I had enough high school French to know is not French. Inside was in English. Poetry. I couldn't make much sense of it, but I wouldn't mind if he gave me something like that to show how much he loves me. It's still right there on the shelf. I don't have to look at it because I memorized right what it said. Not the whole book, just the writing inside the cover. "I bought this because Mary said it reminded her of me." I could hear him pause before he wrote the rest. "I didn't like it." It was in his handwriting. In pencil. No date. "Who's Mary?" I wanted to know. He knows perfectly well I never gave him any book. I don't know if he and I have ever even *read* the same book unless it was the Bible, and I'm not sure about him.

"I bought it," says. "She didn't give it to me."

"That's worse," in my opinion. "It means you cared enough about her *to* buy it."

"I said right there, I didn't like it." He was pointing at the book after he gave up trying to get it away from me. That's about the most romantic idea the man ever had. I could tell just from the way he said that how much he cared about her. He wouldn't have bought the book and read all the way through it if he didn't care about her, would he? It's obvious to me he'd already lost her or he wouldn't have had to buy the book. But that's the worst way—to love someone who doesn't love you. Otherwise he wouldn't have kept the book. And in our marriage. Even if his sister did get divorced before she went on with Joe, that's no reason I should sit still for him. What would possess a man to write something like that? He may be deep, but he lacks common sense. One time he tried to explain music to me and got into this business about A's and B's and said it was like if Lee Greenwood changed the chorus of one of his songs a little bit with each verse. Called it a rondo, I think. He played the trombone in high school and took music appreciation when he majored in general studies at Carolina. He knows I think Lee Greenwood is good-looking, but I don't care that much about music. If it was in pencil he could have erased it. He must have wanted me to find it and feel sorry for him. Which I refused to do. I did find the book, but here I am trying to keep the skin around my eyes smooth and not wrinkly, and who does he think I'm doing that for?

I could have erased it myself, but I'm not that ugly. If a thirty-two-year-old man wants to be in love with some girl he thinks is nineteen but is as old as he is whether he likes it or not, that's his business. But I don't have to like it. He's from here, same as I am, so I don't know where he gets his ideas. One time I said to him, "What you think about when you're out there at the pond?" expecting him to say "nothing." But says, "I'm just trying to imagine what goes on in your head. I can't tell from what comes out your mouth." And I said, "What on earth?" and he laughed and said, "You knew I was cuckoo when you married me," and I laughed too and we kissed, and that may have been the beginning of where I am now.

Maybe if I could lay down for a few minutes I'd feel better, even if we don't have a cucumber in the house. I could at least take out my contacts. And another thing is I don't know what that smoke does to a baby. He's out there and I'm in here and he's going to come in here and want his supper and it won't be fish or cucumbers, because he'll look at me in that certain way because he doesn't want to fight, he just wants to be a big heavy thing in front of me I can't look around. And when he droops his head a little the way he does I know I'll tear into him because all I want to do is hug him and say, "Bob, Bob," and talk about the baby and let him listen to my stomach, which doesn't come from cucumbers.

After living for fifteen years in South Carolina, Thomas David Lisk moved to North Carolina, where he is a Professor of English at North Carolina State University. His poetry, fiction, and essays have appeared in many newspapers and literary magazines.

Deno Trakas

THE CENTER OF THE UNIVERSE

The center of the universe barges into the guest bedroom, my office, and says "Dad," even though the door
is mostly closed, even though she can see I'm trying to
grade papers.

I answer without looking up. "What?"

"You said you'd help me with a story for extra credit,
remember?" When I don't answer immediately, she adds,
"To pull up my grade."

"Can it wait?"

"I've kinda got other plans later."

"Okay, just a minute." She surveys her freckles in the
mirror over the dresser while I write a comment on the
paper in front of me. When I finish and turn to face her,
she looks fuzzy, so I take off my glasses and hold them out
to see if they're dirty or if my sight is getting even worse.
Now she looks fuzzy and far away. "Okay, what do you want
to write about?" I put on my glasses and pull a legal pad
out of my briefcase on the floor beside me.

"I don't know. You're the writer." She sits on the corner
of the bed and begins to fidget, rocking, keeping time with
the fast music under her teenage skin.

"I won't do this by myself, Ruthie."

"Okay, Okay, but I don't know how to start."

"You need a character and a problem. What's your

character's name?"

"Andrea."

"Let's not write about your best friend."

"Okay, Simone."

"Simone what?"

"Jenkins."

"Sounds like a French redneck. How about DesChamps?"

"I can't even spell DesChamps."

"I can." I write it down. "What's her problem?"

"She doesn't know how to spell her name." Leaning back on her elbows, she gives me her look, a tease, a slight squeeze of the eyes, mostly her left eye because her right is hidden behind a wave of red hair. She gives the look without grinning, and it always defeats me.

I sigh. "What else?"

"I don't know."

"Boys?"

"That's so boring."

"Boys are boring?" I'm about to ask why she spends every waking minute of the day talking to them on the phone if they're boring, but she says, "Boys aren't boring. Boy problems are boring."

"Oh. What then?"

She sits up again, tugs at the cuffs of her sweatshirt and presses them to the bed with her arms stiff, as if she's bracing for takeoff. "Maybe the girl could get kidnapped at the mall."

"Who would want her?"

"Daaad."

"Okay, who would kidnap her and why?"

"She's rich and these guys want her money."

"Oh, I didn't know that." I jot it down.

"She's like the daughter of the guy who owns Wal-Mart, and these guys, one of them's the janitor at her school, it's a private school."

"Sam Walton died."

"Jeez. He's like Sam Walton. He owns Richland Mall, Okay?"

"Okay. But why can't we write about a normal girl with a normal problem?"

"Yeah, right. Poor Susie doesn't have a date for Homecoming. Wow. Thrills a minute."

I sit back and imagine. "Maybe Poor Susie has a younger sister she doesn't get along with, and because they live in a tiny house, she has to share a room with her, and she can't stand it so she runs away to live with her best friend."

She rolls her eyes and says, "Bor-ing. What's wrong with a kidnapping?"

I write KIDNAPPED! across my pad. "It's too sensational. And you don't know anything about it. How many kids do you know who've been kidnapped?"

"The same number that've run away from their little sister."

I sigh again. This time she is grinning, or smirking, it's hard to tell. "Okay, it's your story, it's your grade."

"Maybe this isn't such a good idea." She slouches and pulls a strand of hair in front of her left eye to check for split ends.

"Don't give up already, Ruth."

"I didn't know it was going to be this hard. I mean, we haven't gotten anywhere. How long does it take you to write a story?"

"Sometimes days, sometimes months." I look at my watch. "I don't think I've ever done one in twelve minutes."

"Yeah, but yours are, you know, serious."

Yeah, serious. Literary. Bought for two figures, published in journals with circulation in three figures. But Ruth knows and cares nothing about that, so I just say, "We have to be serious about this one too or it won't be good."

"But I told Andrea I'd go with her to the soccer match."

I slap the pencil down, give her my look, the parental disapproval look, "Go then. Forget the whole thing."

She hesitates, studying her hands as her red fingernails drum her kneecaps. I want her to say, You're right, Dad, let's get back to work. Instead, she rises without saying a word and leaves.

The story was Ruth's teacher's idea, but it was my idea for us to do it together. It's not a bad idea, really. In the first place, Ruth needs to bring up her grade. You can't imagine how embarrassing it is for me, a college English teacher and so-called writer, to have a D-in-English daughter. But the more important reason is that I crave to understand the teenage stranger who lives in my house. I know: My friends who have teenagers assure me it's normal—there's no more reason for me to understand Ruth than for me to understand a Mid-East terrorist. But I can't accept that, and I hoped this project would bring us closer. Writing is, after all, the most personal thing I do, except for occasional repartee with my wife.

My wife. We have our habits of peace, and she has a separate peace with Ruth. She expects Ruth to be moody, rude, egotistical, and worse during adolescence. It's a phase, she says. I went through it, too, she says. Chill out, she says. My wife can even talk like our daughter.

I'm chilling out here at my desk, which I refinished with Ruthie's help, when she was five and into helping. Back then it was me, not her, who thought she was the center of the universe. Staring at the wavy grain in the maple wood, I think of Ruthie and turn her into Poor Susie. Poor Susie lives in a trailer with her mom and sister June near Fort Jackson, near enough so that they hear artillery practice almost every day. Boom. It drives Susie crazy. Boom. It shakes the Revlon bottles on her dresser. Boom. That and her mother's nagging and her sister's pestering drive her crazy. Drive. If she could drive, she'd take the car tonight, after her mother falls asleep, and she'd disappear. Maybe she'd go look for her daddy in North Carolina. Daddy. Four years ago he was transferred to Ft. Bragg and simply refused to take them along. She doesn't know if she loves him or hates him. Maybe she'd go to Atlanta, lie about her age, get a job.

I'm in Poor Susie's head, picking up her thoughts, examining them, putting them back, when my wife comes home from work, still wearing her white lab coat. "Hey," she says as she passes my door on the way to our bedroom to change. "Where's Ruthie? I thought y'all were going to work on a story."

"She and Andrea had a prior engagement to ogle the boys at the soccer match."

"Hmmm," is my wife's response, as if Ruth probably made the right choice.

Maybe her mother spoke to her, or maybe she is more embarrassed by her grade than I think, but the next night Ruth returns. She doesn't apologize or grovel. She just nudges the door and appears, one shoulder leaning against the doorjamb. "Dad, will you help me with the story some more?"

I put down my copy of Julius Caesar and think about giving in. "I guess I can spare another twelve minutes," I say to let her know that if she expects my help, I expect her commitment. She plops down and leans against the headboard of the bed, arms folded over the flat chest that is one of her constant preoccupations, along with her thin lips, ski-jump nose, Biblical name, and so much more. Today she has crimped a two-inch star into her wave of hair, and I remember hearing her mention the instrument of such desecration to her mother, but I don't remember hearing them say they might actually buy it. I push away my book and pull out the legal pad on which I jotted our notes. "Okay. I thought up some ideas for Poor Susie—do you want to hear them, or do you want to stick with Simone The Kidnapee?"

"Simone."

I'm disappointed, but it's her story. "Okay. You said her dad owns Richland Mall. What does her mother do?"

"Nothing. They're rich."

"What about in her free time—does she play tennis at the country club or volunteer for Meals on Wheels?"

"She plays tennis."

"Mall-magnate Dad, is he ever home, and what's his relationship with his daughter?"

"I don't know. How am I supposed to know all this stuff? What does it matter, anyway?"

"This stuff is the background that will make your character believable. But we can get right to her if you think parents aren't important." Pause to let that sink in. "Okay, what does Simone want?"

Ruth gives her look and says, "She wants to get away from the kidnappers."

"I mean besides that, before she gets kidnapped."

"She wants to have fun."

"What does she think is fun?"

"Going to the mall with her friends."

"That's her goal in life, to go to the mall with her friends?"

"Daaad."

"That's what you said."

She sulks or thinks. Then, without looking up she says, "She wants to be happy."

The way she says it, simply and sincerely, without the usual sneer, trips my heart. She wants to be happy. I see Simone hiding behind a wave of red hair. "But why, honey?" The term slips out of the past—I used to call her honey all the time but don't anymore. "Why is Simone unhappy?" I try to catch her gaze, but she keeps her head down as she tugs at a rhinestone on her T-shirt.

"She doesn't know."

"Is she ugly?" I ask.

"No."

"Unpopular?"

"No."

"Do you know why she's unhappy?"

"How should I know when she doesn't know?"

"Exactly," I say. Ruth doesn't hear or else ignores me. I press on. "Does she have a boyfriend?"

"What about the kidnapping, Dad?"

"Okay, do the kidnappers have boyfriends?"

"Dad, you're such a dork."

"Is that good or bad?"

"I can't handle this, Dad." She gets up and walks to the door. "I've got to study math."

"Stay, Ruthie. I won't joke around anymore."

"I've got a test tomorrow, or do you want me to make a D in that, too?" She knows I'll have no smart answer to this.

"Go then," I say, and she does.

I follow Ruthie to the mall on Friday night because I want to see what happiness she thinks she finds there.

She and her friends spend most of their time in Flickers, the arcade. I can't go in because they'd see me, but I assume, I hope, they're playing video games. Finally, as I watch, fifty yards away, from a bench partially hidden behind a planter of scheffelera, they emerge, one girl and boy holding hands, another boy chasing and tagging Ruthie. She seems to be complaining, but playfully, and when he isn't expecting it, she tags him back hard on the shoulder.

Ruthie's boy takes a pack of cigarettes out of his shirt pocket and offers them around—the other guy and girl accept, but Ruthie, I'm relieved, does not. The other couple drifts to the benches in the center of the aisle, as if smoking is hard work and they need a rest. Ruthie and the boy she tagged hover near the entrance to the arcade. She leans back against the wall—she's taller than him but leaning back brings her down a few inches. As he moves in close to her, her arms encircle his waist. They kiss, seriously if clumsily, mashing their bodies, oblivious to the turning heads of shoppers.

I get up and take a step toward them so I can kill the boy.

But I stop, knowing that to break them up, even to show myself, would be disastrous for my relationship with my daughter. I sit back down. We can both live with her thinking I'm a dork—I probably am one—but she'd never forgive my being a spy or policeman. Policeman. That's how I feel, here to make sure there's no trouble. Trouble. This scene looks like trouble, feels like trouble, but why?— because she's too young—is fourteen too young to kiss?— no, but it will lead to sex—am I sure?—yes, no, not sure but worried. Worried. She's my little girl and if that boy… I watch his hands, one of which is down at his side, holding his cigarette—thank God he smokes—but the other is on the side I can't see. Paralyzed, I watch.

Although I lose all sense of time, I'm pretty sure the kiss does not last long before Ruthie pushes the boy away. Silently I cheer her on to kick him and gouge his eyes out, but she merely catches his jacket sleeve and drags him across the aisle to the music store.

I breathe again and wipe my foggy glasses. I feel tired as if I've been chasing someone for miles. Thrills a minute. Happiness. Is this what she wants: clumsy kisses from a short boy with cigarette breath?

Go then, I say to her in my head, You can handle this trouble, and you'll outgrow it soon enough.

Feeling useless, I turn to leave. As I glance back one last time to check on my daughter and her boyfriend's hands, I see a door to a storage room and think, that's where it would happen, that's where Simone would be kidnapped. On the way home, I plot the story of how Simone's father arranges a kidnapping to shock his daughter into loving her life again. I wonder if Ruthie will be happy with it.

Deno Trakas is Professor of English and Director of the Writing Center at Wofford College. He has published fiction and poetry in magazines such as The Denver Quarterly *and* Oxford American. *He is one of four writers featured in* New Southern Harmonies, *named Best Book of Short Fiction by* Independent Publisher *magazine in 1999.*

Acknowledgements

The South Carolina Arts Commission is grateful for the invaluable assistance from Betsy Teter, Angela Kelly, John Lane, Mark Olencki, and Lisa Isenhower of the Hub City Writers Project, who made this anthology possible; Jim Johnson and Edna Horning of the South Carolina State Library; and Gwen Boykin of the Arts Commission. Special thanks to Bruce Lane of the South Carolina Literary Arts Partnership.

The Arts Commission would like to acknowledge its former Literary Arts Director, Steven Lewis, who initiated the South Carolina Fiction Project in 1984; the National Endowment for the Arts, whose support helped launch and develop the program during the early years; Christine Randall and *The Post and Courier*, which has co-sponsored the Fiction Project since 1993; and Claudia Smith-Brinson and *The State* newspaper, which co-sponsored the Fiction Project prior to that time.

SOUTH CAROLINA
FICTION PROJECT WINNERS
(1984-2000)

1984
Starkey Flythe, *North Augusta*
Douglas Freeland, *Newberry*
Jeffrey Helterman, *Columbia*
Doc Johnson, *Pomaria*
Thomas Johnson, *Pomaria*
John Lane, *Spartanburg*
Thomas David Lisk, *Sumter*
Jasper Neel, *Florence*
Susu Porter, *Columbia*
Jay Reeves, *Charleston*
Lee Robinson, *Charleston*
Michael Taylor, *West Columbia*

1985
Roberta Beck Connolly, *Columbia*
Scott Gould, *Greenville*
Vera Kistler, *Darlington*
Wayne Kyzer, *West Columbia*
Elizabeth Langland, *Spartanburg*
Thomas Lisk, *Sumter*
Wesley Moore, *Isle of Palms*
Kent Nelson, *Sullivan's Island*
Lee Robinson, *Charleston*
JoAnne Simson, *Charleston*
Faye Smith, *Irmo*
Deno Trakas, *Spartanburg*

1986
Johnny Beavers, *Kingstree*
Mary Cartledge-Hayes, *Spartanburg*
Mary Dana, *Prosperity*
Marion Doren, *Mt. Pleasant*
Virginia Dumont, *Greenwood*

1986 (continued)
Melanie Gause Harris, *Summerville*
M. Elizabeth Littlejohn, *Columbia*
Jonathan Lowe, *Greenville*
Jan Millsapps, *Columbia*
Andrew Nolan Poliakoff, *Spartanburg*
Sue Summer, *Newberry*
Greg Williams, *Charleston*

1987
Gilbert Allen, *Traveler's Rest*
Alice Cabaniss, *Columbia*
Ruth Butler, *Columbia*
Bret Lott, *Mt. Pleasant*
Liz Newall, *Anderson*
Robert Poole, *Columbia*
Lee Robinson, *Charleston*
Elizabeth Wakefield, *Anderson*
Wayne Wall, *West Columbia*

1988
Neuman Connor, *Columbia*
Jean Cooper, *Columbia*
Dianne Threatt Evans, *Lancaster*
Laura Floyd, *Lake City*
Keller Cushing Freeman, *Greenville*
Sarah Gilbert, *Columbia*
Rebecca Godwin, *Pawley's Island*
Sharyn Layson, *Leesville*
Liz Newall, *Anderson*
Ron Rash, *Pendleton*
Jay Reeves, *Mt. Pleasant*
Lynn Jordan Stidom, *West Columbia*

1989

Gilbert Allen, *Traveler's Rest*
Martha Alston, *Rembert*
Nicholas Boke, *Columbia*
Starkey Flythe, *North Augusta*
Jeffrey Helterman, *Columbia*
Sharyn Layson, *Leesville*
Thomas Lisk, *Sumter*
Wesley Moore, *Isle of Palms*
Liz Newall, *Anderson*
Rebecca Parke, *Walhalla*
Jack Turner, *West Columbia*
Kathleen Vereen, *Charleston*

1990

David Burt, *Florence*
Jeff Chasteen, *Columbia*
Wayne Addison Clark, *Rock Hill*
Andrew Geyer, *Columbia*
Cecile Hanna Goding, *Florence*
Scott Gould, *Greenville*
Thomas Johnson, *Columbia*
Sharyn Layson, *Leesville*
Thomas David Lisk, *Sumter*
Tish Lynn, *Charleston*
Aileen McGinty, *Hilton Head*
Harriett Richie, *Anderson*

1991

Peg Alford, *Columbia*
Elise Freeman, *Lugoff*
Phillip Gardner, *Florence*
Deborah Clawson Johnson, *Hopkins*
Thomas David Lisk, *Sumter*
Tish Lynn, *Charleston*
Liz Newall, *Anderson*
Anthony Owens, *Coward*
Rebecca Parke, *Walhalla*
Rosa Shand, *Spartanburg*
Debra Mihalic Staples, *McBee*
Sue Summer, *Newberry*

1992

Gilbert Allen, *Traveler's Rest*
William Baldwin, *McClellanville*
Cathy Smith Bowers, *Rock Hill*
Deborah Reid Cooke, *Liberty*
Debra Daniel, *Blythewood*
Andrew Geyer, *Columbia*
Mary Hills, *Greenwood*
Leslie Rankin Ragsdale, *Easley*
Rosa Shand, *Spartanburg*
George Singleton, *Greenwood*
Merry Speece, *Columbia*
Mary Ann Thomas, *Fort Mill*

1993

Cynthia Boiter, *Chapin*
Curtis Derrick, *Columbia*
Jeffrey Helterman, *Columbia*
Deborah Clawson Johnson, *Hopkins*
Sue Monk Kidd, *Anderson*
John Lane, *Spartanburg*
Rebecca Parke, *Lancaster*
Mark Reeves, *Charleston*
Rosa Shand, *Spartanburg*
Rush Smith, *Columbia*
Lynn Jordan Stidom, *West Columbia*
Deno Trakas, *Spartanburg*

1994

Cynthia Boiter, *Chapin*
Debra Daniel, *Blythewood*
Cecile Hanna Goding, *Florence*
Jeffrey Helterman, *Columbia*
William Moredock, *Columbia*
Barbara Pinkerton, *Fripp Island*
Sandy Quick, *Mt. Pleasant*
Leslie R. Ragsdale, *Easley*
Ron Rash, *Pendleton*
Melodie Starkey, *Florence*
Deno Trakas, *Spartanburg*

1995

Anne Creed, *Hopkins*
Debra Daniel, *Blythewood*
Laura Floyd, *Lake City*
Beth Harrison, *Charleston*
Dan Huntley, *York*
Lori Wyndham Jolly, *Moncks Corner*
Sue Monk Kidd, *Anderson*
Lucy Nolan, *Columbia*
Harriett Richie, *Anderson*
Rosa Shand, *Spartanburg*
Lynn Jordan Stidom, *West Columbia*
David Tillinghast, *Clemson*

1996

Martha Oliver Alston, *Rembert*
Lucy Marie Arnold, *Darlington*
Mignon F. Ballard, *Fort Mill*
Cynthia Boiter, *Chapin*
Cynthia Carver-Futch, *Georgetown*
Debra Daniel, *Blythewood*
Mildred Barger Herschler, *Landrum*
Laura Dieter McGregor, *Mt. Pleasant*
Diane Moore, *Charleston*
Sandy Lang Quick, *Sullivan's Island*
Fred Thompson III, *Sullivan's Island*
Collin Tobin, *Greenwood*

1997

Patricia Ann Benton, *Hilton Head Island*
Anne Creed, *Hopkins*
Sue Monk Kidd, *Anderson*
Laura Lance, *Aiken*
Lori Lewis, *Murrell's Inlet*
Margaret McGinty, *Pickens*
Lucy Nolan, *Columbia*
Nichole Potts, *Fort Mill*
Ron Rash, *Pendleton*
S. Paul Rice, *Conway*
Shannon Richards, *Charleston*
Fred Thompson III, *Sullivan's Island*

1998

Gilbert Allen, *Traveler's Rest*
Cynthia Boiter, *Chapin*
Charlie Geer, *McClellanville*
Timothy K. Hicks, *Rock Hill*
Mike Johnson, *Beaufort*
Janna McMahan, *Columbia*
George L. Mina, *Orangeburg*
Kate Salley Palmer, *Clemson*
Rosa Shand, *Spartanburg*
George Singleton, *Dacusville*
Mary Ann Ruhl Thomas, *Tega Cay*
David Tillinghast, *Clemson*

1999

Peg Alford, *Columbia*
Peter Fennell, *Mt. Pleasant*
Starkey Flythe, *North Augusta*
Virginia Tormey Friedman, *Charleston*
Robert W. Heaton, *Anderson*
Susan Beckham Jackson, *Spartanburg*
Harriet McBryde Johnson, *Charleston*
Kelly Love Johnson, *Charleston*
John Lane, *Spartanburg*
Ron Rash, *Pendleton*
Cameron Sperry, *Charleston*
Robert Stribley, *Greenville*

2000

David Burt, *Florence*
Debra Daniel, *Blythewood*
Jonathan Fenske, *Anderson*
Mindy Friddle, *Greenville*
Phillip Gardner, *Darlington*
Beth Webb Hart, *Charleston*
Stephen Hoffius, *Charleston*
Michelle R. Simpkins, *Edgefield*
Nona Martin Stuck, *Columbia*
Fred Thompson III, *Sullivan's Island*
Deno Trakas, *Spartanburg*
Tobias Van Buren, *Mt. Pleasant*

The Hub City Writers Project is a non-profit organization whose mission is to foster a sense of community through the literary arts. We do this by publishing books from and about our community; encouraging, mentoring, and advancing the careers of local writers; and seeking to make Spartanburg a center for the literary arts.

Our metaphor of organization purposely looks backward to the nineteenth century when Spartanburg was known as the "hub city," a place where railroads converged and departed.

At the beginning of the twenty-first century, Spartanburg has become a literary hub of South Carolina with an active and nationally celebrated core group of poets, fiction writers, and essayists. We celebrate these writers—and the ones not yet discovered—as one of our community's greatest assets. William R. Ferris, former director of the Center for the Study of Southern Cultures, says of the emerging South, "Our culture is our greatest resource. We can shape an economic base...And it won't be an investment that will disappear."

Colophon

Inheritance was designed during one of the South's most bone-chilling, recording-breaking, power-consuming winters to date. Technology update, January 2001: This *was to be* the last Hub City project to be "processed" on the trio of original (and still reliable) 1992 Power Macintosh© 7100/80s. Two speedier, beige desktop G3s lie in wait on the floor, hoping to be configured for book publishing and image manipulation very, very soon. This eleventh HCWP title is released in a first printing of 3000 soft-bound and a limited edition of 300 case-bound copies. The text typeface is Italian Garamond BT, and the display face is Engravers Roman. Numerous shots of Mr. Boston's Rock & Rye helped the designer and his graphic cohorts through the massive manuscript and the long, wintery nights.